YOU NEEDED ME

A LOVE STORY

SHVONNE LATRICE

ABOUT THE AUTHOR

Other Works by Me:

Good Girls Love Thugs 1-5
Falling for a Hood King 1-4
Married to a Distinguished Thug 1-3
She's Gotta Have It 1-2
Me & My Dope Boy 1-3
Yazir & Nina 1-3
Forbidden Love with a Thug 1-3
You Needed Me 1-3
Shorty is in Love with a Real One 1-4
I Got Your Back 1-2
My Baby Is a West Coast King 1-4
Our Love Is the Realest 1-3
She Got It Bad for a Heartless Gangsta 1-4
She Got It Bad for a Heartless Gangsta: An AK Christmas
Hood Boyz Fall In Love Too 1-3
Nobody Can Love You Like Them Roughnecks Do 1-4
She Gave Her All to the Hood's Finest 1-5

Visit www.theshvonnelatrice.com for paperbacks!

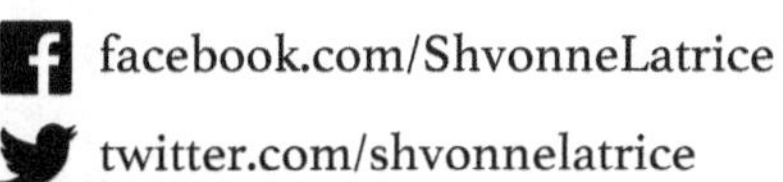

facebook.com/ShvonneLatrice

twitter.com/shvonnelatrice

instagram.com/shvonnelatrice

$17.99

ISBN 978-1-966375-14-2

Chapter 1

KIMBERLYN HARREY

"What did he say?" I chuckled as I stared at my cousin Matikah's phone over her shoulder. We were on this dating website fucking around with niggas' heads for fun.

"He asked if I was into strap-ons!" she squealed as we burst into laughter.

"Ewe, for him or for you?"

"Let me ask."

It was summertime in May, and we were in the park just relaxing since college classes were out of session. It was around 6:30pm so the sun was going down just a bit, but was still out. I loved summertime in Boston, simply because the sun stayed out much longer than usual.

"He said for him," Matikah finally answered and we laughed in unison. "So are you coming tomorrow night?"

"I didn't want to at first, but since I'm twenty-one and can drink, I wanna party."

I'd just finished my junior year in college studying art design, and I'd turned twenty-one this past March, so I was ready to have some fun. I had yet to go out drinking, and this party tomorrow night was the perfect way to start.

The event was being thrown by this guy named Gang, or better known as the 'King of Boston'. He sold drugs, and he was pretty much the man around here; he and his cousin Peel. Gang had a bit of a crush on me, and since he was fine as fuck, I couldn't wait to go to his party and chill with him. He and I were definitely on to something.

"I bet you can't wait to see Gang," Matikah nudged me and I shrugged.

"Not really, I just wanna have fun," I lied.

"Well let's go home because you know Grandma is cooking, and she wants niggas to eat as soon as she's done."

"Okay."

Matikah's mother Janine, and my mother Stephanie, are sisters, and although they hated one another, they had one trait in common: being trifling. You see, my father was Matikah's mom's current boyfriend when my mom got pregnant by him, so naturally they became enemies. They hated each other up until the day my mother died. My parents were shot while sitting in the car talking one night, and that was all I knew about their deaths. Many people believe Matikah's mom was behind it, but no one really knows. I was just happy that our moms' relationship had nothing to do with ours. Matikah and I were best friends and nothing would turn us into enemies.

We made it home from the park about fifteen minutes later, which was tiring on foot. Matikah and I lived with our grandmother in Roxbury, not the best neighborhood I guess, but I still fucked with it. Although Matikah's mom was alive, she lost custody of Matikah when she was four years old, and never tried to get her back either. She pops in every now and then when one of her new boyfriends aren't taking her across the world. And when she does, she only spends about ten minutes with Matikah before going out with her childhood homies. As for Matikah's father, I think he was just a one-night stand. He probably doesn't even know he has a daughter. However, despite the slightly bad hand we'd been dealt, I was very thankful for my life and the people in it, especially Matikah and my grandmother.

"Y'all got here just in time," my grandmother hollered as soon as Matikah and I walked through the door.

"We did that on purpose," I smiled as I walked into the kitchen. "Ooh, my favorite, fried chicken."

"Don't fuel the stereotypes, Kimberlyn," Matikah taunted and I playfully rolled my eyes.

"Ain't nothing wrong with being black and liking fried chicken, Matikah," my grandmother said as she set our plates down.

Steam streamed from the chicken, mashed potatoes, and spinach she'd made, making my mouth water at the smell. My grandmother was one of the best cooks in Boston. After she placed our drinks down, she made herself a plate and sat at the table with us. Eating dinner together was something we all enjoyed.

"What are your plans for the weekend?" my grandmother asked after we said grace.

"We're going to a party," Matikah answered.

My grandmother wasn't the type to have a strict hold on us. She said girls who had strict parents always turned out to be little hoes. That's not to say that she didn't discipline us because she did, but she didn't trip off of us talking on the phone with boys, or going to parties and shit; especially now that we were twenty-one.

"A party? Whose party is it?"

"It's Gang's," I answered.

"Kimberlyn, don't get caught up with that boy, he's bad news. Now I know he's sexy and all that stuff, and he has a lot of money, but he's no good for you."

"You don't like him because he's a criminal?" I quizzed.

"No, I don't like him because he's a *dumb ass* criminal. How many times has he been arrested and shit? It's ridiculous. Now I would much rather you be with a man who earns his keep legally, but if you have to be with a bad boy, get an intelligent one. A dumb one will just bring you down too."

"I hear you."

"Matikah," my grandmother smiled and looked in her direction.

Matikah gulped her drink down and said, "I know that already,

Ma. Kimberlyn is the one who wants to be Mrs. Gang. I'm trying to marry a veterinarian."

The three of us laughed and I asked, "Why a veterinarian?" I frowned and sipped my juice.

"Because I love animals, and what's better than a man who helps to keep them healthy and alive. And even better, he will be rich."

"Thanks for that," my grandma said, making us giggle.

After we finished our food, our mutual friend, Goldie, came over. My grandmother didn't care too much for Goldie because she said she was fast and sneaky. Goldie proved my grandma's strict theory to be somewhat true, because her parents were as stern as they came, yet she had always found a way to have sex with her now ex-boyfriend, Ethan. I remember she couldn't wait to start college and live in the dorms, and as soon as she moved in, she let loose with him. She wasn't a hoe, but she was much more experienced than Matikah and I.

Goldie was beautiful with smooth light skin, and brown hair with golden highlights. She had light honey colored eyes, a small frame, and full lips. Her nose was kind of big, but it went along with her face so it wasn't bad at all.

"Let's go to my room," I said and stood up. Matikah, Goldie, and I went into my bedroom, and I closed the door behind me. "Now what did you have to tell us?" I plopped down onto my bed along with Matikah, as Goldie sat on the La-Z-Boy in my room.

"So I found out some important people are gonna be there at the party," Goldie grinned as she pulled out some weed and began to roll up for us.

"Who?" Matikah frowned.

"The brothers from QCF," she nodded.

QCF or the Quinton Crime Family was just that, a family full of criminals. Although Gang was the King, the boys from the Quinton Crime Family reigned supreme. I'd never seen them before, but I'd heard about the many men they've killed, and the many women they'd smashed. Bitches who'd slept with them acted as if they'd had the best dick ever bestowed upon them. I guess tomorrow night would be the first night I saw them in person. They were like folktales almost though, because no one had solid proof of the shit they did, but you knew they weren't to be fucked with. I honestly couldn't tell you what they were into, nor could anyone else.

As far as their looks, I'd only had descriptions given to me by thirsty bitches. According to them, three of them were caramel, and one was brown skinned. Their father, the head of QCF, was Russian with deep blue eyes that he'd passed down to his sons. Their mother was a beautiful and youthful black woman, and I believe they had a sister who people claimed always stepped out looking like she was from a page in a magazine. I've heard she was so pretty that it was scary to look at her.

"You're lying, Goldie," Matikah covered her mouth.

"Nah I ain't bitch, and you know what I'm gonna be on when I get there. My initial plan was to get at Gang's friend, Tyrice, but now I wanna try to get with Britain, or if not him, then TQ."

TQ was the name of one of the Quinton boys, and I was tired of hearing about him and his brothers Rhys, Britain, and Lendsey. I wasn't sure how Goldie planned to get with Britain or TQ, because I'd heard he and his brothers were picky since they had the right to be. Shit, if they weren't picky they'd be fucking all day with all the hoes that wanted a taste. That's not to say that Goldie wasn't beautiful because she definitely was.

Frankly, I don't even know how girls got close to them, because it wasn't like you saw them on the streets. I mean some people have said they saw them at burger joints and such, but who knows. One of my classmates, Anya, said she saw Lendsey once, but was too scared to speak.

"And how exactly do you plan to get with Britain?" I asked as Goldie lit the blunt.

"You just worry about Gang and watch me work. Next time you see me, I may be rocking a Rolex."

"Bitch, please, you think your pussy is that good?" Matikah raised a brow.

"I know it is. Y'all bitches wouldn't know anything about that. Let me know if you need some tips for Gang, Kimberlyn."

Yeah, Matikah and I were some old ass virgins. We didn't like telling people because muthafuckas acted like we were some science objects. I remember one guy didn't want to date me anymore because he said if he took my virginity I would get too attached to him. I found that funny because I was barely attracted to his ass. Then another guy proposed to me, hoping that would make me bust it open. So see, either boys were turned off by us being unseasoned, or too turned on by it.

It's not like Matikah and I were squares or some shit, it's just these niggas out here weren't about shit, and none of them made me want to let them fuck; same for Matikah. Shit, the Quinton boys weren't the only people that were fastidious.

I think a part of me was so caught up in the movies and how my first time was supposed to be. I knew none of the guys I dealt with would give me that experience so it never happened. Only one guy came close, Ezra, but by the grace of God, I found out he'd gotten some bitch pregnant and was obviously cheating on me.

"I don't need any tips, I'm sure I will be perfectly fine," I said, and Matikah nodded in agreement.

Losing my virginity to Gang was definitely something I'd thought about on more then one occasion. We would have to see though.

Chapter 2

TARENZ "TQ" QUINTON

"Arnoldo Fuentes." My father handed me a folder with some pictures and details. "He's gonna be at Glitter tonight, and I want you to make sure you catch his ass."

"Pop, Rhys don't need me for this shit, he can do it alone," I frowned while looking over at my older brother. I usually liked to go along with my him, but this Arnoldo cat wasn't shit, so he didn't need my help.

"I know, but since this is a public establishment, I need you to look out for him," my father responded.

"Plus, who gon' fuck some of them bitches with me," Rhys leaned over and said to me in a low tone, making me laugh. This nigga knew he wasn't about to fuck no bitches with his always gotta be faithful ass.

"Business before bitches," my dad chuckled and sat behind his large wooden desk.

My father, Tracy Quinton, better known as Stony, is the head of the notorious Quinton Crime Family. There ain't shit we don't have our hands in, and although me make good money, we live very dangerously. I love the shit, but sometimes I did wish I were just a regular nigga. The job was a bit stressful and vicious at times, and believe it or not, there is a such thing as too many women.

Anyway, my mother is black and my dad is a full-blooded Russian cat. We inherited deep blue eyes from him, but smooth deep pigmented skin and kinky hair from my mother. I was a good-looking ass nigga, so they were the perfect mix. The bitches agreed with me.

My dad was born Anatoly Verenich, hella Russian. He changed his name upon entering America, and met my mother, Josephine, soon after when he was just a common criminal. I still don't even think my dad is legally in the United States to this day, but we've been here in Boston for all of my twenty-six years, and he's never had a problem making moves like a citizen. Plus, his marriage to my mother validated him anyway.

My parents had five children: my oldest sister, Saya, then my older brother Rhys, me, Lendsey, and then my youngest brother, Britain. We all work for my father, committing all kinds of crimes all day, and making plenty of fuckin' money from it. I wasn't rich, I was wealthy as fuck, and those are two totally different things. Ask somebody.

My dad has a business relationship with a guy named Alejandro in South America. He gets drugs for very cheap and in large quantities brought into Russia, which I then fly into the states. We serve distributors in Pennsylvania, New York, and our home state of Massachusetts. My dad made sure I got my pilot's license at fifteen, by helping me lie about my age, and ever since then I've been transporting drugs for him. I make at least one million dollars or more per trip, and I don't plan on stopping anytime soon.

My older brother, Rhys, is a highly paid hit man. He can kill anyone at anytime and no one will ever find out who'd done it. He's killed so many people that he doesn't even blink at the sound of gunfire. My dad groomed him from childhood, had him shooting guns in our backyard at eight years old. He actually had all of us doing that shit, but he focused a lot on my brother.

My younger brother, Lendsey, worked for my dad's unemployment company. He processed fake passports, immigration papers, green cards, and anything else you needed to look like a legal U.S. citizen. He mainly helped Russian and Ukrainian ones, but there were a couple other types too. He also provided new names and identities for Americans who needed to change shit up.

As for Britain, he was the personal loan officer for QCF. He kept track of anyone who owed my dad money, how much it was, and how long they had to pay the shit back. If they took too long, or tried to get over on my pops, we took care of it; mainly Rhys took care of it. If it were more convenient though, Britain would just pop the nigga himself.

My mom, Josephine, wasn't your typical wife of a criminal. She didn't sit at home enjoying the fruits of my father's labor. I mean she could, but they fell in love because of their fondness of crime. She and my older sister, Saya, ran a high-end prostitution ring. They provided bitches for niggas who made no less than one hundred thousand dollars a year. Every chick made at least $1,000 an hour, and my mom and sister took 40% of the money they made. There were about fifty girls in the ring, so you can just imagine how much money my mom and sister were making.

So like I said, our whole family was full of muthafuckas who made a living off of doing illegal shit. However, my brothers and I did have a couple carwashes all over Boston, and we made really good money from that due to it being an upscale car wash. I enjoyed running a business, even though it started out as just a way to clean our money. Having something legal made me feel good, and it gave me a sense of relief sometimes when this illegal shit became overwhelming.

"Alright let's be out," I said and stood to my feet with the manila folder in my hand.

Tonight, my brother Rhys and I were gonna murk this nigga named Arnoldo Fuentes. He was a registered nurse who my dad hired to assist our doctor when nursing our team back to health. Everything was all good until the nigga agreed to help the FEDs take my dad's empire down for a couple hundred grand. Little did he know, we had people working for us every damn where, and they snitched on his ass. My dad was too smart of a man which is why he'd been doing all this shit for over twenty years and hadn't been caught. Anyway, Arnoldo was found out and we'd been looking for his ass for a good week. Now that he felt the need to step out and party, we were gonna take his bitch ass out.

Rhys and I climbed into the black Escalade parked out in the lot of my dad's warehouse, and headed to Glitter. Glitter was a strip club located on Centre Street in a neighborhood called Jamaica Plain. I grew up over there so I knew it like the back of my hand. Glitter was a place where I'd had plenty of good memories smashing plenty of sexy ass strippers, and sometimes the women who just came to watch.

"Aye, so I'm just gon' slip in and pop that nigga. Right when I do, we gon' slip the fuck out," Rhys said as he lit up a blunt. As it hung from his lips, he loaded his gun.

"Got you. I know you wanna scope on some hoes for a bit, but let's not take too long because if that nigga sees us and gets wind of us being there, he's gonna flee and go back into hiding."

"Nigga, I was joking, I ain't looking for nothing, you know me. But I do wish the bitches weren't so thirsty sometimes though, a nigga can't never be low-key with shit."

Rhys wasn't lying. As soon as we walked in anywhere, women just flocked to us like squirrels to nuts. It made it hard when we just wanted to relax somewhere and enjoy ourselves. However, I did enjoy it when the women were beautiful and desperate, because I wasn't the type of nigga to do too much for pussy. Either you were gonna give it to me, which I'm sure you were, or you were gonna keep it pushing. I wasn't about to be moonwalking and matrixing for no fuckin' pussy. All pussy was the same it just depended on what type of bitch it was attached to. And since a nigga like me wasn't in the business of giving any woman my last name anytime soon, I didn't give a fuck. As long as she wasn't a prostitute and hadn't been tossed around by too many niggas, she was good in my book.

I had different bitches for different things. Some I only hit for head, and some I only hit for pussy. It was rare that a girl could do both well, but when I found one that could, I would keep her around; maybe. Until then, TQ was gonna continue to stick and dip.

We pulled up in front of Glitter and just peeped the scene for a little bit before I pulled around back by an alley. Rhys looked to make sure we were by the exit of the club, and then I slowly pulled over and parked by it. We got out of the car, and came back around from the other corner so we could throw someone off in case they were being nosey.

"Hey TQ," some bird waved to me while walking with her friends up to the entrance of Glitter. I ain't know much about weaves or hair period, but I knew the shit wasn't supposed be all high and bumpy like that.

"What's good, ma?" I stated nonchalantly, and Rhys laughed when I shook my head 'no' to him.

"Hey Rhys." She glanced at him, then looked back to me. "You and your brother want some company tonight?" she asked once all of us reached the entrance.

"Take care of yourself, ma," was all I said.

"What?" she yelped, not understanding me. That was my point, I didn't care that my answer wasn't a sufficient one. Looking the way that she did meant we had nothing to talk about.

"He's right over there, getting a lap dance like everything is all good," Rhys pointed to Arnoldo as we stood up against the wall of the dark club.

"Bitch ass nigga," I shook my head.

"Hey," I heard a sweet voice say. I looked down to see the home girl, Hayden.

Hayden was beautiful with brown skin, long hair, and she was thick in all the right places. I loved fucking her and I had no plans on stopping. She was fucking with this dude named Peel, and he worked for one of my distributors named Gang. I didn't give a fuck about her being his girl; the pussy was cool, but the head was even better so I was gonna continue to fuck with her.

I met Hayden in high school and we used to fuck around a lot back then. She got mad because I wouldn't be her nigga, so she got with Peel to make me jealous. Only I wasn't the jealous type, so that shit didn't work for her at all. Now here she was, years later, stuck with him but still chasing me. I had no idea if he knew that I was smashing his bitch or not, and honestly I didn't care.

"Sup Hayden," I hugged her close to me.

"What you got going on tonight?"

"Aye, go to my crib and I will meet you there in a little bit, some shit is about to pop off," I told her once Rhys let me know it was time.

"Okay baby," she squealed with excitement almost, and rushed off to grab her belongings.

Once I saw her slip out, Rhys and I discreetly made our way closer to Arnoldo. He was sitting on the side in the dark, with some chick popping her ass in his lap. Rhys and I stayed close to the wall, then when I gave him the head nod, he took his silenced gun and popped him on the side of the head. His body slumped, and the stripper continued dancing lazily in his lap, not even realizing it. By the time she did and began screaming at the top of her lungs, Rhys and I were already out the back door and speeding off in the Escalade.

"Too easy." Rhys shook his head as he lit another blunt for us.

"I don't even know why niggas cross us. It's rare, but they still do it for some reason."

As we got farther away from Glitter, the police sirens faded more and more. We didn't have shit to worry about because Glitter had no cameras, and even then, niggas were too scared to run their mouths on a Quinton nigga.

"Drop me at the hotel."

"Nigga, Summer gon' fuck you up if you don't come home tonight," I chuckled referring to Rhys' girlfriend.

Rhys and Summer had been together since she was in ninth grade and he was in twelfth, a decade ago. Rhys loved Summer, he really did, but he barely spent the night at their crib because they fought too damn much. He was nothing like me and my younger brothers, Lendsey and Britain, but shit, they were worse than me. Those niggas smashed a different bitch for every day of the week it seemed. They were always dogging bitches out. I can't tell you how many times chicks have gotten into fights over them. Britain was the worst of us all, then Lendsey, and then me.

Rhys only fucked around on Summer once with some bitch named Lisa, and he refused to let it happen again. Especially because the bitch he fucked with turned crazy and has been harassing him ever since. I couldn't lie though, his determination to remain faithful was commendable. I just hated that Summer refused to believe him, which is why she fussed so much. He really loved her ass though, was straight crazy about her. Only bad thing about Rhys was his temper. He was hot headed and would blow up over the smallest shit.

"Man, Summer is gonna go off on me whether I come home or go to the hotel. I really don't know how I can convince her insecure ass that I'm all about her."

"Well start off by making sure Lisa stops calling your phone constantly."

"Lisa is like a fuckin' harmless fly. I barely have my personal phone like that, so it don't bother me," he shrugged.

"But it bothers Summer."

"What doesn't bother Summer?" he looked over at me before we both chuckled.

"True."

I dropped Rhys off at the hotel he damn near lived at, and then sped home so I could have Hayden suck me to sleep. Once I got to my apartment in Brighton, I saw her standing outside waiting like a dummy.

"Fuck you standing outside for like niggas wouldn't rape and kill you?" I hissed as I pulled the door open to the building for her. Brighton was by no means the hood, but muthafuckas acted crazy everywhere.

"I knew you were coming soon."

"Yeah, aight."

As soon as we got up to my apartment, I opened some Hennessy and poured it into two glasses. I went and changed into some black jogger sweats and socks, leaving myself shirtless, then returned to the living room.

"I heard you and your brothers are coming out to Gang's party tomorrow," she sipped her drink and removed her shoes.

"We are. It's Lendsey's twenty-fourth birthday so we wanna celebrate for him."

"How are you gonna go to Gang's party and let Lendsey take over?"

"Watch and see. If I hit you tomorrow night for some good, you better come."

"I will, TQ, you know I would rather be with you than Peel anyway. I think he's gonna propose, and if you keep up your bullshit I'm gonna say yes."

"Ma, if you're looking for marriage and shit, say yes to that man because that ain't me and you know it."

"I think you can be that way, TQ, you just need some work."

"You may be right, but like my mama said, don't waste your time waiting for a man to become what you want him to, when you can go out and find a man who is already everything you desire. And Peel is the nigga for you, Hayden, not Tarenz Quinton," I palmed my chest.

"I'm not letting you fuck me anymore if I marry him."

"Yeah right, and speaking of fucking, come here." I pulled her ankle and she giggled.

When she was close enough, I reached under her dress and began pulling on her panties while kissing on her neck. I threw her thong to the side, and then turned her onto her knees before sliding a condom down.

"I love you, Tarenz," she cooed as I slid into her from behind.

I pressed her face into the couch pillow and asked, "Even after you get married I'm still gon' get this pussy, right?"

"Ye-yesss TQ!" she whimpered as I pounded into her.

I smacked her ass, and then gripped her waist before slamming into her a couple more times. I then pulled out, flipped her over, took the condom off, and let her suck me up until I busted.

"Come shower with me." I pulled her up off the couch, and she smiled because she knew what was up. I picked her up, and then went to fuck her in the shower once more before sending her back to her nigga. Good head didn't mean you could spend the night.

Chapter 3

KIMBERLYN

THE PARTY…

Tonight was Gang's party, and I was so excited to just let loose and actually get drunk. Matikah and I let my grandmother know that we would be having plenty to drink, so she agreed to come get us if Goldie was incoherent, as long as it was no later than 2am. I loved that my grandmother gave us our freedom; it made it hard to make bad decisions because we didn't want to disappoint her. But she'd raised us well anyway, so we weren't in the business of being trifling and scandalous.

I brushed my fresh press down, and let it lightly sweep the middle of my back. Tonight I was wearing a long sleeved crop top in gray, with skinny jeans, and sandal stilettos. I parted my hair down the middle, and wore gold for my accessories. I wanted to be cute but not too flashy, and Gang was already interested, so there was no need for me to go all out.

"Cute." Matikah walked into my room with my grandmother right behind her.

Matikah had her long dark hair in its naturally curly state, and she was wearing a black tube top with the matching pencil skirt. She wore sandal stilettos as well, except hers were black and mine were a pewter color.

"Thank you," I winked, and then slipped my big gold hoops into my ear. "You look cute too. Is Goldie on her way?"

"Yeah, she'll be here in about ten minutes."

Goldie lived in a neighborhood named Mattapan, so she was about ten minutes away from us. It was convenient as fuck because she was the only one of the crew who had a car. I just hated that she controlled our trips sometimes, because she loved to do hoe shit. And if you didn't want to be a part of it you either had to catch the bus, find a ride, or suck it the fuck up.

"Make sure that girl takes y'all straight to the party, and do not let her drive y'all home unless you know she's sober. Call me if she's not," my grandmother stated as she stood in the doorway of my room.

I nodded my head and sprayed my Juicy Couture perfume all over my body.

"Do me," Matikah walked in and spun around as I sprayed her with the perfume.

HONK!

"That must be Goldie's ignorant ass." My grandma shook her head and walked away as Matikah and I laughed.

I grabbed my little clutch, gave myself one more look in the mirror, and then left out to go party.

We pulled up to the venue on Boylston Street, and you could hear the loud music all the way inside Goldie's car. It was literally drowning out what we were listening to.

"There is a park," I pointed, and Goldie zoomed to it and swooped in.

"Let's smoke one before we go in," she smiled and reached into her glove compartment, crossing over me.

"Nah, I'm not trying to roll up in there smelling like a dime sack, let me out," I shook my head, and Matikah scooted to the door closest to the curb, signaling she agreed with me.

"Square ass bitches," Goldie sucked her teeth, put the weed away, and then unlocked the door.

Goldie looked nice in a white dress that I'm sure she bought in a smaller size because it was hugging her small frame like crazy.

The line to the party was all the way down the sidewalk, and I was thankful that I didn't have to wait. Tonight the streets were busy as fuck, and I guess because this was a club street basically, it seemed so crowded and loud.

"I'm Kimberlyn Harrey, I should be on Gang's guest list," I said to the bouncer.

He declined to respond and just looked down at his clipboard for a few moments. He then pulled out this white thing, and waved for my hand before stamping it.

"Says you have two guests?"

"Yes, this is Goldie Taylor, and Matikah Jacobson," I pointed over my shoulder. He stamped their hands, and then pulled the rope away for us.

"Damn bitch, you're already enjoying the perks of being Gang's girl," Goldie nudged me and I chuckled.

The three of us danced our way into the party, moving our bodies to "Still Here," by Drake. I looked around until I saw a big ass VIP of niggas, but I didn't see Gang. I saw there were four guys dressed really nicely, but in dark colors. They were drinking, smoking, and getting lap dances from some girls, all while their homies partied up too. They stood out from their friends though. A sudden feeling of nervousness came over me as I wondered if they were the Quintons. Why was I nervous?

"That's them," Goldie whispered to me.

"Who?" I frowned, halfway knowing the answer.

"Her obsession," Matikah rolled her eyes and checked the time on her iPhone.

"Oh, the Quintons," I nodded and looked back up there.

I couldn't make out their faces, but something about what I could see was very attractive. I loved men who were well dressed, and all four of them were. Their calm demeanor spoke volumes, and although I hated to admit it, I was interested. I wanted to be over there, but I knew it was unlikely that I'd gain entrance.

"There's Gang, Peel, and Peel's girlfriend, Hayden," Matikah pointed upwards.

"Come on," I huffed.

We all held hands in a line, and rushed up to the VIP where Gang was sitting with Peel, Hayden, and a couple of random homies. Gang was the King out here, so every nigga wanted to be his homie, and bitches wanted to be his girl. To make matters worse, he was sexy.

"Sup boo," Gang smiled once I neared him, then stood up to hug my body tightly in his strong arms.

"Hey, you look nice," I blushed.

"Thanks, I try, and so do you." He bit his lip and then pressed his mouth against mine. I never felt sparks when I kissed him, but he was cute, respectful, and had money, so I was gonna work with him.

I cupped his chin lightly as we kissed, and then pulled away to see his friend Monica glaring at me as she danced in some nigga's lap. I was sure she didn't like me, but Gang said that wasn't true. Something told me she had a crush on him despite them both denying it.

Goldie, Matikah, and I then sat down, and started making ourselves different drink combinations with the free liquor.

"I think I'm gonna go over there," Goldie said as she stared into the Quinton's VIP.

"And get turned away," Matikah scoffed, making us both laugh.

"Yeah right, bitch, do you see me? Them niggas would be fighting over me." She then leaned into us to whisper, "Gang is small potatoes compared to them niggas. Look how they got signs saying *Happy Birthday Lendsey Quinton*, when it was initially Gang's party. Gang don't run shit but the dummies who are fooled by knots of cash and nice cars."

I looked over at the Quintons along with Matikah and Goldie, while taking in what Goldie said. I mean it had to have some truth to it. When this party was announced, it was just a little bash that Gang was throwing together. Then when word got around that the Quinton boys would be in attendance, that's all people talked about, and now, the party wasn't even for Gang anymore.

I turned to Gang who was bobbing his head to the music and

asked, "I thought this was your party? Why is *Lendsey Quinton* everywhere?"

"It's his birthday and since we're cool, I let him use this as his birthday party," he shrugged.

I nodded and then looked over at Peel and his girlfriend, Hayden. She was grinding her ass in Peel's lap, but her eyes were locked on the Quinton boys. I wasn't sure which one, but I could see in her face that Peel was the least of her worries. I just watched her for a little bit more, before explaining to my friends why Lendsey's name was everywhere.

"Gonna go to the bathroom," I whispered to Gang and then said the same to Matikah and Goldie before getting up.

I walked around the couch, and then went into the nice luxurious bathroom in the VIP. After relieving myself, I washed my hands, and then made sure I was still looking good. I was a little tipsy, but I planned to get a little bit more buzzed.

Coming out of the restroom, I bumped into someone and their body felt like steel. My eyes trailed from their torso up to their face, and I swear it was mesmerizing. Smooth deep caramel skin, bluish gray eyes, perfectly lined up beard and mustache, and his cologne smelled like it cost $2000 a bottle. He wore a black baseball cap, but a fancy one, a black long sleeved button up with the sleeves rolled up just enough to show his watch, bracelet, and tattoos. On his bottom half were a pair of dark jeans that weren't too snug or too baggy, and black shoes. He had on a pinky ring, which sounded ugly but just complemented his look.

"You ain't gon' say excuse me?" he grinned and almost blinded me with his perfect smile and white teeth. He could be a tooth model. He rubbed his beard and waited for me to respond, then sipped his drink.

"Actually, you were standing in front of a door, sir, so technically you must've wanted to get bumped into," I spat.

He moved closer to my face, making me back up and hit the wall lightly. He chewed on his gum, and I could smell how minty it was despite him sipping some dark. Looking me up and down, that beautiful smile finally appeared again. He placed his tatted arm against the wall, blocking my right side.

"Maybe I did wanna get bumped into, by you."

"Well then, umm, don't expect me to apologize."

He laughed and threw his head back, before looking down at me again.

"What's your name? I like you."

"Kimberlyn."

"I'm Tarenz, but people call me TQ." He bit his lip and I almost fainted.

My breath seemed to get caught in my throat when he said his name. Had I known who he was I wouldn't have come at him like that. Seeing this nigga in the flesh gave me full understanding of why all the bitches in Boston went nuts for him. If his brothers even looked a teeny bit like him, I knew they were fine as fuck.

"TQ, nice to meet you," I responded in a much nicer tone than before. I was gonna shake his hand, but mine was trembling too much.

"Who you here with, ma?"

"My friends."

I didn't mention Gang. Who the fuck is Gang? I'm a terrible person.

"Come chill with my brothers and me, you can bring your friends."

"TQ, I'm actually here with a guy friend too," I admitted although my pussy, heart, and mind was telling me to forget about Gang.

"What I just say?"

"To come chill with you," I smiled and so did he, as he chewed on his gum with his fine ass. "Okay, give me a couple minutes."

"Okay, two minutes."

I started off, but he grabbed my small hand into his, and yanked me back to him lightly. Snaking his arms around my small frame, he leaned down to whisper into my ear.

"You better come back."

"I will," I moaned almost, eyes closed and everything.

He let me go, and I rushed back to get Goldie and Matikah. Since

I didn't want Gang to hear, I grabbed their hands and pulled them off the couch.

"What? You almost made me spill my drink, Kimberlyn," Matikah spat.

"TQ just asked for us to come chill with him and his brothers."

"Okay Kimberlyn, I know you had a couple drinks boo, but yeah right," Goldie laughed and nudged Matikah so she could join in.

"Fine, don't believe me but he said I had two minutes and I don't wanna make him wait." I walked off, and best believe their asses were right behind me.

I tensed up once we got close to their area, but a smile tugged at my lips once TQ stood up and waved us three in. He grabbed my hand, pulling me close, and then let his hand rest on my small hip, giving me goose bumps.

"Kimberlyn, this is my brother Rhys, his girl Summer, and my other brothers Lendsey and Britain. This is the homie, Jayce."

"Nice to meet you Rhys, Summer, Britain, Jayce, and Lendsey." When I looked at Lendsey, he was eyeing Matikah like she was piece of moist ass pound cake. "Umm, these are my friends Goldie and Matikah."

"Matikah, welcome to my party," Lendsey stood to his feet and towered over her. I rubbed her back to make her respond because I thought she would pass out.

They sat down next to one another, and then TQ pulled me into his lap, catching me off guard. I was sure he could feel how nervous I was. *Stop shaking, Kimberlyn!* Goldie sat down on the couch across from us, and she was giving me a look that said I needed to be careful. I didn't care though; I just didn't care.

Chapter 4
TQ

I PULLED KIMBERLYN'S PRETTY ASS DOWN INTO MY LAP, AND BROUGHT her closer into me. She was so fuckin' pretty; she reminded me of Aaliyah. She didn't look like her, even though they were the same caramel color and had long, straight dark hair. She had Aaliyah's cool, laid back, demeanor and I liked that shit. I didn't like all that animated shit.

"How old are you?" I whispered to her.

"I'm twenty-one, how old are you?" she touched my beard. I liked that she was getting comfortable with me; maybe it was the liquor.

"I'm twenty-six. You fuck with Gang?"

"No, I'm just here because he invited me. I was on his guest list. We're friends." She was lying, but I had that effect on women. They would dump their boyfriends fast as fuck if they even thought I was interested.

"On his guest list, huh... you sure that ain't your nigga?" I quizzed when I saw her glance over into his VIP. She shook her head no. "You fucked him?"

"I can't believe you just asked me that!" she frowned.

I knew she was appalled but I had to know. I wanted her ass bad for some reason. I didn't know if I just wanted to fuck or if I wanted to be her man. It was a weird feeling for me, because I'd never wanted more than a couple fucks and some head from a girl.

I'd never seen shorty before. She was beautiful *and* I could tell she had her mind right. I'd had my eyes on her from the moment she sauntered into the club, swaying her little body. And as soon as I saw her get up for the bathroom, I got up too. TQ was no thirsty nigga, but she had me a little parched.

"Did you fuck him or not, Kimberlyn?"

"No I didn't." I licked my lips and nodded approvingly. I was hungry for her in more ways than one. "Why?" she inquired.

"Because I'm interested in you but I don't want anyone that he's had. We work together in a sense, and that just wouldn't be cool for you to be on *my* arm, and having fucked *him*. I want something exclusive."

"Who said I wanted to be on your arm?"

"Fine, you can just stay in my lap," I whispered onto her neck and then kissed it gently.

I felt her body stiffen up, so I gripped her tighter in my arms. Sucking on her neck, I set my drink down, and began caressing her thighs.

"Can you leave with me?" I pulled back to look up into her face, waiting for an answer.

She nibbled on her full bottom lip for a bit, and then nodded her head 'yes'. I was happy as fuck, so I quickly moved her off of my lap and then stood up. I felt a pair of eyes on me, and when I looked to my left I saw it was Gang and Hayden, watching with hate in their eyes. I understood Gang being mad, but Hayden had seen me leave with plenty of women so I didn't get it. I think she didn't want me leaving with Kimberlyn in particular for some reason.

I took shorty's hand into mine, and then looked down at my brothers.

"Aye, we about to leave," I announced.

Her friend Matikah looked at her, and she just shrugged one

shoulder then smiled. The Goldie chick shook her head; I guess she was the cock blocker of the group. Every group of women had that one cock-blocking bitch who didn't get any play so she didn't want her friends getting any. Goldie was cute as fuck though, so I'm not sure why she was a cock blocker.

"Bye, bro." Rhys put his fist up and I dapped him. Lendsey, Britain, and Jayce did the same. I hugged Rhys' girl, Summer, then led Kimberlyn out of the VIP.

Gang and Hayden's eyes followed us the whole time in the huge club, and I saw Kimberlyn look at him before swiftly looking away. To fuck with him. I let go of her hand and then hugged her from behind, placing kisses all over her sweet smelling neck. Her body felt good against mine and she wasn't even naked... yet.

We made it out to the parking lot, and I hit the alarm to my Maserati before opening the door for her. I got in on my side, and saw she was scoping my car with her purse in her lap. She was hugging that purse like she thought I was about to rob her ass.

"This is really nice, TQ," she nodded and smiled, before pushing her hair behind her ear.

"Aye, honestly," I cranked my car up, "I swear you're the prettiest girl I've ever seen out of everywhere that I've been. You from Boston?"

"Yes, and thanks," she chuckled and shook her head at me.

"What?"

"You don't have to say all that, I'm hip to game."

"I don't need game, shorty, I only speak the truth. I promise I've never seen a girl as pretty as you, and I've been almost everywhere."

I was dead serious; she could choose to believe me if she wanted to or not. One thing she would learn is that I didn't need my words to get me some ass. One smile and a wink usually did it for me if my name didn't.

A little bit later, we pulled up to my condo building in Brighton. I parked my shit and got out, jogging around to open the door and help her out of my car. We entered the building, then I led her straight to my bedroom.

"You thirsty? I have vodka."

"What makes you think I want vodka?" she smiled that beautiful smile of hers.

"Because all bit- all women like clear shit."

"All bitches?" she grinned widely and we both laughed.

"No, I meant women."

"Sure, mix it with some kind of juice please." She began walking around my huge room, admiring things.

"Yes ma'am."

I went to grab a bottle of Grey Goose, along with some apple juice since it was all I had, and all a nigga bought outside of liquor and water. I looked down because my dick was rock hard just from talking to her ass. That was not like me.

Grabbing some glasses, I went back to my bedroom to find her sitting on the couch in there. She'd thrown her hair over to the other side, giving her this Victoria Secret model look. I just shook my head at her beauty, before handing over the glass.

I filled them both with vodka and juice, then we began sipping.

"What is a girl like you doing with a square like Gang?" I was really confused. Then again, people out here believed all that shit he barked. Real niggas didn't need to talk so much and so loudly.

"I told you I'm not with him, with him. And a square? Gang is the king of the city for your information."

"Oh yeah, but you left with me."

"I know."

"Gang is cool, but you can do better."

"Are you better?"

"I think you know the answer to that, ma." I sipped my mixture and so did she. "Why so nervous?"

"Your reputation precedes you."

"What have you heard?"

"You're mysterious, ruthless, a womanizer, and fine."

I just shrugged and finished my drink.

"Come here."

She set her glass down, removed her shoes, and then walked

closer to me. I grabbed my remote to dim the lights, and then pulled her into my lap so that she was straddling me. She placed her soft hands on the sides of my face, and our lips finally met. Sucking her lips, I reached my hands down the back of her pants and felt her thong. I then brought my hands to the front of her body and up her shirt. When I realized she wasn't wearing a bra, my dick got even harder. I pushed her little top up to expose her perfectly round breasts, and then began sucking her nipples. I stood up, still holding her, and then carried her to my bed. She laid there looking up at me as I took off my button up, shoes, and jeans. I then began removing her jeans, and yanked them down her legs before rushing between them.

We were kissing hungrily, and only stopped so that I could remove her shirt past her head. Her body was beautiful, toned, but soft, and her skin was the most beautiful shade of caramel. I began kissing down her stomach, and tugging on the waistline of her thong.

"Tarenz, stop," she pushed my head.

"What? Why?"

She scooted her body away from me, and further onto the bed, grabbing her top. I could see in her eyes that she wasn't feeling this.

"I'm not gonna be one of your little hoes that you fuck for convenience."

"Who said I wanted you to be?"

"That's what you do, I know already. When I came into the club you had a girl in your lap, TQ."

"Kimberlyn, it wasn't my intention to make you some one-night stand shorty. I can get pussy from anywhere, but I want you."

"Why?" she frowned and pulled her shirt over her head.

"I don't know honestly, I just do."

I yanked her ankle so that she was closer to me again, and then got back between her legs to kiss her soft lips. They were red from how hard we'd been kissing seconds prior.

"I'm not trying to hit and quit," I said in a low tone as I kissed her neck and groped her body that was so unbelievably sexy to me.

"It's not supposed to be like this."

"What is it supposed to be like?" I stopped kissing her neck.

"We're supposed to go on a date or something. You probably don't even know what that is, do you? You're used to fucking the first night."

"I do know what a date is but you're right, I haven't been on many."

"I thought so."

She moved me off of her and then got off my bed. She grabbed her jeans from the floor, but I hopped up and pulled them from her before she could put them on. I don't know why, but I didn't want her to leave.

"Look shorty, just stay here with me tonight, we don't have to fuck. I will take you on a date."

"Really?" she moved her hair from being in her shirt.

"Yes."

"Don't take me if it's just to fuck me."

"It's not. I promise. Come lie down with me, without your shirt. We can keep our bottoms on."

She paused for a moment, and then removed her top. I took her hand in mine, and then we went and got into my bed. As soon as we did, I got back between her legs and slipped my tongue into her mouth.

"Promise me you'll eventually let me have you," I said in between kisses, while groping her breasts.

"I promise."

I dipped my head down to suck her nipples, and then let my hands roam her body. I was starving to fuck her right now, which was new for me. Pussy came to me so easily that I never felt the need to be thirsty for it.

"Can I use my fingers?"

"No, I'm a virgin, Tarenz."

I jerked my neck back and stared down into her eyes as if she were an endangered species; shit, she was.

"No one has ever fucked you?" She shook her head no, and

caressed the sides of my face. I pinned her hands to the bed and said, "You're mine, Kimberlyn."

We smiled at one another, before I began tonguing her down again.

"TQ, I have to go home tonight."

"Nah, not tonight ma. Tomorrow, after our date."

Chapter 5
MATIKAH JACOBSON

AN HOUR AND A HALF EARLIER…

I sat down next to Lendsey, smiling at the fact that Kimberlyn was sitting in TQ's lap. I didn't like Gang for her, so anybody that could pull her from him was okay in my book. The only thing was that the Quinton boys were known for doing everything the bad way, especially when it came to women.

"Why have I never seen you before?" Lendsey frowned as he looked into my face.

He was beautiful with blemish free brown skin, full lips, bluish gray eyes, short kinky hair, a muscular build, and beautiful long eyelashes. His facial hair gave him a rugged look, making him overall easy on the eyes.

"Because you only know women that hang out in the clubs."

He laughed and said, "Aye, that's probably true. But I'm glad you decided to come out tonight."

"Why is that?"

"Because I would've never met you."

"Not true. God puts people in other's pathways one way or the other, so if you didn't meet me tonight, you would've met me later."

He smiled and nodded his head.

"You're a know it all, it's cute."

"Thanks, I guess. So where are the girls you had dancing in your lap?"

"They're around here somewhere, why, are you jealous?"

"Jealous of what? I don't even know you."

"I was just asking, but yeah, they're floating around here somewhere. It's my twenty-fourth birthday, I deserved a dance."

"Yeah, I guess. You just took over Gang's party, is it true you asked and he offered?"

"Hell no. My bro, TQ, told that nigga that it was gonna be a celebration for my birthday, and that was the end of the conversation. What you will learn about me, Matikah, is that I don't ask for anybody's permission to do anything."

He moved in closer to me, making me hot all over. I took my hair tie from my wrist, and piled my long curly locks on top of my head; yeah, he had me that hot.

"I see, so you don't need permission for anything?" I couldn't think of anything else to say, he was making me that nervous.

"Nah, only to fuck. I ain't the raping type of nigga. If she don't wanna give it up I don't force it. It's rare though," he looked my body up and down and shook his head.

"Aye, we're about to leave," TQ stood up, holding Kimberlyn's hand.

I looked at her ass like she was crazy, and she had the nerve to shrug at me. This wasn't like Kimberlyn at all, so TQ must've really laid his game down on her. I watched as they walked off, and TQ was all over her, while Gang and Hayden watched from afar.

"You're so bad, I know you got a man," Lendsey said and I shook my head no.

"No, I haven't found someone worthy enough to be my man."

"Oh word? You're picky, I like that."

"Do you?"

"I do."

"Oh shoot, I just remembered I have somewhere to be in the morning. Matikah, are you riding with me?" Goldie stood up.

I knew she was lying and only wanted to leave because Britain was getting head from some random right in the open, and she was mad about it. I wasn't really trying to leave because I was enjoying all this flirting Lendsey was doing. I knew he was bad news, but what girl didn't like bad boys?

"Oh Goldie, now? It's not even that late and we've only been here like two hours."

"I told you I had somewhere to be!"

"Alright, give me a few minutes," I told her and she rolled her eyes.

"I'm gonna go to the bathroom, and when I come out I'm leaving, Matikah."

Once she stormed off towards the bathroom, both Lendsey and I burst into laughter. As it ceased we made eye contact. His eyes were so alluring, just like the rest of him.

"So, since your hatin' ass friend is mad, can I get your number before you leave?" Was he for real?

"What do you want my number for?"

"So I can fucking talk to you, shorty, what else would I need the shit for? I like you and I wanna spend some time with you outside of the club. And I know your little mean ass ain't gon' come home with me."

"You're right."

"Exactly then, so give me that number, ma, this is the last time I'm gonna ask you before I get desperate and take the shit from your phone."

"A Quinton boy getting desperate? That's unheard of."

"Exactly, that shows that you're special, now quit fucking with me." He licked his lips and handed me his iPhone with the caller app up. I typed it in, and then handed it back to him. "Thank you."

I spotted Goldie switching back over, so I got up from the little couch.

"You better call, nigga."

"Look who's thirsty now," he grinned with his fine ass, and sipped whatever was in his glass.

"I'm not thirsty, I just don't like giving my number out for no reason."

"Don't give your number out to nobody else either."

"Or what?"

He set his drink down and stood up to tower over me. He was at least 6'4".

"Because I'm coming for you," he leaned down to whisper into my ear, and palmed the small of my back. I couldn't do anything but nod.

He kissed the side of my face as I palmed his biceps, then I said goodbye to his brother Britain, then Rhys and his girlfriend, Summer. I'd forgotten the other dude's name.

Goldie and I walked through the huge venue so we could get to the exit, and my cheeks were starting to hurt because I couldn't stop smiling.

"Why are you over there looking like a fuckin' Jack in the Box?" Goldie frowned as she buckled her seat belt.

"Why do you think?"

She burst into laughter and shook her head as she cranked the car.

"Because of Lendsey Quinton asking for your number? Matikah, that nigga is a boss and he has a boss's appetite."

"A boss's appetite?"

"A large appetite for the opposite sex. He wants your number so he can fuck you and then never call again. I hope Kimberlyn knows that's why TQ took her home. He's probably fuckin' right now."

"No, Kimberlyn wouldn't do that. She doesn't even know him. And how do you know their intentions, Goldie? You don't even know them."

"No, *you* and Kimberlyn don't know them, I do. They are men who have the world at their feet, you honestly believe that they'd just throw all that away for you and Kimberlyn?"

I processed what she was saying and she was definitely right. I'd be stupid to think that Lendsey and I could foster up any kind of relationship. Maybe we could be cool, but I'll be damned if he tries to make me one of his little bitches.

"I get it. If he texts me or calls me, which he probably won't, I just won't respond."

"And what about, Kimberlyn?"

"I can't control her, but I will try and convince her. She's a smart girl, so I'm sure she won't fuck with it."

I looked over at Goldie and she was nodding.

"Yeah, you should make sure she doesn't."

A part of me felt like what Goldie was saying was very much true. It went along with all the rumors we'd heard over time. The other part of me felt like she was just a hater, and didn't want anybody dating a Quinton if she couldn't.

Chapter 6

GOLDIE TAYLOR

I got home from dropping Matikah off, and I will admit I was a bit bummed. I didn't even talk to Britain, I just sat there staring at him like a fool. He was so much better looking up close, and I wanted to just jump on him. Too bad he had a bitch sucking him off right in the open like a for real hoe. Some bitches really had no self-respect at all!

As I approached my apartment building, I saw my ex-boyfriend, Ethan, leaning up against the wall smiling at me. I rolled my eyes because I was not in the mood for this shit. My night was already ruined, and his nutty ass was just gonna make it worse.

"Damn shorty, you look good. Where was you?" he asked and stood behind me as I unlocked my door.

Ethan was very handsome. He had smooth dark skin, dreads, and always dressed nice. You will learn I have a thing for men with dreads, hence my interest in Britain's fine ass. Although Ethan was good looking, he was no Britain for sure.

"You know where I was Ethan, I was where everyone else was tonight."

"Oh, at that Quinton party? You better not had been letting niggas feel all on you."

"Oh, now you care about other niggas being in my face? I could've sworn you begged me to be in an open relationship when we were together."

"True, but I was still your nigga so it was different." He followed me into the house.

Ethan and I met four years ago when I was seventeen years old. It was during the time when I was still living with my mom and under her strict rules. I barely got out, so when I met bad boy Ethan, I was hooked. He had me sneaking out and missing bible class just to be with him. I thought I was in love, especially because we'd been together for two years. Once we hit that two-year mark though, he came to me with that open relationship shit. He only requested it after I'd found out that he'd been cheating on me with every Sarah, Jane, and Mary in the city of Boston. Because I was dumb and in love, I agreed to the shit, but was miserable the whole time.

About five months into our 'open relationship' I broke it off with him, and had been having a hard time staying strong. Thank God for my best friends, Kimberlyn and Matikah, because without them, I may have reverted. They kept me busy by always hanging out with me, even when I would try to cure my broken heart by going to chill with random niggas. I never fucked them because I just couldn't do it, but it did ruin my reputation a little since I was seen going to their houses and chilling with them. Anyway, here we are two years later, and Ethan is still on my bumper.

I will admit, I did let him fuck me a couple times over the years we'd been broken up, but it was just because I was horny and didn't want some random smashing me. I cut that off about eight months ago though, so now he was buggin'.

"What do you want, Ethan? I'm ready to go to bed."

"I want you. I came to talk. I'm twenty-five now, and I wanna settle down," he pleaded, before moving his dreads from his face.

I stared into his eyes before bursting into a fit of laughter. This nigga had to be fuckin' kidding me. There was no way I would ever believe a word that came from those lips of his.

"I'm serious!" he barked, obviously offended by me taking him for a joke.

"Boy, you must've been at the party drinking, and a lot, if you think I'm gonna be convinced of these lies you tell." I plopped down on the couch next to him and removed my heels.

"Let me prove it to you, Goldie. I swear I'm serious." He dropped down to the floor in front of me. "I really have been doing some thinking, and I realized that you were everything I wanted. I was just childish and didn't realize the goddess I had in front of me."

"Ethan—"

"You don't love me?"

"Yes, but—"

"Aight then. Give me a little trial run, ma. I swear you won't regret it. You know a nigga always loved you, I was just too young to handle my shit like a man, G."

He was pecking my exposed thighs as he stared up into my eyes, silently pleading for me to give him another chance. Truthfully, I missed being in a relationship, and sometimes I did find myself begrudgingly yearning for his no good ass. I mean how harmful could it be for me to give him a trial run? Fuck that, I knew it would hurt me like crazy, but I still had love for him. I didn't wanna miss out on what we could build together if he in fact had changed.

"Okay, but this is just a trial, Ethan, you better not fuck me over," I threatened as he pulled on my panties.

Once they were off, he pressed his face between my legs and began sucking on my clit gently. Damn, I forgot how good he was at giving head. I spread my legs wider for him, and let him go to town on me with his mouth. He was sucking and lapping up my juices like a dog that hadn't drank water in years. My fresh acrylic scraped against the couch as I cried out in pleasure.

"Baby, I missed you," I whined as I gripped his dreads into my hand. "Ahhh, fuck." I released and he cleaned me up with his tongue. He stood up to unbuckle his jeans, but I stopped him. "Thanks, but I'm tired now." I pushed him towards the door as he protested and stumbled back.

"For real, Goldie?" he hissed once he was outside.

"For real, and your trial just started so be good."

And with that, I slammed the door and headed to the back to take a hot bubble bath. At least my night ended with a good ass nut.

Chapter 7

KIMBERLYN

YES THAT SAME NIGHT… IT AIN'T OVER YET…

I WOKE UP IN THE MIDDLE OF THE NIGHT WITH A FULL BLADDER. TQ WAS behind me, hugging me tightly in his arms. I couldn't believe all that had transpired the night before, or early this morning. I went to the party expecting to chill with my crush, Gang, and ended up leaving with a nigga like TQ. I never would've thought in a million years that someone like him would be interested in me. I was still waiting to wake up from this dream. I couldn't say that I wasn't happy about it though.

I moved from his embrace, and then padded to my purse. I took my iPhone out and saw I had some texts from Goldie, my grandmother, and Matikah. I took my phone with me, and then went in search of the bathroom. Once I found it, I went in, closed the door, and sat down on the toilet to pee and text.

Gran: Where are you?

Me: A friend's house, will be home tomorrow.

Goldie: I'm so mad at you. Don't be dumb, Beri.

Matikah: Goldie is a hater because she didn't bag Britain, lol. Goodnight and keep your legs closed hoe.

I chuckled at Matikah's text, and then set my phone on the sink. I wiped myself, flushed, and then pulled my panties up before washing my hands. Grabbing my phone, I padded back to the bedroom, and climbed into bed with TQ. He was even fine when he slept. I'd never seen a man that attractive up close before.

I laid down facing him, and just stared for a little bit. I could feel the air he exhaled from his nose, which tickled mine. I was very attracted to him, but I wasn't sure if I was ready to entertain someone like him. He was a criminal, and not some little petty thief who robbed liquor stores or snatched purses, he was a for real Al Capone type. Gang was no small time crook either, but I could tell he and TQ were worlds apart.

I always thought I would marry a teacher or something simple, yet here I was in the bed of a notorious ruffian. Scared was an understatement.

I caressed his bearded cheek and then kissed his lips. I just needed to calm down; nothing was set in stone. I hadn't even been on a date with him. Then again, I could see the seriousness in his eyes when he told me I was his. My grandfather, when he was alive, told me it takes a man only one hour to recognize the woman he wants for life, but it can take women years. Maybe he was right.

I pushed my half naked body into his, and he woke up just a little to hug me back. His strong arms felt so good wrapped around my body. I could stay in this position forever. I was glad he woke up too, because I wanted to talk to him. I was becoming attached already.

"Are we really going on a date?" I asked lowly.

He kissed me and nodded his head slowly, obviously still tired.

"I don't take women on dates, but I will give you what you want."

"You don't wanna take me on a date?"

"I do, but I don't feel it's necessary in order to sleep with you. But the little things mean the most to women so I understand why you want me to take you out."

"I would feel like a hoe if I let you before we went on *one* date."

He burst into laughter and said, "Shorty, it takes a little bit more than that to be a hoe. But trust me, if I only wanted to smash I would've sent your ass home when you stopped me from kissing you."

I chuckled and kissed him again.

"You don't even know me."

"But I want to. I wanna know you in a couple of different ways." He hugged me even closer into his body. I felt his six-pack prodding me.

"Would you still be interested if I hadn't come to your condo tonight?"

"Yeah, I would. Men don't think the same as women, shorty. You guys base being a hoe or being easy on different criteria, somewhat. A woman with a ninety-day rule is not a saint, just like a woman who sleeps with a man the first night isn't technically a hoe. I know plenty of bitches getting fucked by every damn body, but have a ninety-day rule. All a nigga is gonna do is wait the three months, fuck, and then chuck the deuces. Life is too important and precious to be taken so seriously. Feelings and time have nothing to do with one another."

"I don't know if you're smart or if you're just trying to sleep with me." We laughed in unison.

"Both, shorty. I'm a man so I'm always gonna wanna fuck you whenever I'm around you. All you should worry about are my actions *after* I fuck you."

"What will that be?"

"Well with the way you're holding out on me, right after I fuck you I will most likely fuck you again and again." We both chuckled.

"Do you know how to make love?"

"Of course."

"That's how I want it the first time."

"I got you. I'm a man of many talents."

"I guess I should go to sleep, I have to wake up and go home tomorrow."

"After I take you to breakfast, aight?"

"Okay."

Our lips met and we began kissing hungrily. His hand made its way to one of my breasts, and he began toying with my nipples. My clit throbbed, letting me know I wanted to have sex, but I couldn't. I've waited all this time and I refused to just carelessly give myself up, virgin or not.

"Watch when I get my hands on you," he whispered and sucked my lips.

"Can I ask you a favor?" I pulled from our kiss.

"Anything."

"Don't do all of this just to hurt my feelings in the end."

I woke up the next morning and I could faintly hear TQ talking to someone in the living room. I placed my hands over my eyes, and took a deep breath before peeling the covers off of my body. *I'm gonna miss this bed and these bomb ass pillows.* Last night still seemed like a mirage.

I sat up and then walked over to the little couch in his room to pull my shirt over my head. He had the air conditioner on, and it was freezing cold. After slipping my pants past my hips, I sat down to fasten the buckle of my sandal stilettos around my ankles.

"You ready?" TQ finally walked into the room. He was wearing black basketball shorts, black socks, black Nike slide-ins, and a black t-shirt. The tattoos on his arms were showing, making him look so rugged. He wore a couple of small chains that I knew he never took off because he'd slept in them. A watch was on one wrist, and a bracelet was on the other.

"Umm, I have to go home and clean up before we go to breakfast."

"About that, Kimberlyn, I have some business to take care of, but I promise tonight I will come get you for dinner," he smiled and I realized he had one dimple.

"Sure," I nodded. I knew he was lying. Because I hadn't had sex with him last night, he was over me. I was just happy that I didn't let the way I was feeling get the best of me, because I would be feeling stupid right now. "Actually, I have somewhere to be tonight, TQ, so there is no need for you to come back tonight. Maybe some other time." I grabbed my purse and slipped past him out of the room.

He walked into the living room and pulled his black hat down on his head before chuckling. I stood still by the door, staring up at the ceiling, waiting for him to let me know he was ready.

"Aye ma, I for real have some shit to do. I'm gonna pick your little mean ass up tonight, and you better be ready no later than 8:15pm, aight?"

"I will have to check my schedule."

"Nah, your ass better be ready."

"And if I'm not?"

He grabbed two bottles of orange juice from his stainless steel fridge, twisted the cap off and drank some out of one before saying, "You will be."

Walking closer to me, he handed me the other juice, and I snatched it before pulling his door open. I wanted to go on this date with his fine ass, but I had to stand my ground. I was no idiot, and if he thought he could just push our breakfast date to the side, he was sadly mistaken.

The whole ride home I didn't say anything unless giving him a direction. I just stared out of the window at my city. TQ played his music loudly, and then cracked the windows before lighting a blunt. Even though the smell of the weed was strong, his Armani cologne still overpowered it, making me wet between the legs.

"Thanks," I said once he pulled onto Seaver Street and in front of my grandmother's big white, but dingy house.

"Kimberlyn, don't fuck with me, shorty. Two things I don't like being fucked with and that's my time and my money. If I come here at 8:15pm and your ass is still on this bullshit, wasting my time, we're gonna have a problem."

"Yeah, yeah, yeah," I waved him off and slammed his car door.

I looked back at him, and his passenger side window was all the way down. He had the biggest smile on his face, which in turn made me smile. Yeah, I was going on this date. I'd be a fool not to.

Chapter 8
TQ

I knew Kimberlyn's ass thought I was bullshitting her, and right now there was nothing I could do to prove myself. I really had some shit to do, and I couldn't take her ass to breakfast. Since I'd never been one to feel the need to explain myself to a woman who wasn't my mother, I couldn't think of a way to make her feel better. But oh well, her ass just better be ready when I came back by tonight.

I honestly didn't know what came over me last night at the party. Kimberlyn was beautiful as fuck, so me being attracted to her wasn't what baffled me; it was the fact that I was interested in more than just hittin' the pussy. It was something about her aura that I really liked. Anybody that knew me would be surprised that I didn't have my driver take Kimberlyn home after denying me. Actually, I think people would be more surprised that she denied me.

All my life I'd been around hoes, literally and figuratively. Every bitch that wasn't my mother or sister, Saya, was either a paid hoe, a free hoe, or a bitch that was too clingy and had no idea that she was nowhere near being my bitch. But Kimberlyn was just a regular girl from Boston and I liked that shit. She knew who I was and what I was about, but she didn't seem to even really care. No woman that I fucked with would have ever waved me off the way she'd just done, and I hated it but liked it at the same time.

When she walked into the club last night, my eyes locked onto her and I couldn't pull them away. Her subtle sexiness was something I'd never seen before. She was sexy without trying or having to show too much, and it made me want to see more and know more.

"Man, you need to start driving some of these times," I told my brother Rhys as he hopped into the passenger seat.

"Nigga, you know I don't like to drive."

"Nah, your ass don't know *how* to drive, or better yet, it's not safe for you to," I said making us both laugh.

My older brother Rhys was the definition of a fuckin' maniac. By saying that, he had road rage that was off the fuckin' charts. One time a person cut him off and this nigga switched up his whole route just to follow the muthafucka all the way to their destination. And when he got there, he hopped out on them and pressed a pistol to their head, making them apologize. From that day forward, everyone agreed that letting Rhys take the wheel to drive to business was not a good idea.

"That's because niggas ain't got no fuckin' street etiquette my nigga." He pulled a blunt from behind his ear and lit it.

"Don't I know it. You're still a fuckin' nutcase though."

He shrugged.

"So what happened with you and that little bitch from the club? She was cute as fuck, which probably means her pussy was whack. And if the pussy was good, she crazy."

"I don't even know yet." I shook my head and he immediately began choking on the smoke of the blunt, and beating on his chest.

"Nigga, you got her to the crib and she didn't let you hit?"

"Nah, but I will, you know me."

"Wait, the TQ I know would have sent that bitch home in an Uber, fuck you talkin' about you *will* hit. You gon' still fuck with her?"

"Yeah, I'm gon' see what she about. She wants me to take her on a date and shit first, which isn't too unreasonable."

"You're the worst nigga," he chuckled and so did I. "Taking her out so you can fuck, that's shady man. I'm telling you, you need a real one by your side. Ain't nothing out here but some hoes with their hands out."

"I'd like to think I'm just taking her out so I can fuck, but that ain't true. I'm taking her because I low-key want to."

"What? Nigga, just the other day I told you to settle down and you was barking all that bullshit about how you ain't the type."

"I ain't the type to settle down, my nigga, at fucking all, but shit, I don't know... shorty got me feeling some type of way. She got swag."

"Nigga, you sound like a bitch," he laughed. "But nah," he took a pull, "you need to get like me and get a girl. Shit, you and Lendsey, y'all can't be hoes forever."

"Rhys, you and Summer are not the best people to promote monogamy. Are y'all ever happy?"

"That's because Summer and I can't get along due to her paranoia. And we are very happy in the bedroom. It's just once we come out that muthafucka."

"I just don't know if I'm willing to deal with all the nagging and shit. Plus, I like pussy too much."

"Then don't take her out," he looked over at me with a smirk.

"Maybe I won't," I lied.

Kimberlyn had me feeling some type of way already, like I was some weak ass nigga. I didn't want anyone else gettin' at her either, whether it was Gang or any other nigga. I felt like I'd found a needle in a haystack, and I wasn't ready to drop that shit back in. I was just gonna take it one day at a time. I wasn't ready to be exclusive to anybody, but ever since last night I felt like maybe I was. I'd been fuckin' bitches for a while, and maybe Rhys was right, having something stable did sound much better now that I was twenty-six. Damn, she already had me contradicting myself.

We pulled up to my parents' home in Mission Hill, and I shut the engine off. Rhys ashed the blunt he'd been puffing on, before we both climbed out of the car. I hit my alarm, and then walked up behind Rhys as he unlocked the door using his key.

When we walked in, it appeared that no one was home because it was quiet. Usually you would hear my mom on the phone with one of her old ass predator home girls who thought I wanted to fuck, or she would be handling business. Rhys and I tread through the foyer until we made it to my dad's office. We laughed because as we got closer, we could hear him going in on someone over the phone. My dad was psycho and I think we all got a little bit of his crazy, especially Rhys' ass.

"Have it by tomorrow." My dad slammed the phone down and then stood up wearing a smile. "Sit down boys," he gestured towards the couch.

We both took a seat, and I grabbed a cold water from the ice bucket near me. Rhys gave me a look, and I sucked my teeth before tossing him a cold water as well.

"I need you to meet with a new distributor down in South Carolina," my father said as I twisted the cap off of my water.

"South Carolina?" I frowned.

"Yeah, he's really making a name for himself."

"Who is this dude?"

"His name is Jasper Johnson and he knows we provide the best, which is what he wants. So TQ, go meet with him and take your brothers."

"When? And why do they need to come?"

"Well, Rhys knows why he needs to go, and Jasper has a couple people that he needs to get new identities for, so that's where Lendsey comes in. It's a little favor I'm doing for Jasper. I need Britain to check on a debt that is owed to me by someone out there named Charlie."

"When am I supposed to go? It can't be tonight."

"And why not?" My dad cocked his head and looked down at me with his matching bluish gray eyes before sitting down.

"Because this nigga is in love, Pop," Rhys laughed loudly.

"Really? Who is she?"

"Ain't nobody in no fuckin' love, aight? Shorty is fine as fuck and I want to take her out. Damn, can a nigga take a bitch out without having to explain to everybody?"

"I mean, TQ, you swore you would never settle down, no matter how many times Rhys and I have advised you and Lendsey."

"I ain't as bad as Lendsey. Britain is even worse than me."

"No, they're hoes, but you're bad as fuck too. Shit, at least Britain has a girl," Rhys said before gulping more of his water.

"I will admit that she had me thinking about trying to be in a relationship, but that's it, just thinking about it. I'm taking her on a date, and I can't say what will happen."

"Your mother would be proud. Wait until I tell her," my father grinned.

"Why are y'all acting like I'm getting married or some shit? I'm going on a date and I will probably never even see the girl again after that. Now what date is the meeting, Pop?"

"Well since you have a hot date tonight, how is Wednesday morning, gives you sometime to plan the wedding," he responded, causing he and Rhys to double over in laughter.

"Alright, fuck the both of y'all," I chuckled and stood to my feet.

"No, but seriously son, be in Columbia two weeks from today. I will let him know that you will be calling him once you land to set up a meeting time."

"Cool," I nodded.

I loved and hated my job. It got me big money, but I despised meeting these dope boys who always referred to themselves as the 'king' of their city. This Jasper cat better not be trying to get buck with me at all, because I wouldn't hesitate to pop his ass. I don't give a fuck about how many cities he runs, or how many bells his name rings, my bullets don't discriminate.

Chapter 9

KIMBERLYN

As soon as TQ dropped me off at home, I showered for a long ass time because I was thinking. I knew what I was possibly getting myself into by entertaining him, but for some reason that did nothing to deter me.

Stepping out of the shower, I began brushing my teeth while staring into the mirror. My grandmother and cousin Matikah were asleep when I walked through, and I was sure they were up by now. I did not feel like explaining myself, but unless I planned to move out right this very second, I would have to.

After flossing and rinsing, I darted to my bedroom and closed the door. I'd spotted Matikah on the couch fully dressed, so she must've showered while I was in the other bathroom. Once I put on my bra and panties, I smoothed lotion all over my body, and then put on some jean shorts, a crop top, and some sandals. Twisting my long thick hair up into a bun on my head, I walked out into the living room. Once Matikah and I made eye contact, we smiled at one another.

I sat down on the couch next to her, but before she could speak, my grandmother walked out from her room, tying her robe belt.

"Well look at what the cat dragged in. Please tell me you weren't with Gang."

"No, Ma, I was with someone else, but nothing happened." I put my hands up in mock surrender, making Matikah snap her neck to look at me.

"Who were you with?" my grandma furrowed her brows.

"This guy named Tarenz."

"TQ," Matikah jumped in, causing my grandmother to buck her eyes and fold her arms. I didn't say TQ because my grandmother knew who that was.

"Kimberlyn, be careful; he's not your typical corner boy or gangsta, that's a real life thug right there," my grandma shook her head. "He's nothing to play with. Neither was Gang but they're very different. Isn't he in a Russian mafia or something?"

"No Ma, and there is no need to worry, you know me."

"I do. Are you guys hungry? I'm gonna make waffles and oatmeal."

"Yes," Matikah and I responded in unison.

Matikah watched my grandmother until she disappeared into the kitchen, and then looked at me.

"Nothing happened?" she raised a brow.

"No Matikah, we kissed and got real close to doing it, but I stopped him."

"And he didn't threaten to shoot you?" she chuckled.

"Nope, I told him he needed to take me out first. I wouldn't feel right just losing my shit on some one-night stand. I'm too old for that. I've been holding onto it for this long."

"I get it. Well, what did he say to the date? Fuck no?"

"No bitch," I laughed. "He said he would, tonight. But who knows, he's probably fucking some other bitch right now. He was supposed to take me to breakfast, but something came up supposedly."

"Why supposedly? You do realize who he is, right Kimberlyn? Something coming up isn't odd for him, he's a busy man."

I felt stupid all of sudden. I hoped he hadn't changed his mind about taking me out since I'd been rude to him.

"I guess I was just paranoid."

"So are you gonna let him, tonight?"

"I want to, because I really want to have sex with him. But then I don't want to because I don't wanna regret it."

"Just see how you feel by the end of the date."

"I will. I saw you talking to his brother," I nudged her and bit my lip.

"Yeah, he's cute. I gave him my number, but I don't know, he has a bad reputation."

"What Quinton doesn't have a bad reputation, Matikah? People think too much; sometimes you just have to live your life."

"Where the fuck did you get that from? TQ?" she asked as we laughed together. "Yeah, he must've been really trying to get into your pants."

We ate breakfast in the kitchen and then went to sit down on the porch. The sun was really shining, and it was so beautiful out. The warmth of the air on my exposed skin made me smile as I watched people come up and down the sidewalk. I could never see myself living anywhere other than Boston. I may move out of Roxbury, but Boston—never.

"Hey," Goldie hit the alarm on her car, and sat on the step lower than where Matikah sat.

"Hey," I responded lowly. I didn't know how she felt about me leaving with TQ, so it was a bit awkward. I knew she wanted to scold me for being dumb, as she would say.

"You look tired," Matikah frowned.

"Thanks for the compliment, bitch," Goldie rolled her eyes and then took her purse from her arm. "So what happened last night, Kimberlyn?" She stretched her legs across the step before crossing them, and then leaned her back up against the rail.

"Nothing," I shrugged.

"You went home with Tarenz Quinton and nothing happened? Yeah right, I can see your hips spreading from here."

"Well your eyes are deceiving you, Goldie, because I didn't sleep with him. Well I did, but I didn't fuck him. All we did was kiss, talk, drink, and snack a bit." I leaned back on my elbows and frowned since the sun was in my eyes.

"Shit, bitch, your dumb as fuck. I would've been bouncing on that dick all night, and hopefully with no rubber so I could trap his sexy ass," she joked.

"You're terrible," Matikah giggled and I shook my head. For some reason I felt like TQ was mine now, and hearing her speak of him that way made me angry and jealous, even though I knew she was kidding.

"I need him to work a little bit more before I do all that."

"Work? Who are you, Rihanna? TQ don't work for no pussy and I don't blame him. He's got bitches yearning for him left and right, so if you think he's gonna start changing shit up for you, Kimberlyn, you're sadly mistaken. You should've taken that dick when it was in your face."

"He's taking her on a date tonight." Matikah stared down into Goldie's face.

"Yeah right," she shook her head.

"He is; we're going out tonight. I told him he needed to take me out and he's doing so. So Goldie, I guess you're wrong, TQ does work for pussy, ones he really wants." I cocked my head and she playfully rolled her eyes.

"I told you I was coming for him if I didn't get Britain," she said, making Matikah and me chuckle.

"Didn't you just give her a whole speech about fucking him?" Matikah frowned and pointed to me with her thumb. Shit, I was confused too.

"I don't care if she fucks him, but going on dates, Kimberlyn? It's like you're trying to be serious with him or something, and that's not cool for multiple reasons."

"Which are?" I asked still looking out at the people walking by.

"One-time dick is okay, but not what you're trying to do. And secondly, you're a good girl, Kimberlyn. You want the husband, the kids, the white picket fence, and TQ only wants his dick sucked, some pussy, money, drank, and blunts. That doesn't mix well."

I began massaging the crook in my neck as her words flowed through my mind. She was right in a sense that I wanted a family and real relationship, whereas TQ wanted a freak of the week. Still, nothing inside me was saying not to go on this date. I wanted to go. This was one of those times that I would have to learn the hard way.

"I will let you know how it goes, G," I responded and looked down into her eyes; she had some anger in them. She then looked away from me and shook her head.

"I care about you, Kimberlyn, and I don't want to see you miserable like I was when Ethan and I broke up," she explained. I understood where she was coming from, and I appreciated it, but I couldn't help it. I wanted TQ and bad.

After chilling with Matikah and Goldie for a bit, I left to get my eyebrows and nails redone, before returning home to take a little nap. I wanted to be well rested for my date tonight; if it even happened.

Chapter 10

TQ

This shit was weird. I was excited about taking Kimberlyn out, and that shit had me feeling like a whole 'nother nigga for real. I was not that nigga that took bitches out and shit, but for some reason I was all for it. It couldn't be that I liked her that much, because I just met her. Then again, maybe it was because I liked her little cute ass a lot. As my dad says, time and love have nothing to do with one another. This nigga married my mother only three weeks after meeting her. My dad and I were different though, or so I thought.

I pulled up to Kimberlyn's grandmother's on Seaver Street, and then swooped into a park by the curb. As I was exiting my Maserati, Kimberlyn came out of the door, slamming it behind her. She rushed down the stairs, but stopped once she got to the end of the walkway.

"Hey," she smiled as she walked closer to me but very slowly. She was wearing a red dress that had triangle holes on the side. It was short, but not slutty, it was just really sexy. She had red shoes on to match, and one little skinny watch. "I brought a bag like you suggested." She held the bag up.

"Good, you look sexy as fuck, shorty," I shook my head as I looked her up and down. She was so fuckin' fine and it made no damn sense. "Come on." I opened the door for her, and she slid into my car. After checking out her sexy legs, I closed it and jogged around to the driver's side.

"I like this car, and you look nice tonight as well. I love seeing you dressed up," she said once I got in.

"You've only seen me dressed up twice."

"And I liked it both times, nigga," she chuckled and flashed her pretty ass smile. *Damn.*

"My bad. Why didn't you let me come to the door for you? Now your grandma is gonna be thinking I'm some weak ass nigga."

"No she won't, and why do you care what she thinks? You wanna marry me or something?" she raised her brow. Why was she so bad?

"Nah, not even. Calm your little ass down with that ego, ma, I don't think I will ever get married."

"Then don't worry about what my grandmother thinks. And to answer your question, I came outside because I didn't want her questioning and bothering you."

"Thank you for that," I said, and we laughed together as I cranked the car up.

I drove to a port that was for personal planes, and then parked my car in the underground garage. Grabbing both of our bags, we headed up to the runway so we could board the plane.

We landed in New Haven, Connecticut a couple hours later, then my driver out here took us to my house in Bridgeport.

I kept a house out in Connecticut because it was peaceful. I rarely came, but when I did it was to clear my mind, or for special occasions. Tonight was special, although I hated to admit it, so I thought I would bring Kimberlyn here.

"Whose house is this, TQ?" she smiled as she looked out the window of my driver's car.

"Mine, shorty." I hopped out with her after the driver opened the door. I nodded to him before he got back into the truck and pulled off.

Once in the house, I showed Kimberlyn around, and then took her to the den to chill until the chefs finished with the food I was having them prepare for us.

"Wine or champagne?" I asked.

She smiled as she thought about it. I loved her fucking smile. It was so sincere and innocent, not conniving or seductive like the bitches I was used to. That's what attracted me to her; I was a regular ass nigga in her eyes so she had no interest in trying to seduce or swindle me.

"I want something fizzy, so I would like the champagne, please."

"You got it."

I filled the glasses then walked over to sit with her on the plush rug. I handed over the glass, and she took a sip as I set the bottle on the coffee table in front of us. Sipping my own, I used the remote to cut on the fireplace since it was cold *and* the room needed some light.

"So TQ, why do you have this big place here in Bridgeport, but that condo back in Boston?" she quizzed.

"I work a lot, and I'm mainly in Boston, so I prefer something small. I got this because sometimes I like to have a place to think, and sometimes I just wanna see what I work so hard for."

"I see...well, it is very nice."

"Have you ever had a boyfriend?" I furrowed my brows. She seemed so sinless, so I had to pry a bit.

"Yes, I've had two actually. Have you ever had a girlfriend?"

"Nope," I answered and we chuckled.

"Why not? You don't want a girlfriend?"

"I didn't, but now I'm thinking it may be something I'm interested in." I stared into her eyes, and saw her become uncomfortable. "You swear you've never been with Gang in anyway?"

"I swear. Why do you keep asking me that? You don't want anything serious with me, so why would it matter?"

I scooted closer to her as my eyes roamed all over her petite but alluring body. I pursed my lips because I was trying not to get hard as a rock.

"I'm asking because I want your ass, and even though I'm in denial just a little bit, I can admit it. And since I'm intrigued, I want to make sure Gang hasn't touched you."

"We kissed," she whispered.

"Which lips did he kiss?" I grinned and she shook her head at me.

"The top ones, I told you I'm a virgin." I already knew that since I saw him kiss her in the club the night I met her.

"In every way?"

"In every way."

"Excuse me, Mr. Quinton, the dinner is ready," the chef peeked into the large den.

"Thank you." I stood up, and then reached my hand down to help her up. I gripped her hand tightly, and before we walked out, I leaned down to kiss her full lips. I didn't care that they were covered in lipstick and shit.

"Ah," she giggled when I cupped her round ass in my hands. My dick was so hard right now that you could play the drums with it.

We went into the dining room, and I nodded my head as I took in the scenery. I paid someone to set this shit up because I wasn't the romantic type. Shit, I never had anybody that I needed to be romantic for. I wanted Kimberlyn to think I fixed this up myself though.

"You like it?" I asked as I pulled her chair out.

"Yes, I didn't think you could put something like this together."

"Well you're wrong, shorty, I did, aight?" I walked around and sat down at the table. When I did, I saw she was staring at me, smiling. "What?" I frowned.

"I know you didn't set this up, but the fact that you had someone do it is just as good," she chuckled and so did I.

Chapter 11

KIMBERLYN

"I'm glad you appreciate the thought," TQ smiled. He was so cute, and every time I heard his voice or saw that enticing smile, I just wanted to jump across the table on him.

"I do."

A chef came out and set down two martini glasses holding shrimp cocktails. There was shrimp around the rims of the glasses, with crushed ice and a dollop of marinara sauce on top of it. TQ was about to dig in, but I reached across the table to grab his tattooed hands into mine.

"We have to pray, Tarenz," I said, using his real name.

"Aight," he huffed.

I prayed over our food then we began tearing into the shrimp. Halfway through that, the chef returned with teriyaki glazed salmon, jasmine rice, and asparagus. It smelled good as hell, and I hoped we were able to get seconds.

"Do you like salmon? I wasn't sure, ma," TQ looked at me, bearing an innocent expression. I inhaled sharply just to get another whiff of his cologne before responding. It was so cute that he cared about impressing me and getting the food I liked. I didn't expect that from him.

"Yeah I do, good job."

We devoured the food, and for dessert we had a slice of maple pecan pie with cinnamon ice cream on top. After polishing off our champagne, TQ showed me to the bathroom so I could empty my bladder.

I came back out into the humungous den, and just admired it for a bit. The floors were laminate, but there was a huge piece of plush white carpet covering the middle areas of it. There was a fireplace up against the wall, which was currently burning and warming the room perfectly. Adjacent to that was a huge bay window with no curtains. You could see the whole city of Bridgeport when you looked out of it. There was a bench attached to it, perfect for sitting and just admiring the comings and goings of the Connecticut people.

"Feel better?" TQ asked as he removed his jacket and sat down on the plush carpet area. I walked over to him, and removed my shoes so that I could join him.

"Yes, much better. So Tarenz, tell me something about your family. I only know, or I've heard that you guys are just a bunch of rich ass criminals." I watched as he opened another bottle of champagne and poured some into my glass. His pecan skin glistened every time the light from the fire flickered.

"Well, that part is true. I don't really know what else to tell you. I have three brothers, Rhys, Britain, and Lendsey, and then I have a sister, Saya. Saya is the oldest, and I'm the third to last, with Lendsey and Britain being the baby boys."

"I see, and what do you do to help your family?" I sipped my drink.

"I import narcotics into the U.S., and have them delivered to people like Gang. I do it by plane. I really don't want to tell you this."

"Why?"

"For your safety, shorty. If shit pops off, I don't want you to have any knowledge about this. So that's what I do and I'm gonna stop right there."

"So you work with Gang?"

"Yeah, I do, he gets his stuff from me. I work with him, a cat from New York, Pennsylvania, and soon South Carolina."

"I can tell you make a lot of money from it."

"I do. Now your turn, shorty, I don't like talking about myself too much. I'm not that interesting."

"You are to me."

I moved closer to him, and he pulled me into his lap so that I was straddling him. I could feel his dick hardening under me, and from the feeling I knew it was big. I suddenly became a little bit afraid, and I knew he could tell.

"Don't be scared, Kimberlyn," he whispered and removed the champagne flute from my hand. I hesitantly rested my hands on his broad shoulders as he kissed on my collarbone and squeezed my ass.

He stood up with me still straddling him, and then carried me upstairs to his bedroom. I was so scared that my palms were starting to sweat, and I had no idea what was gonna happen. Once we got to his bedroom, he moved the light slider up just a little so that there was light but the room was still dim. Placing me to my feet, he reached behind me and unzipped my dress slowly while sucking my lips. My dress fell to my ankles, and he stepped back away from me. His eyes danced all over my body as he removed his own clothing.

"Take your bra off," he instructed.

I reached behind myself slowly and unclasped my bra, before sliding it down my arms. I nervously tousled my long dark locks, as he stared at my physique for what seemed like an eternity. He pulled his wife beater off, and his body had my full fucking attention. Every peck in his abdomen was perfectly placed there. It was as if I'd never seen it before. His arms were so strong, and his chest was too. He didn't look disproportionate either. He was perfect, even though hundreds of tattoos covered his body.

He walked near me, and when he got super close and towered over me with his muscular frame, I stepped back a little in fear. He pulled me back close to him and dipped his tongue into my mouth. I loved kissing him. His lips were so soft. I reached my hand up to caress his beard as he backed me to the bed before lightly pushing me down.

We moved to the middle of the bed, and he immediately got my lace panties off. I wasn't sure how he did it so fast. *This nigga is a pro, Kimberlyn, are you ready for this?*

"TQ," I panted as he sucked on my nipples like he was trying to suck the gold out of them. His big, strong hands groped and squeezed all over my small frame as his tongue went to town on my nipples. "Tssss," I whispered as he nibbled on them a little bit. It was painful but pleasurable as well.

He reached his hand between my legs, and began to move them around slowly while he sucked. When he'd had enough, he trailed his soft lips down my flat stomach, and then tugged on my belly ring with his perfect teeth.

"I wanna make you cum," he looked up into my eyes as he began to kiss my lower lips.

He pressed my thighs against my stomach, and then began slowly making love to my center with his mouth. I loved the feeling of his lips on my body. My back arched, and I threw my head back as he began to suck on my button.

"Tareeennzz," I called out his government name. I'd seen this shit in plenty of movies and had heard about it, but if I had have known it felt this good I would have been gotten some head from someone.

"Ooh shit," he smiled and bit his lip as he watched me cum. As soon as I finished releasing, he dove back in and continued feasting.

He had me breathing super hard, and gripping the fuck out of the sheets. My body was covered in sweat, and I knew my press was done for. I tried to move up, but he gripped my small waist tightly into his hands, and continued devouring me like a lunatic.

"Aaaah!" I screamed louder than I knew I could as I exploded yet again. "Please TQ," I pleaded as he kissed between my legs slowly. I tucked my bottom lip into my mouth as I watched him, not knowing what he was gonna do next.

"You want me to fuck you?" he stood on his knees and I nodded. "No, tell me you want me to fuck you, Kimberlyn," he demanded.

"I want you to fuck me, TQ."

"After I fuck you, Kimberlyn, this pussy is mine."

"I know," I nodded.

"Don't even think about letting another nigga fuck you or touch you."

Again, I nodded.

He pushed his boxers down, and his dick popped out immediately. I felt like that shit was gonna poke me in the fucking eye. He got down off the bed to completely remove them, and then came back close to me.

"Sit up," he said. I sat up and he waved me over. I crawled to him on the bed, and once I got close, he began rubbing his dick on my lips. "Think of it as a popsicle. No teeth."

I opened my mouth slowly, and began to move my mouth down. Suddenly, he grabbed a handful of my hair, stopping me in my tracks.

"Watch your teeth, shorty."

He loosened his grip on my hair, and I resumed moving my mouth down. Still clutching my hair loosely, he guided me up and down his long and thick rod, until I began to get the hang of it. Every time I forgot about my teeth, he would grip a handful of my hair tightly to let me know. Soon enough, I was able to suck without thinking, and he began humping my face.

"Just like that Kimberlyn, fuck," he groaned as he moved my mouth up and down his dick, still grasping my hair. "This is the only dick you suck, you hear me?" he added and I just looked up into his eyes as I continued to please him. "Shit baby, fuck," he grumbled again. "Go as far down as you can." He humped my face slowly and began doing so in a circular motion. All of a sudden, he grumbled loudly, and I felt a warm liquid spill into my mouth. "Take it down."

I did as I was told, and since it didn't taste like anything I was fine. He laid me on my back, and reached into his drawer for a condom. I watched as he rolled it down his dick, and the sight of it made my legs tremble.

"You good, baby?" he asked and when I nodded, he laid down on top of me.

"TQ, I wanna be with you." I stared into his eyes, waiting for his response.

"Like my girlfriend?"

"Yeah." I knew this was moving fast, but I was always the honest type, so I had to say what I felt.

He continued to stare down into my eyes and then pecked my lips gently before pulling away.

"Do you know what it would be like, being the girlfriend of a nigga like me?"

"I don't care; I want to be."

He chuckled very lightly to the point where it was almost unnoticeable. He pinned my hands above my head, and I felt him poking at my hole.

"If you wanna be my girl, Kimberlyn, you gotta promise to ride for me no matter what, aight? And I will do the same for you. You know what it is I do, and I need someone who can be by my side and not get scared and shit."

"I can, I'm strong," I responded and he laughed.

"Remember what you're saying, shorty. I'm gonna hold you to it. You stuck with a nigga now, just so you know."

"Good."

He kissed me so hard our noses were pressing into one another. I felt his dick at my opening again, right before he slipped his arms under my thighs to push them back.

"Stay calm, baby, so that we can both feel good," he said before kissing my cheek, and then trailing it to my neck.

"Ahh, ahh, uuuh," I whimpered as he pushed into me. His strong arms were under my thighs, and his hands were pinning my arms down at my side so that I couldn't move a muscle. He kept going into me, and I was wondering how much dick he had left. "Uuuh, aaah, Tarenz."

"Shit, yo," he groaned as he began to move in and out of me. He pinned my arms down harder as he glided in and out. Seeing the pleasure in his face was remarkable. "Your pussy is so tight, I'm gonna be able to feel when you cum," he whispered before biting my lips.

Although it was super painful, it somehow felt good too. I knew I was gonna have another orgasm any minute now. He began sucking and biting my nipples again, before speeding up his thrusts a bit. I exploded so hard that I was sure I wet up his bed sheets. He removed his arms from under my thighs, and immediately pinned my hands behind my head. I locked my legs around his waist, and he went to town before calling out and cumming himself. He began kissing my sweaty neck, so I lifted his face and brought his lips to mine.

"Am I yours?" I asked.

"You've been mine."

I woke up the next morning, and rolled over to see that TQ was gone. An uneasy feeling immediately came over me as I scanned the bedroom. I blew out hot air, and then climbed out of the bed slowly. My vagina was in pain from him fucking me all night until 5am. I grabbed my duffle bag, and then went into the bathroom within his room so I could take a shower.

I set all my stuff down on the sink area, closed the door, and then sat down on the toilet to pee while admiring the huge ass bathroom for the hundredth time. When I urinated it burned a little, and when I wiped, there was a little bit of blood there still. I flushed, washed my hands, and brushed my teeth before climbing into the shower.

As soon as I stepped in, the warm water cascaded down my body, soothing my aching muscles. I was worried about where TQ had gone, and was hoping he hadn't just been saying bullshit to me. I know we just met, but I felt something strong with him. I wasn't that girl who fell in love easily either. It would be reason to stop the presses if I even liked someone, hence the reason I was twenty-one and still untouched. Anyway, if he did call himself playing me, we were gonna have a big ass problem.

I finished washing my body, and then got out to wrap myself in a towel. Coming out of the room, I still didn't see him, so I sighed heavily.

"Ah!" I screamed when I felt someone grab me from behind. "TQ, what the fuck!"

"You thought I ditched your little ass?" He started kissing on my neck and removing the towel from my body.

"No," I lied.

"Right." He pushed me down onto the chaise lounge so that I was on all fours. He then pressed my head down so that my ass was in the air, before removing his boxers.

"TQ, be gentle, I'm still sore."

He paused and then sat down on the chaise. Yanking me into his lap gently, he placed my legs on the outside of his, and pressed my back against his chest. Lifting me just a little, he slowly brought me down onto his dick, making me wince in pain. He reached his hand around to play with my clit as he slowly bounced me in his lap, and despite my soreness, it felt bomb. I gripped the armrest of the chaise lounge for leverage, as he pounded into me feverishly yet with precision.

"You look so sexy," he whispered and sucked on my neck from behind.

I couldn't talk because I was cumming too hard to do anything else. He wrapped his strong arm around my midsection, and then humped upward until he came inside of me.

"Are you on birth control?" he panted while cupping my breasts and sucking my shoulders.

"I will get some."

"Cool." Moving me off of his dick, he then gripped my neck to kiss me nastily. "Get dressed, Kimberlyn."

"You're taking me home already?"

"Relax shorty, I'm gonna take you out for the day. You're my girl, ain't you?" he raised a brow. I just nodded with a wide ass smile.

Chapter 12

MATIKAH

I HADN'T SEEN MY COUSIN IN ALMOST TWO DAYS, AND I WAS HOPING HER ass was okay. She slipped out of the house to go on her date with TQ, and the bitch hadn't been back since. She wasn't answering her phone either, and I was starting to worry. Kimberlyn never ignored me, and I just prayed that she was enjoying herself and not thrown into a ditch somewhere. TQ wasn't exactly a church boy.

"You ain't seen Kimberlyn?" Goldie quizzed as we walked down her street, headed to the liquor store.

She'd been pressing me about finding out where Kimberlyn was, because she didn't want my cousin hanging with TQ. And with the way shit was right now, I didn't want her with him either.

"I told your ass I hadn't seen her." I shook my head and turned my lip up.

"You think she's still with TQ?"

"Where else would she be? If she wasn't with him she would be home."

"I told her not to go with him. I bet you he fucked her and threw her out on the road somewhere," Goldie burst into laughter so I pushed her ass. Her foot slid out the side of her sandal, and she wobbled a bit to catch herself.

"Stop saying shit like that, damn."

"Calm your ass down, Matikah. You push me like that again we're gonna be fighting in this bitch!" She dusted herself off as if she needed to, while subtly looking around to make sure no one saw.

"Whatever." I waved her off while laughing.

As we were about to enter the liquor store, a navy blue Porsche Panamera with super dark tint slowed down beside us. Goldie and I looked at one another, and then back at the car. It seemed as if I stopped breathing as I waited for the driver or passenger to reveal themselves. The window slowly rolled down, building our anticipation, and finally Lendsey Quinton's beautiful mug came into view.

He was grinning widely, right before hopping out of his car to jog onto the sidewalk. His car was still running, with the music playing loudly from his sound system. His smooth brown complexion was glistening, right along with his jewelry and bottom grill. He was rocking a white and gray crew neck, black jeans, and some white and gray Adidas.

Turning his baseball cap to the back, he said, "Matikah, why the fuck you ain't been answering my texts, ma?"

"I, umm, I've just been busy," I lied.

I unfortunately let Goldie get into my head, and I didn't want to entertain Lendsey at all. I knew he was no good, and I refused to let myself get caught up in that. But seeing him right now, and being in his presence again had me feeling the opposite of what I'd been feeling these past few days.

"Well you ain't busy now, so come on." He waved me over and then walked to get into his car as if I was supposed to just come.

"Lendsey—"

"Get yo' ass in the car, ma."

"Bitch, you better not go. I told you he ain't shit," Goldie gritted under her breath, gripping my bicep into her hand.

"I'm just gonna chill with him, aight?"

"Matikah!" Lendsey barked from inside of his car. He'd turned his music down and was staring at me, stroking his beard. This nigga was gorgeous.

"Talk to you later, G."

I rushed to Lendsey's car, and then held my dress at my thighs while sliding in so that it wouldn't rise up. I low-key checked my appearance in his side mirror to make sure my low curly ponytail was still slicked down and intact.

"You good shorty, chill out," Lendsey chuckled before peeling down the street. I guess I wasn't too low-key.

His windows were all the way down, and he was driving so damn fast that the wind was stopping me from breathing. He dipped through the streets of Mattapan, until we were out of the neighborhood. I glanced over at him every now and then, admiring how fine he was. Because we weren't talking, I pulled my phone out and began to scroll on Instagram, hoping I would see a post from Kimberlyn. Nothing.

Finally, we pulled up to a condo on Colborne Street in Brighton. It was pretty nice, but not what I expected from someone like Lendsey. I thought he would have some huge mansion with naked hoes walking all around it and carrying silver trays.

"This is your home? Or is this just where you're taking me?" I looked over at him as he pulled into his parking space.

"Both," he replied before slipping out.

He came around to open my door, and then we went inside his condo. Now the inside was more of what I expected. Everything was furnished beautifully, and looked just like those houses in the *Home* magazines. The air was even fresher and much cooler than it was outside. Boston was usually windy, but this summer it was scorching, so feeling this air against my skin was a blessing right now.

"Sit down, ma, you hungry or thirsty?"

"What, you were gonna cook me some food?" I raised a brow before sitting down on his L-shaped gray couch. It was so soft that I thought I was gonna sink into it.

"No, have you ever heard of take out? Or are you too busy in the library studying?" he grinned as we both laughed.

"Fuck you, what, you trying to call me a square, nigga?"

"Nah, I'm not, actually. I can tell you're a good girl though, am I right?"

"Maybe, but I will take some water please, I'm dehydrated from it being so hot outside."

"Got you."

He went into his kitchen and returned a few moments later with some water. I cracked it open and then downed it for longer than I'd intended. He stared at me for a couple moments, and then set his water on the coffee table in front of us before speaking.

"So tell me why my texts went ignored?"

"Do you want me to be honest?"

"That's preferred."

"Because I know what you're like and I want no parts of it." I gulped some more water, trying to calm my unexpected nervousness.

"Word? I don't know you, so I'm not sure how you know me. But please, inform me, Matikah." He draped one of his arms across the back of the couch, hitting me with a whiff of his cologne.

"Well, you're a player and you have no idea what fidelity is," I said and looked into his eyes. I could tell by how big his perfect smile was that I was right. His bluish gray eyes were like pretty pools of water as he searched my face with them, trying to think of something clever to sway me. "See, I knew I was right." We chuckled in unison.

"I mean, so what. Yeah, I get around, but I'm newly twenty-four and I don't have a girl. Why should I not enjoy myself with the many beautiful women who throw themselves at me?"

"Because it's disgusting. I hope you wear condoms."

"Aye, I like to fuck, but I ain't no nasty nigga. Bitches are just as promiscuous as niggas, and I would never slide up in them easies with no cap."

"I'm glad you're smart about it," I smiled.

"So what's your story? Are you some man-eater or what? You look like you fuck with niggas heads, I think that's what made me like your ass."

"I'm no man eater. I've had a couple almost boyfriends, but it just didn't work out. I ain't really looking for anyone."

"What if someone is looking for you?" He tilted his head to the side, as his eyes took in my body. His bottom lip was tucked into his mouth, and by the way his eyes were glazed over, I could tell he had all kinds of lustful thoughts floating around in his dome.

"Someone like you?"

"Yeah someone like me, girl, why the fuck you think I got you up in my crib? I like your ass, and despite what you have heard, I'm really not that bad," he palmed his chest.

"Oh, you're not?"

"Nah, I'm not."

As if it were a coincidence, his cellphone rang and the name Dania flashed across the screen. Jealousy overcame me, even though I didn't know him at all and had no right to be jealous.

"Can you take me home please, I forgot I promised my grandmother I would help her cook tonight's dinner." I rose to my feet.

"Matikah, that's just a friend th—"

"No, I promise it's not that, I really need to help my grandmother. Could you just give me a ride home? Thank you." I started towards his door, but not before hearing him sigh.

I wasn't about to fuck with Lendsey's ass at all.

Chapter 13

LENDSEY QUINTON

The whole ride to Matikah's grandmother's house, she didn't say shit to me. I knew she was mad about seeing Dania's name, and to me that was perplexing. I mean, I just met her ass and she really had no right to be mad about shit. I'd just explained to her ass that I was no saint, so she shouldn't have expected me to have zero bitches hittin' my damn phone.

"So are we ever gonna chill again? Or did big daddy scare you off?" I asked as I pulled up to her grandma's house that she'd directed me to.

"Nigga please, I told you I had to help my grandma so calm down."

"What kind of fool do you take me for, ma? You saw a bitch calling my line and got pissed. The shit is all in your pretty ass face."

She looked away from me, and then back into my eyes. I knew I was right. I knew women like the back of my hand. They stayed getting mad about shit that they shouldn't have been getting mad about, and then they wanted you to fix it even though you didn't even know why they were mad. Besides the fact that I loved to get my dick wet, that was a reason why I stayed on my bachelor shit.

"We can be friends, Lendsey, but don't be trying to flirt and shit because it won't go there. I like guys who can be with one girl, and that's not you, so don't waste my time."

"Aye, don't be acting like you know me, shorty. Go help your grandma before a nigga spring that good shit on you and make you fall in love."

"Right," she giggled and then grabbed the lever to open the door.

I watched her walk up the steps as the words she'd just spoken circled my mind. She was right about everything she said, but something in me wouldn't let her go that easily. If only a nigga lived in Africa or some shit where I could have fifteen wives. Then again, I would never marry any of these hoes, except Matikah.

I pulled off, and headed towards the hair salon that Dania was at. I knew she was calling me because she was ready, and it made me wish I'd never promised to pick her ass up. But being a man of my word, I had to do what I'd said.

"Damn, Len! What the fuck took you so long!" she spat, throwing her Louis Vuitton bag into my back seat.

As soon as she got in, the smell of hairspray and shit hit me in the face. I swear I loved the way she looked with her hair like that, but I hated that burnt chip smell it came with on the first few days.

"My bad, I was busy."

"Busy doing what, Lendsey? Because Rosie told me she saw you dipping through Mattapan with some bitch!"

"Aye! Quit all that muthafuckin' yelling in my fuckin' car, Dania! Firstly, Rosie is a hoe that wants to suck my dick, and secondly, you ain't my damn girl so I do what the fuck I want!" I barked as I sped down the street.

Dania was like my super unofficial ass girlfriend. We spent time together, but she was not my girl in any way, shape or form, in my eyes that is. On her end, we were in love and building, but over here, she was just some constant pussy. Dania was sexy, could fuck and suck, and she was smart. She wasn't like the normal gold digging bitches who wanted me to break them off all the time. Dania had a job. She worked as an insurance agent selling policies and shit, and she made a nice amount of money.

My problem with Dania was her mouth, and the fact that she was sneaky. She was always trying to check me, knowing that she and I weren't even like that. She'd fought plenty of girls that I'd dealt with, and once fought my cousin because she thought she was a bitch I was fuckin' with. I'd cut her off plenty of times, but every time she would threaten to kill herself, and the pussy was hella good so I would find myself backpedalling.

On top of her acting like a wild banshee on occasions, she would try and do little sneaky shit. She would attempt to get drunk together so that I would hit raw, or one time she lied to me and said she was on birth control so that I would. When I asked the bitch to show me the pills, she couldn't come through. I could never, and would never wife a bitch like Dania. I planned to be single my whole life, but Matikah had me wondering. I knew if I messed with her, however, she wouldn't allow me to continue on with my lifestyle. Maybe she was worth it, who knows.

"Hello, nigga!" Dania snapped in my face, causing me to come up out of my head.

"What the fuck I tell you about snapping at me, Dania? You know what, I'm taking yo' ass home, I ain't got time for this shit."

"Who was the bitch, Len?"

I stayed silent as I raced through Boston to get her ass to her home in Jamaica Plain. I couldn't get this hoe out of my car fast enough. She and Matikah were so damn different, and I enjoyed that. I loved that Matikah was so calm and not all loud and boisterous like Dania's ass.

"Get out," I pulled up to her condo.

"Babe, I'm sorry, you know how I am," she stated in a calmer tone, and then ran her soft hand across my dick.

"Get the fuck out, shorty. I'm a millisecond away from knocking your teeth of ya mouth, now get out." I stared straight ahead, waiting for her ass to exit stage left.

"I swear I didn't mean it. Call me later, baby, and I will make it up to you. I love you." She leaned over and kissed my cheek before getting out.

Once the door closed, I looked in her direction and cringed at the tattoo of my name on her left breast. Dania was like that single strand of hair that took the most just to get off of you.

Chapter 14

GOLDIE

Since Matikah's ass ditched me, I decided to just get some food so I could go home to chill. Not having to attend class was cool for the summer, and since I only worked on Mondays and Wednesdays, I had a lot more free time.

I walked into Tasty Burger on Boylston, and my mouth was already watering at the thought of tasting that burger. I couldn't wait to bite into it and see all the cheese in it. I was a naturally small girl, so I could eat how I wanted. My mom claimed she used to be the same way, so now that she looked like a triple scoop waffle cone, I tried to make sure I worked out here and there to prevent that from happening to me down the line.

I placed my order, getting the big tasty burger and a side salad, then I sat down to wait. I was gonna have water to drink, so I didn't need to get anything here. I knew it was weird to get a salad as a side with a burger, but I was eccentric like that.

As I sat in the steel chair, my phone chimed, and I saw it was a text from Ethan. He'd been doing a great job, but I was thinking it was only because I hadn't let him fuck yet. He talked to me a lot, and came over almost every night unless I told him he couldn't. I don't know though, for some reason I wasn't feeling it like I had been in the past. I used to love being around him all the time, but lately I found myself becoming annoyed upon seeing that *on my way* text. A couple times I pretended not to see it, and just didn't respond. He wasn't stupid enough to just show up, and if he did, I wouldn't answer the door anyway.

Ethan: *Hey, see you tonight?*

I sighed as I reread the text, just as a figure stood in front of me. When I looked up, there was a skinny girl who was lighter than me, and had a short ass ponytail. She was pretty, but the fact that she felt it was okay to rock that comma ponytail took away from her looks.

"Is there a problem?" I quizzed, confused by the scowl she bore on her face.

"I came to let you know that Ethan is taken and you need to get over the relationship, boo," she rolled her neck as she spoke each word.

I stared at her and couldn't help but to laugh. Was she serious? I'd never seen nor heard of her, and I'd seen plenty of bitches that Ethan fucked with. The way she was coming at me, you would think that I would know who the fuck she was. The fact that I'd *never* seen her showed how low on the totem pole of Ethan's hoes she was.

"Girl, don't nobody want Ethan like that."

"I beg to differ, I've seen your name pop up on his phone many of times and I'm tired of it. I've been looking for you for a while now."

"To do what exactly, boo? Like I said, don't nobody want Ethan. And you should delve deeper into your investigations, because then you would see he always texts me first." I stood up. She was about 5'10", so she was a nice amount taller than me who stood at 5'4", but I didn't care. I was no punk.

"That's funny, because he was just telling me that he couldn't get rid of you."

"Oh really? Was it before or after he cleaned my pussy juice from his beard? Because not too long ago he was eating me out like it was going out of style."

She immediately shoved me back, and once I caught my balance we began going at it. We were flying all over the place as we swung at one another. She gripped my hair in her hands and began pulling so hard that tears came out of my eyes.

"Hey!" someone inside yelled. I assumed it was a worker of Tasty Burger.

I couldn't take the pain of her pulling my locks any longer, so I assaulted the only thing I could; those double D cup tits in my face. Chomping down on one, I gritted my teeth causing her to scream out and let go of my hair. She began screaming while pushing my head away, but I kept my grip on her boob as if my life depended on it. Finally, I was pulled off by some random bitch who I snatched away from.

"Take your food and go!" the employee yelled to me, handing me my bag. She then turned to the bitch and told her to leave as well.

As I turned to walk out, my heart fell into the pit of my stomach when I spotted Britain in the doorway. He was with some girl, and they were holding hands. We made eye contact, before I rushed past them both in embarrassment. Tears spilled down my cheeks as all kinds of emotions ran through me. I was upset with Ethan for playing me yet again, and then I was ashamed that Britain had witnessed me acting like some local hood rat.

I ended up passing my car, so I turned around to go back. As I walked, some girl switched up into the parking lot holding a baby.

"Here Juanita, he's wet." She handed the baby to the girl I'd just fought who was massaging her sore boob. "You out here actin' crazy over that nigga when you know he ain't shit!" she added as they walked to their car. They didn't notice me staring nor eavesdropping.

"I got his baby, so I mean more to him than these bitches, aight Aisha?" Juanita snapped before climbing into the car.

The mention of her having Ethan's baby was like a dagger to my heart. Although my love for him had dwindled severely over time, that bit of information still hurt. I loved him, at one point deeply, but he clearly didn't feel the same and he never would.

When I got into my car, my phone rang and I saw it was him. I decided to answer because I wanted to see if he knew what happened, and what he had to say about it.

"Hello," I picked up.

"Hey baby, I was thinking we could go to the movies tonight."

"I met Juanita," I stated dryly.

"Hello? Goldie? Hello?" he responded after a few moments of silence, and I just scoffed and hung up. That was the best he could come up with? Pretending the phone was going out?

Right when I dropped my phone into the passenger seat, I spotted Britain walking out of Tasty Burger with that girl whose hand he was holding. She was all over him like white on rice, yet he seemed to not be as interested as she was in whatever they had. He glanced over and caught me looking, so I promptly turned away and cranked my car. I was better off staying my ass in the house.

Chapter 15

KIMBERLYN

A COUPLE DAYS LATER…

TQ and I had just left The Paramount on Charles Street where we had a nice big lunch. He promised to take me to the mall, but he got a call and had to tend to some business. I really liked being with him, but I just hated that he was like a doctor on call or something. He was always answering his phone, sighing, and having to leave.

"You promise you're gonna come back to get me?" I looked over at him with my arms folded across my chest. I hadn't even known him that long, yet I felt so needy.

"I promise. Have I lied to you yet?"

"No," I smiled and tousled my hair from one side to the other.

"Aight then, I'm gonna be back. Pack clothes for the week."

I nodded as I hit the seat belt release button. I then leaned across the center console, letting my lips meet his. Once they did, I gripped his face lightly in my hands to introduce our tongues. I couldn't help but to close my eyes as we kissed one another like we'd just been pronounced man and wife.

"Go on, ma," he chuckled and nudged me back lightly. I pecked him once more, before grabbing my duffle bag and getting out.

Rushing up my grandmother's porch steps, I turned around to watch him speed down my street, and hook a right on Columbia Road.

"Well, well, well," Matikah came out onto the porch, and when I turned around I saw Goldie standing behind her. I knew she was about to get in my ass about spending all my time with TQ. I hadn't been home since our date, and they'd both contacted me but got no response.

"Excuse me, ladies," I half smiled and walked past them.

"Kimberlyn, I thought your little ass had died or something!" my grandma came out wearing her favorite apron.

"Nope, just had a very nice date. Excuse me, Grandma, I'm gonna take a nap." I rushed to my room, and I could hear Goldie and Matikah right on my heels. I tried to close my door behind me, but Matikah put her foot there before she and Goldie slipped in, shutting my door behind them.

"I want every fucking detail, hoe." Matikah sat in the chair in my room while Goldie sat on my bed with me.

"He flew me to his big ass house in Bridgeport, and he had a professional chef serve us a full course meal, dessert included. After that, we drank champagne and we talked. The days after that have been just as good."

"Kimberlyn, did you fuck him? That's what the fuck we really wanna know," Goldie looked at me with a semi happy face. I chuckled lightly at her excitement.

I glanced from her to Matikah a couple times, and then nodded my head 'yes' making she and Matikah squeal loudly.

"Did it hurt?" Goldie frowned.

"Yeah, a lot, and he's so freaky," I replied while laughing. I looked over at Goldie, and she was laughing but her jaw was on the floor.

"I can't believe you let him play you, Kimberlyn. I thought you were smarter than that, boo." Goldie shook her head, coming down from her temporary joy.

"How exactly did he play me?"

"He got in your pants and you haven't even known him for two weeks! This is TQ, all he wants is sex, and once he gets it he's done with you, I told you that!"

"He took her out though, Goldie. That should mean something," Matikah chimed in, defending me.

"He took her out, in another state and inside a home. He wouldn't dare take you out around Boston, and you should be happy he didn't. If word gets out that you have any connection to Tarenz Quinton, these hoes will make your life hell."

"He took me to lunch this afternoon in Boston, aight? So he ain't hiding shit. And I don't care about these bitches. That's my man and ain't nobody gonna get me away from him."

"Your man? Really?" Matikah bucked her eyes as she played with one of my fuzzy chair pillows.

"Yeah, he told me we were together. He said I needed to be strong, and that I had to be his rider," I stuck my tongue out and playfully popped my ass, making Matikah giggle.

"You have to be strong because of all the bitches he's gonna smash," Goldie scoffed and sighed, but I just rolled my eyes.

"No, he meant because of the business that he's in. He didn't say shit about me turning a blind eye. And if that is what he meant, we would not be together."

"You already gave him your v-card, you can't just leave," Goldie frowned.

"Oh yes I can."

"Both of you are gonna give me a heart attack. The Quinton brothers are only good for one thing, and that's getting some dick. Trying to be in a relationship with them, is like trying to stir oil and water together," Goldie attempted to explain.

She was gonna give herself gray hair if she kept worrying about us the way she did. I loved her though, and although she was annoying sometimes, I caught her drift.

"Both of us? What do you mean?" I turned my attention to Matikah.

"I went to Lendsey's condo a couple days ago to chill. It was cool until some bitch called his phone, so I asked him to take me home."

"Why did you get mad? He's not even your man, Matikah?"

"Because I already know how he is. Why would I even dabble with that?"

Matikah was right. TQ, Rhys, Britain, and Lendsey all had reputations with the ladies, but Lendsey and Britain were notorious. They'd smashed so many girls, that it was a surprise that they didn't have any children. I didn't blame Matikah for stopping while she was ahead. I'd even heard that Lendsey had a girlfriend who claimed him, but he only claimed her behind closed doors. To make a long story short, he was just a mess.

"So I have something to tell you guys, but you can't get mad," Goldie glanced back and forth between Matikah and I.

"No promises," I said as we waited for her to spill.

"Ethan showed up and I agreed to give him a second chance."

"Why—"

"Wait, let me finish. So we were doing okay, but for some reason I wasn't feeling it like usual. Then one day while I was getting some food from Tasty's, some hoe walks in and presses me. We got to fighting, but the Tasty employee broke it up. But get this, he has a son with that bitch, and worst of all, Britain Quinton witnessed me acting like a Jerry Springer guest," she exhaled heavily and shook her head at herself.

"This nigga has a kid? You know what, I'm not even surprised about that shit. He was always a slut, and I hope you got an STD test," Matikah scoffed.

"I didn't let him fuck me," Goldie turned her lip up as if the mere thought disgusted her.

"Good. Fuck Ethan, Goldie. I know you loved him, but it's time to move on. Even you said yourself that this short lived hundredth chance you gave him didn't feel the same," I said.

"Yeah," she nodded slowly.

"Kimberlyn, you have a visitor," my grandmother peeked into my bedroom.

"Who?" I frowned.

"Saadiq," she responded, using Gang's real name.

"Ooooh shit!" Goldie and Matikah said in unison once my grandmother left out.

I stood up, but slowly, because I was still in pain from TQ fucking the shit out of me all night. I walked out of my room, through the living room, and then out the door to see Gang sitting on the large porch steps with his back to the door. I crept up behind him, and then sat down next to him.

After staring straight ahead for a couple moments, he looked to his right at me and said, "You look nice."

I was wearing some blue skinny jeans, with a heather gray crop top and sandals. My long dark hair was hanging down my back, and I had on some gold hoop earrings.

"Thank you."

"Where have you been, Kimberlyn? I haven't seen you since you left my VIP to hang with umm, them Quintons." I could hear the anger in his tone even though he was trying to mask it.

"That was just two weeks ago."

"I know, but I've dropped by a handful of times since then and you were gone every time. I came by the night of the party, a couple times after that, and then I came by yesterday evening," he looked at me and then back out into the street. I felt so bad every time we made eye contact.

"Gang, I—"

"Don't lie, Kimberlyn."

"I was with TQ those times you came over." Before I'd even finished, Gang was laughing and shaking his head.

"With TQ, huh? You know he's just fucking with you to piss me off, he don't really want you like that, Kimberlyn." I felt him look at me, but I just stared into the street.

"I thought you guys worked together, why would he do something like that to you?"

"I don't know, but he saw you ned I were kicking it, and now all of a sudden he wants you? Come on now."

"Gang, it wasn't like that, he likes me for real and he and I are together. You have to go because I don't want people telling him I was talking to you." I stood to my feet. TQ made it clear that I needed to cease all contact with Gang.

"Wooooow Kimberlyn, are you fucking serious? Do you know who the fuck I am? Boston is my muthafuckin' city! You need to be thankful that I even wanted your hoe ass!" he barked and stood up as well.

"Then as the *King*, you should have no problem getting a new girl to fuck with, Gang." I turned around and he grabbed my arm, but not roughly.

"Kimberlyn—"

"Gang, you have to go, I told you I don't want anyone to see us. I'm sorry, I really am, but I wanna be with him."

"Aight," he nodded and bit down on his lip roughly. "Did you fuck him?" he asked, causing me to stop in my tracks.

"See you around," I said before slipping back into the house, and closing the door despite him still standing there. I didn't want to answer that because it'd be like squeezing lemon juice onto an open wound.

Gang was right, he was the king of this city, which is why him finding someone else would be as easy as pie. I just wanted him to stay away from me, because I was sure TQ would not have that shit at all. I hadn't known this dude a month, and he already had me gone.

Chapter 16

SAADIQ "GANG" RONSON

I sat back down on Kimberlyn's grandmother's porch for a few, before finally standing back up and walking to my car. When I made it to the back seat of the black customized Chevy Suburban, my driver hopped out and opened the door for me. I slid into the back seat, and just let out a huge sigh, expressing my disappointment.

"I can't believe I sat in the car while you did that shit," Monica snapped.

I'd been fucking her for much longer than I knew Kimberlyn, so I really couldn't blame her for being salty. She thought she was gonna be the one, and so did I, but when I met Kimberlyn it seemed like no one else mattered, including Monica.

"My bad, ma, you know how I feel about shorty, and I just had to see what was up with her," I explained.

I loved Monica because she was like my best friend, but I just didn't want her like that. I racked my brain on the daily trying to figure out why she didn't satisfy me enough, and I always came up empty. She was cute, had her own money, was smart, great in the bedroom, and she wasn't with me because I was Gang, she was with me for Saadiq. She had her moments where she got out of line, but what woman didn't? Every woman every now and then became overwhelmed with emotion and back talked, so that wasn't a negative about her in my opinion.

And then there is Kimberlyn, someone I have strong ass feelings for, and planned to marry and make the Queen of my throne. I'd never met a bitch who didn't want me, let alone one who would dis me to be with another man. I wasn't sure who I was madder at, TQ or Kimberlyn. I mean TQ and I weren't homies, but I worked for him so I thought we had some sort of loyalty to one another, but I guess not. Then Kimberlyn, we were good, we really were, and it's like the nigga snapped his fingers and she'd forgotten all about me.

I met Kimberlyn in a liquor store almost a year ago. We were in it at the same time, and she was so damn pretty. I loved women who had at least one imperfect feature on their face, and she had that. Kimberlyn had the prettiest dark brown eyes, the perfect nose, long dark hair, and a slim thick body. Her imperfection, if you will, was her mouth. She had a huge ass Kool-Aid mouth like Aaliyah. It made her smile very captivating. Her home girl Goldie was fine too, and funny enough, her big ass nose made her bomb. I tried smashing her on the low, but she shut me down so badly I almost had her killed for embarrassing me. To keep her from running her mouth to Kimberlyn, I had to pay her five grand. Matikah was cool too, but she looked too perfect and pretty like a doll. All her features were flawless, and for some reason I didn't like that. We all had our own little things that we liked, I guess.

Anyway, I got Kimberlyn's number and we got to know each other for a little over a year. We would hang out a lot, but she would only let me kiss her. I didn't mind because I knew I had her in my pocket. Little did I know, her little ass was gonna leave me high and dry. Me, Gang, the king of Boston, got ditched by some regular bitch from Roxbury. But damn was she pretty.

"Does she know that I've basically been your girl, even before you knew her? Does she know you haven't stopped fucking with me?" Monica quizzed as she stared out the window with a lone tear traveling down her light cheek.

"Nah, she don't. Of course she don't, and I appreciate you keeping quiet about that shit, shorty. Don't cry," I pulled her over to me, in which she hesitated at first, but finally gave in. "I love you, don't even trip. You know you gon' be my wife, especially now that she's out of the picture."

"For real, Saa? Or are you just blowing smoke?" She looked up into my eyes with her hazel ones.

"I'm for real. I just need to get out this funk. I don't even think it's necessarily her that got me tweakin', it's that my ego is a little bruised."

"To be honest, I think it was karma."

"Karma? How?"

"She did what you did to me."

"Get off me, man." I moved my arm from around her, and she sucked her teeth before scooting back over to her side. "I ain't even really leave you like that. I explained that I just wanted to fuck, and that I did have love for her but I didn't love her like I love you," I lied. "So how is it that it's karma? You knew once I fucked I was gonna be right back to you."

"It's still fucked up, Saa, I should be enough for you."

"And I told you I was a nigga with needs, and you said it was cool as long as you were the main."

"Well I don't know if I feel like that anymore. We're twenty-eight years old, Saa, it's time to progress or just separate."

"Well if you keep trying to come at me sideways and change who I am, we're gonna fuckin' separate and that's on everything I love. Moose, take Ms. Jordan home, please."

"Really, Saa?" she snapped her neck to look at me after hearing what I'd instructed my driver to do.

I declined to respond, and we didn't say shit to one another the whole ride to her house. I didn't feel like hearing all the bullshit she was talking about. Like I said, I would love to give Monica the world because she deserved it, but something was keeping me from feeling that for her. I couldn't move forward with her until I figured it out, and that was the end of it.

After dropping Monica off, I had my driver pick Peel up because he said he had some shit to tell me. We made it to his crib in Backbay, and pulled over. I text him to let him know I was outside, and he promptly came out and jogged to the car.

"What's good?" he dapped me up and shook his head once he got inside.

"Same shit, gettin' money and dealing with this TQ and Kimberlyn shit. But what's up with you? What did you have to tell me?"

"Man, I think Hayden is fuckin' around on me."

"What, nigga? Why?"

"Well I think she wants to. A couple of times I caught her checking social media for TQ."

"That nigga don't have social media."

"Yeah, but bitches that's on his dick do, and they be posting shit about him, even Kimberlyn posted once or twice. Anyway, she be searching his name in the tags. I caught her three times, and both times she was stammering over her words."

"Damn, did you ever take the time to see exactly what she looks at? Or you just saw her searching and said something?"

"I saw her searching so I said something. One time I did see her on Kimberlyn's page, and she was reading the comments under a picture Kimberlyn posted of this fancy ass dinner. TQ wasn't in the picture though."

"I don't know, man, Hayden is the homie. Maybe she's just looking out for me."

"I hope so bro, because if that nigga is smashing my bitch, we gon' have to kill his ass."

"Shit, that don't sound too bad, it's just that I would need to find a new distributor if we did. His dad, Stony, has the connects, but TQ is the one who gets it over here. Without him, we ain't got shit."

"True... well, we will just wait and see what's going on. For his sake, he needs to find his own girl and keep it pushing. He can't have both of our bitches."

"Ain't that the truth. Hold up, this nigga Jayce is calling me." We smirked at one another before I answered the call.

Chapter 17

TQ

I'D JUST WRAPPED UP A MEETING WITH MY BROTHERS, FATHER, AND BEST friend about the trip to South Carolina. We would all be leaving in a couple of weeks, minus Jayce, and I was not excited. Every fucking time my father acquired a new distributor, it took away more and more of my time. I loved the money aspect of it, but damn, at the rate he was going, I would only have time to eat, shit, shave, and shower. I will admit it bothered me more now because it took time away from being with Kimberlyn.

"Mama and I are about to cook a big ass feast, it should be ready in a couple of hours," my sister Saya said as she walked into the den of my parents' home.

"Oh, I'm gonna have to take a rain check, sis, I got somewhere to be," I replied as I took the blunt from my best friend, Jayce.

"Yeah, this nigga got him a bitch that he's sweet on. He be trying to play that shit down, but we know the deal," Rhys laughed and lit another blunt.

"Oh really? Is this a good time to be getting into relationships, TQ?" Saya raised a brow and folded her arms.

Saya was the spitting image of my mother, with smooth chocolate skin, and a small shapely frame. Only difference was the fact that she had bluish gray eyes like the rest of us. The one thing I hated about my sister was that she was always meddling in some shit, especially relationships. I think she thought since she was the oldest that she was supposed to. I paid her ass no mind though, usually.

"I have time for whatever I choose, Saya."

"So it's true, she's your girl? Nigga, you just met her ass at the club like two days ago!" Lendsey chimed in while sipping on some mixture in his glass.

"Give the bro some credit, it's been almost a week now," Britain smiled at me.

"Aye! I'm a grown ass fucking man, and I'm not about to be discussing my personal life with a bunch of hating ass niggas. Whomever I choose to spend my time with is my muthafuckin' business. Shorty is fine, I like her, and that's it. Don't worry about what I got going on if it don't have nothing to do with work, aight?" I hissed and then took a pull on the blunt, making Saya exit the den.

These niggas were gettin' on my nerves. I knew that Kimberlyn and I were moving hella fast but I couldn't help that shit. It was moving and I couldn't stop it because I didn't want to. I hadn't known her that long, but I had a stronger connection with her than any other bitch I'd ever 'dated'. I agreed to be in a relationship with her because I'm grown and I do what the fuck I wanna do. Right now I wanted to be with her, and that's what I was gonna do. If I changed my mind then so be it, but for now, shorty was mine and that was the end of it.

"Damn nigga, chill out. Did you cry after you nutted?" Rhys chimed in, and I shoved the fuck out of his ass as he and the room roared with laughter.

"What y'all need to be doing is worrying about your own damn bitches."

"My girl is good, my daughter is great, and so am I," Rhys said before blowing smoke out of his mouth.

"Nigga, Summer is about two seconds from leaving yo' ass, shut the fuck up," my little brother Britain said to Rhys, making us chuckle. "You better start making amends with Lisa so you'll have some back up."

"That's what Summer wants y'all to think, but she ain't going no damn where. She knows I love her. I just got some problems. And Lisa is *not* a problem we have," Rhys lied through his teeth.

"You got a lot of problems my nigga. But mainly you need anger management or some shit," Lendsey shook his head with a smile at Rhys.

"Nigga, I know you ain't talking, you need a sex addict course. That's why shorty left ya crib when she saw one of yo' clients calling," Rhys taunted Lendsey.

"Wait, what shorty?" I asked, while laughing.

"Yo' girl's best friend, or cousin, or whatever the fuck she is. Light skinned, long ass curly hair, and them sexy lips," Rhys reminded me.

"Matikah." Lendsey shook his head. "She had me feeling dumb as fuck. I thought we were about to chill and kick it, but she straight up told me to take her little ass back home."

"All because a bitch called your phone?" Britain frowned.

"Yep."

"What you thought, you were gonna fuck?" Rhys quizzed Lendsey.

"Shit, that would be cool, but I knew she wasn't gonna let me that quick. I'm gonna get her ass though, watch."

"Nigga what about Dania?" I poured myself some of the Hennessy that we had out, while waiting for Lendsey's response.

"That psycho bitch," Britain commented.

"Man, Dania gon' be aight. She's good, but I ain't worried about her right now, I'm worried about Matikah. And Britain, worry about Tekeya, not what I got going on."

"You're a mess my nigga," Jayce shook his head, as Rhys and I nodded in agreement.

Britain seemed to be in deep thought about his bat shit crazy ass girlfriend, Tekeya. Tekeya and Dania were a lot alike in the sense that they would cut anyone who got close to their men. However, Tekeya was actually Britain's girlfriend, not some consistent smash buddy like Dania.

"Aye, let me talk to you real quick, TQ." My best friend Jayce stood up and went into the little side area of the den.

"What's up?" I quizzed once I got to where he was.

"I was thinking that your dad could put me in charge of the gun transport. I know he said he was looking through the roster, and I was just wondering if you could put in a good word for me and shit. I'm tired of just being a tag along, I want my own shit like you and your brothers."

"Jayce, man, I can't influence my father like that, and honestly I don't think you're ready. You're just now getting to the point where you can go a day without drinking."

Jayce's wife got murdered two years ago by some bitch he was fucking with. That shit took a toll on him, a major one, and he started drinking. The judge went in on his ass, and blamed his infidelities as the reason for his wife's death, and I think that shit made it worse. He was just now getting to the point where he wasn't drunk twenty-four hours a day.

"TQ, come on, you're supposed to be—"

"And he don' already chose Solomon, he told me this morning. There ain't shit I can do." I patted his shoulder and walked back to join my brothers. I saw him staring at me for a bit, before he joined us as well.

I would love for him to be able to have his own area in QCF like my brothers and me, but Jayce wasn't ready. And if he fucked up with something like that, my dad would surely murder his ass, or have Rhys do it. I didn't wanna see him go out like that.

10 P.M. THAT NIGHT...

I was lying in my European King bed, with Kimberlyn's head on my chest. We'd just gotten done fucking about an hour ago, but I was already ready for round two. I didn't know what I was doing with her, and I think it was because all of this shit was so unfamiliar to me. I didn't do relationships, yet somehow I found myself in one with someone I'd only known over a short amount of time.

"TQ, I saw Gang earlier today," Kimberlyn whispered as we watched the lone candle flicker on the dresser in front of us. Without it, the room would be dark.

"I don't want you around him, Kimberlyn."

"I know, and I told him to leave right away."

"Fuck did he want?"

"He was just wondering where I'd been all this time. He'd come by to see me a couple of times, and I wasn't there," she replied as I reached for my glass of water to take a sip.

"If he comes to see you again, don't come outside, and I mean it. I got eyes everywhere, and I don't want anyone coming to me about seeing you with that nigga."

"Okay." I could feel her head nodding against my chest. "I don't wanna hear about you with other girls either," she added in a low tone.

"You won't. I'm with you, right?"

"Yeah."

"Then don't worry about that."

I gripped a handful of her long dark locks, and then pulled her head back so that I could kiss her. Her small hand rubbed up and down my chest as I kissed her roughly while playing with her clit. I quickly towered over her body, and then spread her legs open to stare at her center for a bit. I then dipped my head down, and began to suck on her clit with my eyes closed. Her taste was so good, making it possible for me to stay down there for forever it seemed.

"Tarenz," she moaned and caressed my fade.

I held her legs apart with my hands, and continued to devour her pussy like it was my last meal. Listening to her moans, and feeling her body move slightly every time she panted was perfect. She exploded and cried out, and I just licked it up and kept going. We made eye contact as I feasted, and she bit down her lip. Seeing how much pleasure I brought her made me go harder. We intertwined our fingers as I devoured her middle, and watched her chest rise and fall rapidly.

"Baby, uuuh, mmm," she whimpered as I pushed my face further in between her legs.

I reached up to play with her nipples as I gave her this tongue lashing, and after cumming two more times, I could tell she was spent. I could hear her nails scraping the sheets as she gripped them into her hands while crying out. My dick was so damn hard, so I came up from between her legs, and kissed all the way up to her soft full lips.

"I want you on top," I whispered into her mouth right before our tongues became entangled.

After kissing for a nice amount of time, I laid on my back to roll a condom down. Once it was on, I tugged on her wrist. She mounted me, then I guided her down onto my dick, loving the way her face twisted up as she took me further and further inside of her.

"Just move up and down, and make sure you go all the way down, Kimberlyn," I explained to her and she nodded.

I placed my hands behind my head, and watched as she moved slowly up and down on my pole. Every time I felt her warmth at my base, she bit her lip and whimpered lightly. She was so damn beautiful, and watching her move up and down on my rod with her snug wet walls was something I could look at all day.

"Aaaah, uuuh," she called out as she hit the base of my dick again. She sat there paralyzed, and damn did it feel good. After a couple moments, she resumed her movements.

I sat up to grip her ass and suck on her nipples hungrily. I began slamming her down on my dick, making her scream out. I flipped her onto her back, placed her legs onto my shoulders, and went ham. I sucked on her lips, and kissed her nastily as I pulverized her pussy.

"Fuck!" I hollered out into her mouth as I continued to beat it up with her legs on my shoulders.

I kissed her harder, and then finally I was filling the condom up with my seeds. I threw my head back, panting heavily, and then slid out of her. Falling to the side, I removed the condom, and placed it into the trashcan nearby.

Looking over at her, I saw she was still breathing hard as hell. Her golden complexion was covered with beads of sweat. I leaned over and kissed her flat stomach, before pulling her closer to me.

"Who's your man?" I sucked on her lips.

"Tarenz Quinton," she panted and rubbed my biceps. "And I'm your girl."

"Yep." I got in between her legs, pinned her hands above her head, and kissed her passionately and sensually.

Chapter 18

RHYS QUINTON

THAT DAMN DINNER THAT MY MOM AND SISTER COOKED WAS OFF THE fuckin' chain. I ended up chilling and talking with my siblings, minus TQ, all damn night. That nigga TQ was on some other shit, and it was funny to sit and watch. He didn't want to admit that he enjoyed having someone to keep the other side of the bed warm. Most niggas liked new pussy every now and then, but there was nothing like smashing pussy that you knew was yours. My days of stepping out were way behind me though, so hunting for that new new wasn't my thing.

I knew TQ was trippin' when I saw how his eyes were locked on shorty from the minute she walked into the venue that first night. The nigga watched her for an hour straight, until she went to the bathroom. It seems like they've been attached at the hip ever since that night too. I was happy for my little brother, and now all we needed to do was get Lendsey's ass some act right. Britain had a bitch, but he would never change.

I walked into my condo on Glenville feeling tired as fuck. I was full as hell and it was late, so all I wanted to do was knock out. I was even too tired to fuck, which was rare because Summer always kept me in the mood, unless she started running her mouth too much. Tonight though, I was just gonna check on my daughter, Bryleigh, and then knock out in the living room.

As soon as I made it to my couch, I plopped down and began to remove my shoes. I was gonna sleep out here because I didn't feel like showering, and I had to shower before getting into my bed and lying on my nice ass Egyptian cotton sheets. So since I was damn near dead right now, I would have to sleep on this comfy ass couch.

I got my shoes and crew neck off, then slipped my jeans down before getting a blanket from the linen closet. I laid it across the couch, took a piss, washed my hands, and then went and laid down after kissing my daughter. As soon as I began drifting off, I could tell someone turned on the living room light; that someone in particular was my girlfriend, Summer.

"Summer, please, I'm tired as fuck," I grunted as I listened to her small feet pad towards me.

"Where the fuck have you been, Rhys?" she folded her arms across her chest and frowned down at me with her pretty face. "Bryleigh wouldn't even go to sleep for the first hour because she was asking about you."

My phone buzzed as Summer went on and on, so I looked down to check the text.

+1 (617) 555 - 7133: I miss you.

+1 (617) 555 - 7133: We need to talk.

I ignored the text from this girl named Lisa, and then silenced my phone before looking back up at a fuming Summer.

My girl was bad as fuck, and was cool as hell too, which is why I made her my girl. At one point in my life I was like my little brothers, not wanting to be in a relationship, but that was until I met Summer. Like Kimberlyn, she showed me how good it felt to have that one person for you at home. Summer was not only gorgeous with her smooth pecan brown skin, long brown dreads, and sexy ass frame, but she could hold a conversation and had goals. The pussy and head was on some other shit too.

I met her when I went to the mall to purchase some sneakers. I thought it was cool that she was so sexy and feminine, yet knew so much about tennis shoes. And, of course, because I'm a good-looking ass nigga, she came up out of them digits quick, fast, and in a hurry. We got off to a rocky start because I was still on my player shit, but once she made it clear that she wasn't having it, I had to decide what was more important, her or other bitches. Of course she won, but despite my faithfulness she accused me constantly.

"Baby, I was with my family all night, please turn the light out," I stated calmly, hoping she backed the fuck up. Summer knew my temper was bad, and I was not trying to go there with her little ass.

"With your fucking brothers, fucking bitches you mean!" she hollered, making my ears ring, and that shit pissed me off.

I hopped up off the couch and towered over her ass wearing a scowl. Just like I knew she would, she cowered under me.

"Be quiet before you wake up the baby! I told yo' muthafuckin' ass I was with my family! Get the fuck up outta my face accusing me of shit! I'm tired and I have a long fucking week ahead of me!" I barked and she jumped back.

"Okay," she nodded slowly, before walking over to the light and cutting it off.

I threw my head back and sighed, before saying, "Aye, Summer, come here, man." I plopped down on the couch.

She walked back over to me, fidgeting a bit, and then once she got close enough, I pulled her into my lap. Kissing on her neck, I groped her thighs and inhaled whatever she'd used to wash her body some hours ago.

"I ain't mean to yell at you, but I swear to God I was with my family tonight. I love you and I am not fuckin' around on you, okay?"

"So you don't speak with Lisa anymore?" she raised her brow and I shook my head 'no'.

Lisa was a girl that I cheated on Summer with almost a year ago. Summer and I had been together eight years at the time, and we'd hit a huge snag. We decided to break up for a little bit, and when we did, I met Lisa. The problem was, when I got back with Summer I fucked

Lisa a couple more times, and Summer found out. I haven't touched Lisa since then, yet Summer felt the need to question me about her. I mean, yeah, Lisa was low-key still obsessed with me, but her and I have been over for some time.

The most I did now was text other bitches here and there, but I would never fuck them. I may come over to the crib to chill, but that was it. I wasn't built to cheat, so no matter how bad I may have wanted them right then and there, I couldn't do it. Cheating on Summer was a one-time thing, and it would never happen again. By saying that, me texting and chilling with other girls here and there was nothing big in my opinion, since I wasn't touching them. Even though I felt that way, Summer could never know about it.

"Why didn't you come to bed?" she asked, pulling me from my walk down memory lane.

"Because I'm dirty and I was too damn tired to get in."

Summer reached down into my boxers while keeping her eyes locked on mine. I knew she wanted to fuck in order to tell if I was lying. She knew I would never disrespect her and fuck her after I did it to another bitch. I just shook my head as she removed my rod from my boxers. How many times did we have to go through this for her to see I was serious about being only into her?

I yanked her little body closer to me, and then pulled her panties to the side before slipping into her.

"Mmm," she tucked her bottom lip in her mouth. I hadn't hit in about a week, and damn was her pussy snug.

"I know what you doing, ma, and now you see I wasn't lying."

I guided her hips as she bounced on my dick slowly. This shit was about to have me crying out like some hoe ass nigga. This was one of the top five reasons I'd wifed Summer's ass. I threw my head back, enjoying the feeling of her. She cupped my face and began kissing me hungrily as I started slamming her down onto me, pounding her spot.

"Aaah, uuuh, uuuh!" she whimpered as I bit her bottom lip.

We both released together, and continued to kiss one another while panting heavily.

"I told your bratty ass I was behaving myself." I pecked her and she grinned widely.

I loved seeing that smile. She had deep dimples like myself, and every time she smiled it made me feel some type of way. One day I would marry this girl, but we needed to get some trust back up in this shit first.

Chapter 19

SUMMER GILLIES

THE NEXT MORNING...

Here I was lying in bed alone, just like the night before, and the night before that. Thinking about it alone made me cry. I was so in love with Rhys Quinton, but I hated the way he treated me sometimes. I just hated how angry he got over the smallest things; it was really scary. Not to mention the fact that I knew he was cheating on me.

I couldn't leave though, it seemed. It was like he knew he had the upper hand, and that I loved him more than anything in the world. I wish I were stronger, strong enough to go against his stupid ass even when he got his angriest.

"Fuck," I mumbled as my alarm went off.

It was 5am and I had to be out of the door and off to work in an hour and a half. In addition to that, I had to get my daughter Bryleigh up and off to my mom's so she could take her to preschool later.

I was a make-up artist, and I worked for a modeling company. I would have to be at the shoots earlier than the damn models, and then sit and do their makeup while they ordered everyone around, begging for lattes. My job paid extremely well though, and I loved doing makeup so that was the only thing that kept me going. I had more than enough money to move out of Rhys' spot, but for some reason other than Bryleigh, I didn't want to.

Peeling the covers off of my body, I got out of the bed and grabbed my iPhone. I dialed Rhys' number and waited as the line trilled. His voicemail picked up like usual, and I was tempted to go off on him and tell him that it was over, but I knew I didn't want that. Leaving him would hurt me more than it would hurt him, and that was bad all in itself.

I got out of the bed, and then brushed my teeth after having my morning tea. I then got into the shower, and once I was clean, I threw on some light blue skinny jeans, a white t-shirt, and some black flip-flops. The weather in Boston was perfect right now, so I was taking full advantage of it since it was rare. I pulled my dreads into a bun on top of my head, and then after putting on my gold watch that Rhys bought me, I went down the hall to wake up my baby.

I bathed her, supervised her teeth brushing, and then took her to the kitchen to make her a small but hearty breakfast after doing her hair.

"Waffles for the princess," I smiled and slid the plate in front of her.

"Thanks, Mommy. Where is Daddy? I got up like I do every night and I couldn't find him." She put some food into her mouth as she stared into my eyes with her pretty blue ones, waiting for an answer. She was only four, but very smart.

"He had to work, Bry, you know daddy's job causes him to stay out all night sometimes." My stomach turned with every word that I spoke.

"I know. I wish it didn't though. I want him to read me a bedtime story."

"I read you bedtime stories!"

"Yes, but you don't change your voice to be like the characters like Daddy," she chuckled and so did I. Rhys was a horrible boyfriend, but he was a pretty great father.

"Well, I will make sure he gets back to reading for you. Hurry and finish, baby."

Once Bryleigh finished her waffles, eggs, bacon, and juice, we were out the door and headed to my mother's.

"Good morning, Summer, the models will be here soon. There are pastries in the break room," my boss, Paul, walked up to me and said. Paul was gayer than gay, and he was super nice although a very rich man. I loved working for him because he didn't hesitate to get the models in check if he felt they were too entitled.

"Thanks, and good morning," I sighed, and walked to the back with my huge suitcase of makeup.

I ate one of the pastries, and before I could even finish, the models had shown up. They were already giving their Starbucks orders to my co-worker, Renee, poor thing. My other coworker Nia and I started setting up, then gave each other knowing looks as we waited to beat faces.

"Ladies, this is one of the new models for today's shoot, his name is Hakim," Paul introduced one of the guys.

He was perfection, and he reminded me of the actor Robert Ri'Chard from *Chocolate City*. This nigga was so damn fine that it gave me a headache. The last dude I saw that was this fine was Rhys.

"Nice to meet you ladies," Hakim smiled and shook both my hand and Nia's hand.

"Let me show you to the dressing room, Hakim." Paul pulled him away and began talking to him. As he walked away, Hakim looked back at me and winked.

"Girrllll, you have a man, let me get in on him."

"I do not want him, Nia. You are right, I have a man and I plan to stick with him, thank you."

"Speaking of Rhys, is his sexy ass still giving you problems?"

"When does a man with blue eyes, caramel skin, and a perfectly shaven bald head with a beard *not* give you problems?" I half smiled and she chuckled.

"True, you need to hook me up with one of his brothers or something. You know I don't care about the rumors," Nia leaned in and whispered the last part. If only she knew the rumors were true.

She used to mess with Rhys before he and I got together. She was his age, so she'd met him before I came to their high school. Nia was simply a fuck buddy of Rhys', so she knew nothing of his life, nor what his father was into at the time. Like everyone else, she just knew the name Quinton meant something.

No one was sure if the Quinton Crime Family existed or not, but people just knew the Quintons weren't the people to fuck with. It's crazy that people feared them and didn't know why they feared them.

"Darling, his brothers are dogs. Every single one of them."

"Girl, have you seen TQ? I don't care. I can tame him. You know I used to want to be a veterinarian!" We both burst into laughter as the models came out.

Hakim rushed to sit in my chair, and when I turned him to face the mirror, he smiled at me and bit his plump bottom lip.

"Are you contracted with Paul? Or are you just on this job?" he asked as I began to prime his face.

"I'm contracted."

"Damn, so that means I will be seeing more of you, right?"

"I guess so, if he hires you again."

"He will, I'm contracted too, which means we will be spending a lot of time together you know. I look forward to it, ma," he opened his eyes and smiled up into my face.

I just paused for a moment and then picked up the foundation to start matching him. He and I didn't talk for the rest of the session, he just flashed me flirty smiles and winks and shit. I knew he was the type who was used to women giving him whatever he wanted, but I was not like those girls. I wasn't even interested. Plus, Rhys would hang him from a tree by his intestines. My baby was not only crazy— he was a professional killer.

Chapter 20

KIMBERLYN

TWO WEEKS LATER...

TQ pulled up to my grandmother's house as I reached into the back to grab my duffle bag. It seemed like we'd been Siamese twins ever since we met. I'd only known him for a month now, and he was already my boyfriend. I'd never moved this fast before. Because he was so attractive and sought after, it was still a little bit hard to believe that he'd chosen me to be his first real girlfriend as he would say.

"Aight shorty, I should be back in town in a couple days." He squeezed my thigh with his tattooed hand, making goose bumps rise on my arms.

I leaned over and pressed my lips against his, then draped my arms around his neck to caress the back of his head. I hated that we had to be apart, but I think it was healthy for me to have a break from him, and he did have to go do some work down in South Carolina.

"Okay, call me as soon as you can."

"I will call once I'm settled into my hotel suite."

I nodded, then exited the car wearing this new casual chiffon dress by Jeremy Scott that TQ had purchased me. It was $445, but he still got it for me anyway. I didn't want it after I saw the price, but since he'd bought it, the least I could do was wear it.

It was a Wednesday morning, and since it was summer the sun was shining brightly. Summer was my favorite time of the year. I stood at my grandmother's porch steps and just admired the heat from the sun against my skin, before walking into the house.

As soon as I got in, I saw my grandmother sitting on the couch. We'd talked a little on the phone, but not long enough for her to speak her mind. I knew she had things she wanted to say to me, and while away I just wasn't interested.

"Hey, Ma."

"Good morning sweetie, come sit down." She gave me a warm smile and patted the couch cushion next to her. The couch was a three-seater, so I sat on the third pillow, leaving space between us.

"Where is Matikah?" I quizzed.

"She went to the nail shop; she should be back soon."

"Oh, okay," I nodded as my grandmother looked me up and down, taking in my appearance. I had mink nails, a new gold watch and necklace, not to mention my dress, and I was sure she could smell how expensive my new Chanel perfume was. I forgot to mention that my necklace was a small gold chain with the letters TQ hanging from it.

"You've been with TQ this whole time, huh?" she asked, and again I nodded in response. "Did you give him your body, Kimberlyn?"

I sat there breathing a bit heavily, wondering if I should tell her the truth. I was always honest with my grandmother, but then again I never had anything to hide. Telling her that I'd lost my virginity to a man that I barely knew would surely break her heart. Let alone the fact that I'd lost it awhile back.

"Kimberlyn, just tell me. I already know the answer, but I wanna hear it from you. There is no way a man would buy you all of the nice things you walked in here with unless he's gotten in between your legs."

I pushed my freshly styled hair behind my ears, and looked into her eyes. I could see she was disappointed and I hadn't even spoken yet.

"Ma, I... I did but I'm sorry," I grabbed her hand into mine.

"Kimberlyn, did you want to do it?"

"Yes," I let her hand go.

"Then don't be sorry, sweetie. If you wanted to do it, then I'm fine. As long as he didn't make you do anything you didn't want to, I won't be angry. And if he did, I would be angry but not with you."

"Really?"

"Yes, Kimberlyn, you're a twenty-one-year-old girl, it was bound to happen. The fact that you weren't doing it at thirteen like your mother is good enough for me," she smiled and so did I. "So you really like him?"

"Yeah, I do. He's a criminal, but he's smart. He's not like Gang at all," I attempted to sell her on TQ. "He has businesses too; Quinton Car Wash, he owns it with his brothers."

"Oh, I can tell he isn't like Gang. And yes, that car wash is where the rich folk go. What is his real name? I know it's not TQ."

"It stands for Tarenz Quinton, I told you, remember? His name is Tarenz Aakil Quinton." I felt myself smiling, so I placed my hands on my face to stop it, causing my grandmother to crack up.

"Wow, you really really like him, huh?"

"Yeah, I do. And he wants to meet you, Ma. I told him I didn't know if you would do it, but he said he still wanted me to find out."

"Of course I want to meet him. Anybody smooth enough to have Kimberlyn Harrey smiling, is someone I have to meet. You're tough to crack. I feel bad for Saadiq," she chuckled, referring to Gang.

"I know. I didn't mean for stuff to happen the way that it did. All of this took me by surprise."

It was true. I was really into Gang until TQ came and stole the show. I'd never liked someone so much in my life. With Gang, I really liked him but if he stopped talking to me I wouldn't have cared too much. If TQ stopped talking to me I would care a lot, and may be miserable for some time.

I enjoyed everything about him, from his commanding demeanor to his goofy jokes. I liked that he wasn't as serious with me as he was in the streets, unless he needed to be. I also liked how experienced he was in the bedroom. I enjoyed learning all the new things he showed me how to do, and I enjoyed the orgasms he brought me to. He was fluent in Russian as well, and had a pilot's license, which I thought was so sexy for some reason.

"You don't owe Saadiq anything, Kimberlyn, so don't sweat it. Be with whoever you wanna be with, okay?"

"I will. I'm gonna go take a bath and lie down."

"What? You're spending the night here?"

"Yes, TQ had to leave town for a couple days. He offered for me to stay in his condo while he was gone, but I wanted to come home to you and Matikah."

"Well I'm glad you did, sweetie, I missed you."

I rushed to my room and grabbed my caddy so I could go take a bubble bath. Once I finished, I changed into some boxer shorts that I took from TQ, and then a tube top. It was a bit warm in the house, so I wanted to make sure I didn't wear too much. I wasn't going anywhere anyway. I was beat because TQ and I painted the town red last night, and then went to his condo to have sex until three in the morning. I was riding high right now and I loved it.

I dozed off, but then was woken up by my cousin, Matikah. She was standing over me, wearing a big ass smile. I sat up slowly and looked around for my phone, before snatching it from by my pillow.

"You're going back tonight?" she asked and plopped down on the chair in my room.

"No, I am not. TQ has gone to South Carolina, so I'm gonna just chill tonight."

"Cool, wanna make it a movie night? I can call Goldie over here?"

"Yeah, call her, I miss her and I wanna make sure Ethan hasn't crawled his ass back into her life."

"Yes, he needs to keep his Doberman ass far away," she responded before we burst into laughter.

My phone buzzed as I was getting off the bed to follow Matikah to get snacks. I picked it up and saw I had a text from TQ, making my body get warm, and butterflies consume my stomach.

TQ: I miss you already. Just landed, will call around 11pm, cool?

Me: I miss you too baby, and yes that's fine.

This nigga had my head spinning... already.

Chapter 21

TQ

My brothers and I landed in Columbia, South Carolina about two hours ago, and were now getting ready to go meet with this Jasper nigga. I really wasn't in the mood to meet with anymore kingpins who thought they were the shit. Most of them were dumb as hell and loved to floss on you as if they made so much more money than you. Do you not realize that you pay me for product *and* I get a cut from your profits? In addition to that, you're only one of my many distributors who also give me a cut. Dull ass niggas. I wiped my ass with the shit they brought in monthly, but because I wasn't too much of a flashy guy, you would never know.

POP!

A light gunshot was heard from the room Rhys was sleeping in, prompting my brothers and I to become alert. Rhys walked out frowning, and then sat down on the loveseat like nothing happened.

"Fuck was that?" I asked.

"Damn doorknob hit me in my dick!" Rhys spat.

"Nigga, you shot the doorknob off because it hit you in the dick?" Lendsey quizzed with a frown, after coming back from looking at the door.

"Hell yeah, that shit hurt like fuck."

I told y'all this nigga was crazy and easily angered. This nigga had beef with an inanimate object.

"Aye, I met some cute ass bitches downstairs in the lobby," my youngest brother Britain laughed and dapped Lendsey up.

"You take them hoes to your room my nigga, you know I ain't with that shit," Rhys responded and lit a blunt.

"What about you, TQ? You gon' come to my suite? It's seven of them, and I swear they're all bad," Britain chuckled.

I continued fastening the button on my sleeve, as all kinds of shit went through my fuckin' head. I didn't know how I wanted to answer him, so I just decided to keep my words to myself. I was content right now, but who knows how I would feel upon seeing what Britain had actually scraped up.

"Hello?" Lendsey chimed in.

"Let's handle business first, and then we can discuss leisure activities." I pulled my Balmain tuxedo jacket onto my back, and checked myself out in the mirror.

"This nigga sprung off that young pussy he's been getting these past few weeks," Rhys chuckled and popped some gum into his mouth.

"He gotta be, because any other time he would've been calling dibs on five of them bitches that I invited," Britain added.

"Would y'all bitch ass niggas shut the fuck up. Each and every one of y'all better be ready to walk out this muthafuckin' door in two point five seconds. If not, ya ass is getting left!" I barked and then started towards the door of the hotel room.

The four of us left and climbed into the all black Escalade we'd rented while being out here. Rhys was in the driver seat unfortunately, and I was in the passenger directing him, while Lendsey and Britain smoked a blunt in the back seat.

We pulled up to a nice ass mansion, and both Rhys and I nodded approvingly. This was a big, nice ass house, but I knew this Jasper cat was an idiot. For starters, the nigga had us come to the place he laid his head at. You never wanted anybody in this business that wasn't family, knowing where you lived. It was too dangerous because things always changed, and the person you once called your friend could easily become your enemy.

"Aight, come on knuckleheads," Rhys said to Britain and Lendsey as we all exited the car. There was no need for the four of us to come along, but right now I didn't care to speak up.

The four of us tread up the walkway, and Britain rang the doorbell. We waited about one minute before a beautiful ass girl answered the door. She was thick in all the right places, and not afraid to show it off. I could tell by the menacing look in her eyes, and the sensual way she shifted her weight from one hip to the other, that she was fucking more than just Jasper.

"Good evening, you must be TQ?" she smirked and nodded.

"I am, and these three are my brothers. Is it cool if they come in?"

"Of course," she licked her lips with her eyes locked on Lendsey. I knew he was gonna fuck her, and I just hoped it didn't mess with my business. "I'm Jataria by the way, Jasper's wife." And this nigga let us meet his wife? He had to be a rookie in the game. I did feel bad though because dude for sure had a straight up skeezer for a spouse.

"Nice to meet you, Jataria."

We walked into the home, and she led me to the area Jasper was in. She then took my brothers to the kitchen so they could eat whatever she'd made for dinner. I swear I hated when these niggas came on jobs with me, but they insisted. That's just how we were because we didn't want shit happening to the other. Most times when it was this many siblings, there was some animosity involved, but not with the Quintons. You fucked with one of us, you fucked with us all, including Saya.

"TQ," Jasper got up from his couch.

I walked down the three short steps into his den, and admired the scenery. It reminded me of my home in Bridgeport, which then brought on memories of all the shit I did to Kimberlyn's sexy ass body while out there. Damn, shorty had fucked my mind up.

"Jasper, nice to meet you." I shook his hand, and then we both took a seat.

Jataria then walked in carrying a tray, holding two glasses of some sort of brown liquor. I wasn't in the mood to chill like that, so I put my hand up to decline. I didn't like drinking during meetings of this kind anyway. Niggas thought if you indulged in conversation, and threw a few drinks back that they could swindle you up out of a good deal.

"Come on man, you can't deny a drink, that's rude," Jasper chuckled and took both glasses from the tray, handing one to me.

"I won't be long, Jasper. Now my father explained to me that you wanted four shipments per week?" I frowned. That was a lot, and I'd never seen anybody move that much, not even Gang.

"Yeah, I can do that shit. I don't care how much it costs. Y'all got that good shit and I'm sure I will have no problems."

"And you know the terms?"

"I think so."

"Money is to be paid upfront when picking up, and on time when returning profits. There won't be any redistributions, and if so, we will be forced to handle you."

"Oh yeah?" he chuckled but I didn't crack a smile so his faded.

"Now, I'm not gonna bring product down here four times a week. I will deliver in full, and you must in turn pay in full."

"Man, that's a lot of fuckin' money up front." *Didn't he just say he didn't care how much it cost?*

"Take it or leave it," I stated sternly and waited for his answer.

He turned to look through the huge ass bay window ahead of us, before turning his attention back to me.

"That's cool."

Jasper and I discussed some more details, then he gave me the name of the individual he would have picking up the product, and I did the same. I didn't like him for some reason though. He gave me a bad taste in my mouth. He seemed like he was a snake or a snitch, and all it would take was a cold barrel to his dome for him to sing. But it was up to my father to decide who to give product to, so I couldn't say much in that department. The only time I could deny a distributor was if they didn't agree to the terms.

I left out of the den area, and then went to fetch my brothers. Just like I thought, Lendsey was flirting with Jasper's wife all up in his house. I shook my head and then tapped my ring against the counter to snap him out of it before Jasper entered.

"Let's go, niggas." I left out of his house with my brothers following me.

We made it back to our suite, and as promised, Britain brought about ten hoes through. The nigga said seven, but clearly he was lying. I made myself a drink as I unwillingly listened to Britain get some head from one of them in the rooms. I just shook my head and chuckled at his ass.

KNOCK! KNOCK!

I went to answer the door, and I couldn't help but laugh when I saw Jasper's wife Jataria standing there. I stepped back and let her saunter into the room, then Lendsey came from the room he was sleeping in, and waved shorty over with a smile. She damn near ran, and then closed the door behind herself.

"Hey," some girl walked up to me as "Fight Night" by Migos blasted in our suite.

"What's up?" I grinned. She was beautiful as hell, with a nice fat ass that I could almost see from the front. Shit.

Just then, Britain walked out with old girl, buckling his pants. I wished Rhys had stayed in here, but that nigga went and got his own suite when he saw Britain was serious. I probably should've done the same.

"Can we chill in your room?" the girl reached up to grab my chin, then tilted it down to face her. She raised her brow, letting me know she was feeling frisky.

"Hold up," I told her and then left out to the balcony. I closed the door behind me, and let the cool night air hit my face. I then pulled my phone out to dial my shorty. Yes, she had me calling her instead of sliding up in something scrumptious as fuck.

"Hello?" she answered sweetly. That shit made me smile just from hearing her voice; crazy. I loved how bona fide and sincere she was.

"What you doing?" I asked and then sipped my drink. I was leaning on the balcony, looking over the city of Columbia.

"I'm just watching a movie with Matikah and Goldie. What are you doing?"

"I just got back from that business meeting I told you about, and now I'm gonna go to bed and shit. I guess I should let you go since you're chilling with your cousin."

"No, you do—"

"Hey baby, you coming back in soon?" the girl with the fat ass came onto the balcony and rubbed my back gently.

"Going to sleep, huh?" Kimberlyn quizzed.

"Baby—"

Click.

"Yo, get yo' hoe ass outta my face, shorty! Fuck you coming out here for when you see me on the fucking phone!" I marched that little bitch back up into the suite. I tried calling Kimberlyn back a couple times, but she didn't answer me.

Me: Baby, she's just one of the girls Britain invited.

I texted her but got no response after standing out in the cold for fifteen minutes. By this time, I was furious with her assuming ass.

When I walked back in, two other girls were in my face and looking good as hell. Fuck it, Kimberlyn was on some bullshit anyways. If she would get that mad over nothing, then maybe it wasn't meant. I led the two girls to my room to get it poppin'.

Chapter 22

BRITAIN QUINTON

TWO WEEKS LATER...

This week it was my turn to handle the business of the family's car wash, so I was currently in the office going over the books. Since I was in charge of the money, being the official loan officer of QCF, I was the best at balancing books. I got a certificate in accounting and finance from Massachusetts Community College, a year and some change ago at the urging of my dad. I didn't want to, but oddly I came to love numbers and shit. I took pride in being able to solve math problems in my head easily, even small things like calculating the tip at restaurants.

The office phone began ringing, and I already knew who the fuck it was because she'd been blowing up my cell phone before, so I had to put that shit on *Do Not Disturb*. My girlfriend, Tekeya, was gonna be the death of me, and I was only twenty-three. She stayed on my fuckin' bumper and the shit was tiring. If you asked me why I was with her, I couldn't give you an answer because the good pussy was barely enough anymore.

Yeah, I cheated on her constantly, but she had no proof I was still doing dirt. She only caught me twice, with the second time ending pretty badly, but that was a year ago. Since then, she's had no reason to be on me the way that she was. She needed to understand that I was gonna do me regardless. Either she could get with the fuckin' program or get to stepping.

BRNNGGG!

I picked the phone up and slammed it down, hanging up in her face. If it was someone else, they would have to find another way to get through for right now.

I finished crunching these numbers and smiled because we were consistently moving on up like The Jeffersons. We had four car washes spread over Boston, mainly in Brighton and Jamaica Plain, and they were all bringing in a little over two million dollars a year, each. It paid to have rich niggas come through and floss by having all four of their luxury cars cleaned; especially when some cars came in at $150 per wash.

The car wash was pretty legit all the way around, but TQ occasionally used it to clean money. It was initially for that purpose, but TQ started requesting the distributors to have the money cleaned before passing it over to him. Every now and then if TQ felt the distributor fucked up, he would run it through here though.

I stood up and sipped the milkshake I'd bought earlier, while looking out of the window. I saw some guy who was waiting on his Bentley GT, doing the most to get some shorty's attention. She looked familiar, but I couldn't really remember from where. She was beautiful as fuck, but I couldn't quite place where I'd seen her. I shrugged it off, and then grabbed my things so I could head home to re-shower and get dressed. Tonight my brothers and I were going to the strip club, and I wanted to make sure I had enough time to get ready.

I made it home to my condo on Washington in Brighton, and parked my midnight blue Tesla underground. Getting out, I hit the alarm and then nodded my head to say what's up to this shorty who lived in my building named Faith. She and I flirted a little here and there, and she gave me some head once, but we were nothing major. I liked that she wasn't clingy, and understood her place from jump.

"About time!" Tekeya barked before the front door could even close good.

"Yo, why the fuck are you in my crib anyway? How the fuck you get in here?" I hissed as I put the locks on.

"I had a key made, nigga!" she dangled the lone key before slipping it back into her jean pocket.

I bought a house for Tekeya and I to move into when I was clearly not in my right mind. She moved in, and I kept procrastinating with my shit. I knew I didn't want that shit with her at this time in my life, so I bought myself a condo to stay at. She lived in the mansion I bought, and I lived here. I purposely didn't give her a key, but clearly she caught me slipping.

"Oh my gosh, yo," I mumbled as I made my way to the bathroom to get my shit ready for a shower.

"And where the fuck are you going?"

"With my brothers Key, damn!"

"Britain, we need to talk. I've been living in that big ass house by myself for eight damn months now! When are you gonna grow up and get rid of this bachelor pad?"

"Never with the way you're always sweating me, ma! I can't do shit without you breathing down my neck like some damn dragon!"

Before I could even finish tying my dreads up for the shower, Tekeya was taking off on me. Like always, I had to dodge her heavy-handed ass, and grip her wrists to constrain her. Tekeya was a 5'2" beast, but because I was 6'5" and strong, if I hit her little ass I would surely kill her. And I was taught to keep my hands to myself, with women anyway, but damn did she make it hard.

I stared down at her expressionless as she panted heavily like some wild animal. Tekeya was beautiful with her smooth dark skin, and thick ass body. She had the body of a BBW, except her stomach was flat and toned. She was rocking a four pack, but it wasn't masculine, it was sexy. She kept her hair in a cut Rihanna used to wear in her younger days; I think they call the shit a bob or something. Tekeya was bad, and any nigga that laid eyes on her was always left drooling. But as the saying goes, for every beautiful woman, there is a nigga who is tired of fucking her, and in Tekeya's case, that was me.

I could barely fuck her with the way she acted. I used to believe personality didn't matter when it came to sex, but it definitely did. Every time I tried to get some pussy, my dick just wouldn't do what I wanted because her bad attitude was always fresh in my mind. And when I did get hard by thinking about another bitch I fucked, the sex was still underwhelming. She seemed to still like it thought.

"Britain, please," she began to sob hysterically.

I swear this was the same routine, every got damn day, except it wasn't in my damn condo. I would see her, she would go off on me and then try to fight. Once I stopped her blows, she would glare at me for a bit before crying.

"You're running me low, Key, fuck," I sighed and pulled my shirt off.

"Baby, I know I've been a handful, but it's just that I can't get what you did out of my mind. All I see are those girls you fucked behind my back. And then you won't even move in."

"Key, please move so I can close the door and shower."

She stared up at me, trying to get sympathy but I wasn't having it. I was muthafuckin' tired! As soon as I closed the door, I heard her start to weep loudly. I couldn't get out of here and to the strip club fast enough. But before I did, I was gettin' my damn key.

Chapter 23

MATIKAH

A COUPLE DAYS LATER...

KIMBERLYN AND I WERE SITTING ON MY GRANDMOTHER'S PORCH JUST watching people walk and drive by. It was sunny, but a little bit nippier than usual. Goldie would be coming over in a short bit, and we were all gonna go to the movies since we wanted to help keep Kimberlyn's mind off of TQ.

"Are you gonna keep checking your phone?" I looked over at Kimberlyn.

"I'm trying not to," she chuckled, although I could tell she was sad that he hadn't contacted her ass.

"Why did you hang up on him without letting him explain anyway?" I frowned.

"Because there was nothing to explain. I heard the girl call him baby and ask if he was coming back. He told me he was going to bed with his lying ass."

"So why check your phone so much if you're done?"

She just shrugged and then leaned back on her elbows. Suddenly, we heard loud music coming from a black Lamborghini that had just hit the corner. The windows were dark, and they were flying down our street, making everyone outside stare. Kimberlyn and I tensed up a bit, hoping that this wasn't someone coming to do a drive-by. Our neighborhood, Roxbury, wasn't the safest, and it'd been given plenty of nicknames, alluding to the danger that could be found here.

The sports car swooped in front of my grandmother's house, making Kimberlyn and I stand up and start heading inside.

"Matikah!" a familiar voice called out to me. I turned around to see Lendsey, and was annoyed at how a smile appeared on my face. I hadn't talked to him since I visited his condo, despite his efforts to get at me through numerous texts and phone calls.

"Can I help you?" I walked back to the edge of the porch and poked my hip out, folding my arms across my chest.

"Yeah, you can help me with a lot of things." He licked his sexy lips as he rounded the front of his car to step onto the sidewalk. I loved how much style he had, and even his cocky ass attitude. "Come with me and let's get something to eat, ma."

"Lend—"

"Come on, man, you're tripping on me for no fucking reason. You're really gon' dis me because of some fuckin' phone call?"

I looked off to my left, squinting my eyes at the sun. I then looked over my shoulder at Kimberlyn, who shrugged saying she had no advice for me.

"Where do you wanna eat?" I asked, and the biggest most beautiful grin appeared on his sexy face.

"Wherever you wanna go."

"I want Tasty Burger," I suggested one of my favorite spots to eat. I was obsessed with burgers, and thank God I was naturally in shape or I would be like a hot air balloon by now.

"Aight, bet."

"Tell grandma for me?" I looked to Kimberlyn, and she nodded while holding onto the screen door of the home.

"And you quit giving my bro a hard time, shorty," Lendsey pointed to Kimberlyn, as he held his passenger door open for me.

Kimberlyn just rolled her eyes and went into the house.

"So whose car is this?" I asked as Lendsey pulled from the curb, headed to the burger joint.

"This is my car; I have two of them. I change cars depending on how I'm feeling that particular day, ma."

"Oh, excuse me. I wish I had *one* damn car." I looked out of the window as he made a left turn.

"Maybe I can make that happen for you."

"Oh really?"

"Yeah, but that depends on how you act. All that running off shit ain't gon' get you a car, shorty."

"What makes you think I'd want a car from you? You'd probably hold it over my head for the rest of my life."

"That's not really my style, and who wouldn't want a free car?" he looked at me as he pulled into a park on Boylston Street.

I just smacked my lips, causing him to chuckle lightly before getting out of the car. I pulled the lever on my door, and as I was stepping out, he helped me. I was wearing a dress, and I saw his eyes traveling up my thighs.

"My face is up here, nigga!" I snapped my fingers in his face, which brought out his alluring smile yet again. Why was he so fine? I mean if I were him and that damn good looking, I'd be smashing hoes too.

"My bad," he laughed and then took my hand into his.

I thought about pulling away, but I liked the feeling. I guess it was okay to entertain this madness for now. We went into Tasty Burger, ordered our food, and then sat at a table near the wall. I prayed over my food with the quickness, and then dug right in, closing my eyes to relish in the moment.

"Damn, it's really not that good," he furrowed his brows.

"It is too, I love burgers."

"A girl that loves burgers? I ain't never heard that shit before. You're making me like your ass more and more."

"So you like me?"

"You been knew that, Matikah. When I asked you for your

number you should've been able to see that. I don't ask for girl's numbers."

"Oh what, you hold them at gunpoint and then rummage through their purse for their cellphone to call yourself?" I quizzed and bit into my burger. The look he gave me made me laugh loudly, even though my mouth was full of food. I couldn't help it.

"Fuck you, shorty. Nah, I usually spit my game and then fuck right then and there. Ain't no need for a number."

"You know you are not helping yourself by telling me this."

"I'm being honest. My father always taught me to be honest about shit," he shrugged, and sipped some of his drink.

"That's good. So that means if I ask you a question, you will answer it for me honestly?"

"I will."

"Okay, did you have sex last night?" I cocked my head, eating a fry in the process.

He flashed me his smile, in which his bluish gray eyes lit up.

"Yeah man, I did. But so what, ain't like I could've gotten it from you. I would much rather have you in my bed."

"Unfortunately Lendsey, I'm not like the rest of the female population here in Boston, so I'm not anxious to get in your bed just because you're a Quinton."

"And that's why I brought you out, *and* asked for your number." We stared into one another's eyes, and then resumed eating.

Once we finished our food, we trashed the scraps and left. Sadly, I was not ready to go back to my grandmother's house. I was enjoying Lendsey's company, and I liked how we could joke with one another. I was a person who made rude jokes, and most guys got offended, but not him. I refused to express my interest in him though.

"Would you like to come to my crib?" he asked as he peeled down Boylston. People were already out, ready to turn up since it was now dusk. We'd been in Tasty's talking for hours longer than I'd realized.

"You're not getting any, so that's fine."

"No problem," he snickered and then adjusted his grip on the steering wheel. We made it back to his home on Colborne Road, and then once he parked we headed up inside. "You can chill and cut the TV on, I'm gonna change."

"Don't get too comfortable, you're gonna have to take me home soon."

"Yeah, aight."

I walked slowly and aimlessly around his living room as if I hadn't been there before. I was checking to see if I saw any remnants of a woman; mainly a woman who was more than a fuck buddy. *The bathroom!*

"Hey, Lendsey, where is the bathroom?"

"To the left of the front door!"

I rushed to the bathroom, and was surprised to see it had a very manly touch. I found nothing belonging to a woman, which made me smile for some reason. I did have to pee, so I relieved myself, washed my hands, and then returned to the living room to see Lendsey on the couch texting.

He was rocking some gray joggers, socks, and a white t-shirt. He wasn't wearing a hat, and I could see his short, kinky hair. He stroked his beard as he read something on his phone, before finally looking up to see me nearing.

"Texting one of your trollops?" I sat down on the couch.

"Actually, I was texting about some business," he responded.

He then turned the phone over, removed the battery and SIM, and then slipped a new SIM card into it. That was when I realized it wasn't his iPhone that he'd had earlier.

"What do you do exactly?" I questioned.

"You don't need to know all that."

"If you like me and you wanna date me, I need to know something, Lendsey. I'm not gonna be completely oblivious. And I'm not asking for details and your work schedule, I just want to know what it is that makes it so you can afford such a nice place."

He stared at me for a couple moments and then cut his TV on. Looking back over to me, his pretty smile appeared again.

"I help people who aren't here legally, look like they are. I also help people who have to trash their old identity, and become someone else."

"So you help bad people stay bad."

"Not all the time, shorty, sometimes I help good people stay alive."

"I don't see how that's possible," I chuckled.

"A woman who has an abusive husband or boyfriend is finally able to sneak out one night. She goes to stay at some hotel with her two young children, but she knows soon enough her crazy ass man will find her, and probably do more harm than ever since she ran away. He has people everywhere, and he can find her at the drop of the dime. He pays close attention to debit and credit cards, so he knows where she swipes them and what city she's swiping them in. He knows if she purchased a ticket to somewhere, and where she may be staying. All he needs to do is go to the front desk and ask if they have someone there by that name. What's her only option? To become someone else so that she's untraceable, and I help her do that," he explained to me.

"I guess I didn't think of it that way."

"I know my brothers and I seem like bad people. Everyone sees the Quinton Crime Family as this family and friends of thugs who do nothing but terrorize the East Coast. That ain't it though. We do make our money illegally, but we ain't purposely harming niggas, only the ones who cross us. Don't tell nobody any of this, Matikah. Quinton Crime Family is a speculation and I want it to stay that way."

"I would never tell, just because you trusted me enough to tell me. I'm glad I asked though, I feel like I see you differently now," I half smiled.

"That's good. I've been trying to show you that I ain't some horrible ass nigga, but you only wanna listen to your hood rat ass neighbors or whomever you get your info from," he cheesed, and I just admired how gorgeous he was.

"I didn't want to say this, but you are so fine. It's easy to get lost in your smile, it's so warm despite who you are."

"You ain't too bad looking yourself, Matikah. I just knew you had a nigga who was crazy about you, but I had to come for you anyway."

"I'm glad you did, because I don't have anyone." I looked towards the TV.

Suddenly, he pulled me closer by my wrist, and into his lap. I was straddling him, and my hands gravitated to the sides of his face. I let my thumbs brush across his beard as I stared down into his beautiful eyes.

"You're telling me that I don't have to fight for you, and you're fair game?" he quizzed.

"Pretty much. I told you this already though, the first night I met you."

"I was worried that you wouldn't know what to do with a nigga like me, but I think you got it, ma." He gripped my ass and let me feel his hard ass dick. *Damn.*

"I think I got it too."

"So what's good? You gon' quit playing games and shit? I wanna take you to the movies or something, I ain't never done that before."

"That's fine, but I need a kiss first."

"Say no more. You're gonna stay the night with me or do I have to take you home?"

"I think you should take me home, but I'm gonna stay against my better judgment," I responded, making us both laugh lowly.

"I have an extra room if that's what you feel more comfortable in, but I'd prefer it if you slept in my bed."

"That's fine." I leaned my face closer to his, and our lips pressed against one another. His lips felt so soft and moisturized. I loved that they were full like mine, because I didn't feel like I was swallowing him up or something.

I knew Goldie warned me about him, but I just didn't care to listen. Call me a fool.

Chapter 24

LENDSEY

THE NEXT MORNING...

I woke up and wiped my eyes, before slowly looking over at a sleeping Matikah. The smell of her perfume was still in the air, but very soft. I stared at her for a couple moments, watching her chest go up and down slowly. She was so damn pretty that I could look at her ass all day.

I didn't know what it was about her, but I liked her a lot. From the first day that I saw her, I could feel the difference in the energy she had. I'd been dealing with women for over ten years now, since I was fourteen, and I could eye ball when a woman was a hoe, gold digger, etc. When TQ invited she and her friends over, I immediately began feeling them out by watching their demeanor. Kimberlyn was off limits, but Matikah was the one who caught my eye anyway. I could tell by the way her friend Goldie walked over that she was damaged, so I completely ignored her despite her good looks. Matikah looked way better anyway... to me.

I didn't know what I wanted to do with Matikah just yet, but I knew I wanted her to be mine. Girlfriend was something I'd never really taken seriously, but I knew that Matikah was not the type to allow me to do whatever the fuck I wanted, and for some reason I liked that. I needed that discipline.

After looking at my soon to be wife for a couple more minutes, I rolled out of bed and shook my head at the woody in my boxers. Walking into the bathroom, I pulled my electronic toothbrush from the drawer, and got to work. After rinsing my mouth with some oral rinse, I climbed into the shower and cleaned myself up.

Freshly showered, I sprayed some of my Axe body spray on, and then wrapped a towel around my waist before going to get my phone. I peeked into my bedroom to see Matikah was still knocked out, but now on her stomach.

"Hello?" the female answered.

"What's good? I need some stuff to be dropped off in the next twenty minutes. Get whatever kind of soap women use, a toothbrush, and bring some outfits from Urban Outfitters." I'd seen the tag in Matikah's dress, and it was from UO, so I assumed she liked them.

"No problem, and what size clothes?"

"Numbers or letters?"

"Just give me both, just in case."

"Small, 1's, and early twenties." I remembered the size was a small on her dress tag.

"Got it. Be there in twenty, boss."

I hung up, and then padded back to my room to get dressed. I slipped on some boxers, then some dark jeans, a gray polo, and some gray Jordan Retro 3's. After putting on my watch and subtle chain, there was a knock at my condo door. I peeked out the peephole, and smiled when I saw Dimitria, my dad's assistant. She was really an assistant to the whole family, but her main focus was my father.

"Here is the stuff you asked for, Lendsey. There is some Dove soap, Vagisil, deodorant, panties, a toothbrush, and then the clothes." She handed me a target bag and then two Urban Outfitters bags.

"Damn, I forgot to ask for half of this shit. Good thing you're a woman D," I replied as we chuckled.

"Yes, I know. The total was $488.56 for everything."

"Cool." I reached down into my jeans, peeled off ten fifties, and then handed them to her. "Oh, here's an extra fifty just for being prompt."

"Thanks honey, let me know if you need anything else." She turned on her heels and switched down the hall.

I rushed to my bedroom, and then sat on the edge of the bed to tug on Matikah's toe. My mother used to always wake me up that way, and I hated it so I wanted to try it on someone else. Matikah opened her eyes, and when they landed on me she smiled.

"Get up so we can go eat breakfast." I lifted the bags in the air for her to see.

"What time is it?" she wiped her eyes.

"It's 8:30am, so hurry up so we can eat at Thornton's. You know they close early as fuck, shorty, and I'm starving."

She nodded and then peeled back the covers to get out of bed. Her dress was up a little, and the glimpse I got before she pulled it down had my dick hard as a missile yet again. She pushed her long curly locks to the other side of her head, and then reached for the bags. She looked into the Target ones, and then grabbed the Urban Outfitters one.

"How did you know I liked them?"

"Saw the tag in your dress."

"Wow, a man who pays close attention, I like that." She bit down on her lip, and then sauntered to the bathroom to get ready.

While she showered, brushed her teeth, and got dressed, I pulled out my laptop to handle some business. I'd processed a couple new identities, and wanted to check my system to make sure they'd gone through already. I made about $6,000 per identity that I created, and I created about sixty per week. The only time I charged less was when it was a single mother who didn't have that kind of money. In that instance, I took whatever they could spare. I got a pretty nice income from this shit, and on top of that, I got paid from helping my dad run Quinton Workforce Solutions, an unemployment agency. All in all, I was doing very well.

"I'm ready," Matikah walked in, and I could tell her hair was a bit damp in some areas.

"You washed your hair?"

"No, you forgot to get me a shower cap, but it's cool. It's time to redo it anyway. Let's go eat." She walked over to me, and then kissed my lips slowly.

I gripped her ass in my hands, and squeezed so hard I thought I would burst it. I then hugged her small frame in my arms as our kiss became more passionate, but she finally backed way.

"Come on, Lendsey," she tugged on my wrist, so I got up from the chair in my room so that we could leave.

We got to this place called Thornton's, and I swear I ate breakfast here almost every morning. Because I always woke up early, I enjoyed the luxury of sitting down and enjoying a big ass meal before starting my day. The staff knew me around here since I came so much, and because I did, Matikah and I were seated immediately and in my favorite spot.

"You ever been here?" I inquired as Matikah looked over the menu. I already knew what I wanted because I got the same thing every day.

"No, I usually just go to McDonalds, I'm obsessed with the McGriddle. But I can see you love it here."

"I do," I smiled, just as a waitress came to our table to take our order. "Can I get my usual?" I said to Deanna, the waitress who always took my order.

"Sure, the French toast with chocolate, and the omelet?" she asked as she wrote it down.

"That's right."

"And for you, pretty lady? I've never seen Lendsey bring someone with him in the three years he's been coming, so you must be special." I told her to say that if I ever brought a girl here, because if I did, it meant I really liked them. Deanna would be getting a nice tip for doing what I'd asked.

"I must be," Matikah grinned. *Yep, I got her little mean ass.* "I will have the breakfast burger please, but I'd like Swiss cheese on it instead of cheddar."

"You got it, and orange juice for the both of you?" Deanna questioned and we both nodded our heads 'yes'.

"I'm starting to like your ass," Matikah spat and twisted her full lips once Deanna walked away.

"Of course you do, I'm Lendsey Quinton."

"Negro, bye!" she threw her hand up as she laughed.

As I reached across the table to take her small, soft, hands into mine, I felt someone staring at the side of my face. People were piling in already, so I waited until a couple walked passed the person eyeing me, before looking over discreetly. *Dania, fuck.*

Dania knew she was on thin ice ever since she took off on my cousin, so she wouldn't dare act a fool right now. The most she may try to do is run off at the mouth, but she would keep her hands to herself, I hoped. If she decided to get buck in this restaurant while I was working on Matikah though, I would dead her ass and sleep like a baby at night. I let her slide with bullshit in the past because honestly I didn't care about them other hoes, and usually by the time Dania had fought them, I'd already fucked. But Matikah was different, and she'd better realize that without me having to tell her.

"So when are we going to the movies?" Matikah asked as I kissed the backs of her hands and then let them go.

"I got some shit to handle tonight and tomorrow, so what about Sunday night?"

"That's fine. Since it's summer I don't have to worry about waking up for class in the morning on Monday." I liked that she went to school.

"What are you in school for?"

"I'm in cosmetology school."

"Oh you do hair, or am I wrong? I think that's hair, ain't it?" I frowned and sipped my juice that Deanna had set down.

"It's all things beauty, but no, I'm there for massage therapy and to be an esthetician."

"An esti what? The fuck is that, shorty?"

"Basically, I'm gonna be waxing people's bodies, mainly women's pubic area. Also, I'm gonna be able to do massages too."

"Oh word? I would love to do the waxing shit," I cheesed, and she playfully rolled her eyes.

"You're disgusting. I don't even think like that. It's just work to me, and I've seen plenty of vaginas already just from learning."

"Well we have that in common because I've seen plenty of pussy as well," I laughed and she playfully rolled her eyes. "So what, you want your own spot or something?"

"Eventually, but right now I was promised a job at a local salon, so I will be a waxing specialist there once I take my final."

"That's dope."

Right when I said that, Dania walked by us, but there were two tables between us when she did. She then went back and sat down, before continuing to stare. I knew she was salty because I'd never taken her here, but she knew I loved it. I also knew she was here because she was hoping to run into me since I hadn't talked to her in a couple days.

I pulled my personal phone from my jean pocket, and then went into my texts to hit her up.

Me: Get the fuck out of here right now. I ain't fucking around and you know that.

Out the corner of my eye, I saw her look down at her phone screen. She looked longer than she needed to, before getting up and rushing out dramatically.

"So are you spending the night again? You have clothes at my condo now," I smirked. "I have to do some work, but I will only be away for a couple hours."

"I guess another night wouldn't hurt."

I was determined to make Matikah mine, and I would clear out anyone and anything who tried to get in the way of that shit. Hopefully, I wasn't the one who got in the way of us becoming an 'us'.

Chapter 25

KIMBERLYN

A FEW WEEKS LATER...

Tonight the Quinton's were having a party. It was the youngest brother, Britain's birthday. Although a big time party, only a select amount of people were invited, which is why this was the first year ever that I'd heard about it, as well as all the other parties they threw. Unfortunately, I wasn't invited by TQ, because he and I hadn't talked in about a month. Lendsey and Matikah had gotten pretty close, so he told her she could bring anyone she wanted. I didn't want to come because technically I wasn't invited, and then to make matters worse, Matikah was coming with Lendsey. But thank God Goldie agreed to come, because she was gonna be my date for the night.

"This is it? Damn," Goldie giggled as she pulled into the driveway of a huge ass mansion. There were a bunch of luxury vehicles parked outside, and a few valet attendants.

"I wonder whose house this is?" I questioned as I stared out the window.

"You would know before me, you're the one fucking one of them. Excuse me, I mean you used to."

"Thank you for reminding me," I said as the valet attendant opened the door for me.

"I don't mean to be like that, Kimberlyn, it's just I told you his ass wasn't shit, and only good for some dick, but you refused to listen to me." She shook her head as we walked up to the door to two big ass bouncers.

We gave them our names, and let them know we were on the guest list for Matikah Jacobson, before he let us into the party. Immediately, we were greeted by some waitress holding a tray of champagne filled flutes. She had on the skimpiest outfit, but she filled it out well. Goldie and I took a glass, and bobbed our heads to "Tongue Out" by Smoovie Baby that was blasting.

Although I didn't want them to, my eyes instantly began scanning the room, looking for TQ. My heart began beating fast, and my stomach dropped as if I were on a big ass rollercoaster when I spotted him with some bitch in his lap. He was saying something to her, and another girl sitting beside him. I watched him grope them both while biting his sexy lip. He looked so good tonight in a black polo shirt, black jeans, black Nike Huaraches, and a black bucket hat. I hadn't seen him in so long, and it was like I needed him. He sported a gold chain link watch with diamonds that I could see from a mile away, a gold bracelet, and a gold chain.

"Let's mingle, don't get caught up in staring at him. You see he ain't tripping off of you," Goldie said. I nodded my head and then polished off the champagne in the glass.

Tonight I was dressed simple but still sexy. I made sure to use the money given to me by TQ to get the works, which included my hair, eyebrows, nails, and even a full body wax. I got a massage too, so I was happy he hadn't snatched his money back out. I was walking on sunshine until I just witnessed his hoe ass. Anyway, I had on a white dress that hugged my slim thick frame perfectly. It was just the right length, giving a perfect view of my smooth golden legs.

"There's Matikah," I smiled and pointed to my cousin who was in Lendsey's lap, smiling and laughing like she was living life. "Heeyyy!" I walked up and she stood to her feet to hug Goldie and me.

"Hey, you guys look nice. Did Grandma say anything about me not coming home last night?" Matikah whispered to me, and I shook my head 'no' as I grabbed another flute containing champagne. I needed all the alcohol I could get.

"Nah, she knew where you were. Did you guys...?" I raised a brow.

"No, almost, but no. No offense but, after the way TQ played you I'm a little scared to go that far. I feel like as long as we don't fuck, if he leaves I will be good."

"Thanks for that, Tikah," I chuckled, although I was real fucking irritated. Not with my cousin, but with my dumb ass choices.

"This party is crazy!" Goldie smiled as she eyed Britain. She liked him way more than she let on, and when she finally admitted that to herself, maybe she would get off my head about TQ.

"It is," Britain licked his lips as his eyes ran amuck all over Goldie's body. He looked like he was a dog, and I knew he was. I was just waiting for him to bark. I mean, why was his girlfriend *never* at these events?

Britain was cute as fuck just like his three brothers. He was light skinned, had dreads, a lot of facial hair, dimples, and those same pretty blue gray eyes. He was about 6'5" like his brothers, and was built like a muthafucka.

"Hi Kimberlyn, Goldie, nice to see you guys again," Summer stood up to hug us. She was so pretty and I loved that she kept her dreads intact.

All of us began to make conversation, and as I was getting to know Summer, TQ came up with a whole new bitch under his arm. She wasn't even one of the girls he was with prior, but she was really pretty too. She had brown skin, a long ass expensive weave, DD-cups, and a big butt that I could've set my glass on.

After dapping his brothers up, this nigga had the nerve to say, "Hi Kimberlyn." He flashed his gorgeous smile at me, and that one dimple appeared. His bluish gray eyes were glazed over, letting me know he was lit, and his caramel complexion was vibrant as always.

"Hey," I waved lazily before turning my attention back to Summer.

"Hype" by Drake came on, and everyone began to dance with someone; even Goldie was freaking on some random, and the other bitch was working on TQ. I was so mad that I knew if I squeezed my glass any harder, it would burst.

I just sat there like a fool, before pulling my phone out to scroll on Instagram. Some guy came and stood by the velvet rope, and flailed to get my attention. He was a nice looking guy, but he was no Tarenz Quinton. Nobody was as good looking as him, except his brothers, and still TQ was number one to me.

"Wanna dance ma?" he asked.

"Sure," I half smiled and got up.

We made it to the middle of the dance floor in the huge ass mansion, and before I could even press my ass against his pelvis good, I was being snatched the fuck up by none other than TQ. He pulled me through the crowd, and down some hallway that had a door, which he closed right after.

"What the fuck? Why did you pull me back here?" I frowned and folded my arms. Little did he know, I was happy to be getting any of his trifling ass attention.

"So you gon' dance on old boy like I'm not here? That's disrespectful as fuck, shorty," he grinned and clasped his hands at his pelvis. Why the fuck was he so bomb?

"Excuse me? Do we really wanna list shit that's disrespectful, TQ? How about the fact that you were in South Carolina with some bitch! Or the fact that you were just all up on three different bitches in a matter of an hour!"

"Aye! Who the fuck you yelling at, ma? Lower your muthafuckin' voice and show me some fuckin' respect up in here! You better act like you know, Kimberlyn, don't nobody raise their voice at me!" he hissed, and the floodgates between my legs broke.

"Sorry," I said as I backed away from him slowly.

"I tried to explain to you what was going on that night, but your hard headed ass wanted to hang up the fucking phone and shit! You lucky I ain't come through your hood and bust a cap in yo' ass for being rude as fuck!"

"I-I'm sorry, TQ," I whined, praying he didn't kill me. His sexy face was knotted up like crazy, so I knew he was mad.

"I was about to go to bed, but my fucking brothers invited some hoes over. One of them was on me and that's who the fuck you heard, Kimberlyn. I told yo' ass beforehand that if you were gonna be mine, you were gonna have to be mature, have my back, and ride for me. Having my back is believing me when I tell you some shit, or at least giving me the chance to! I ain't scared of no got damn body but God, so ain't no reason for me to lie to you, aight?"

"So you didn't sleep with her or anyone that night?"

"Yep! I did! I had a foursome with some pretty ass bitches in that hotel since you wanted to act like a little ass baby!"

"Fuck you, TQ! I knew you would be doing shit like this." I tried to walk around him, but his tall sexy ass kept moving around, blocking me. "Let me by, I'm done here."

"Oh you done?" he moved closer to me, making my breath become shallow.

"Yes."

He backed me into the wall, and ran his strong tattoo covered hands up my dress while kissing me hungrily. I missed the nights we shared where he would show me all the things he enjoyed in the bedroom, and talking to him about the places he'd traveled and the people he'd met. He would even speak Russian for me sometimes.

He gripped my ass, and then began running his fingers across my center. I moaned softly into his mouth as he kissed me, letting our tongues dance. Suddenly, he lifted me up after unbuckling his pants, and then slid me down onto his dick after moving my flimsy thong to the side. He had me pressed against the wall, so I was forced to take every powerful stroke he delivered.

"Who you done with?" he asked me, squinting his eyes as he thrust into me slowly. There was no reason why something should feel this good.

"Nobody," I whimpered like a little child as I felt my orgasm building.

"I missed my pussy," he grunted and sucked on my neck, which made me cum immediately. "I can tell you've been saving it for me."

"I have," I said before planting kisses on his lips.

He sped up his pumps, and soon enough he was filling me up with his semen. Once we caught our breaths, he slid out of me, and let me down slowly. We then went into the bathroom together to clean ourselves up.

"You forgot a condom," I said in a low tone as I wiped between my legs.

"You're coming home with me tonight?" he ignored my statement, as he buckled his jeans back.

"I can, I just need to get some clothes from my grandma's."

"Nah, you got some shit that I bought you still at my crib." He washed his hands.

"I thought one of your new hoes would've taken it or thrown it out," I scoffed. He turned around and backed me into the wall so fast that my foot shifted to the side. That shit hurt!

"What kind of nigga do you think I am?"

"Huh?"

"Seriously, honestly. What kind of punk bitch ass mark do you think I am, that I would allow some bird to be throwing shit out of my condo like she lives there."

"Well, when girls see my Dove body wash, they may not have wanted to fuck with you," I smiled and so did he as he stared down at me.

"Nah, they don't care. I always get the pussy no matter what, except when with you, because you had rules for me. I kind of liked that."

"Can we leave now? I want you to show me some more ways to please you."

He raised a brow in response as if he was saying *oh word?*

Without another peep, I washed my hands and then we left out. I said goodbye to my cousin and Goldie, and I saw they both were giving me half smiles since I was holding hands with TQ's crazy ass.

As we were leaving, I peeped Gang, Peel, and Peel's girlfriend, Hayden, staring at us. Gang was wearing a deep scowl, and funny enough, so was Hayden. I followed her eyes, and they were definitely on TQ. Something was up with them, but right now I didn't care. I wanted to celebrate being back with my boo.

Chapter 26

TQ

I woke up next to Kimberlyn, and a smile spread across my face. I missed her ass but I wasn't about to go begging and pleading and shit like some bitch nigga. Especially when she was the one on that bull. Honestly, I was done with her little pretty ass, but when I saw her at the party I knew I wouldn't be able to end it. It was easier when I didn't see her, but as soon as I did, I knew I had to have my shorty back.

I climbed out of the bed, and grabbed my phone up before going into the bathroom to shower. Once I was clean, I brushed, flossed, and rinsed, then went to pick out my outfit. My dad texted me last night saying to come over ASAP, so that's where I was gonna go, after I ate some Cheerios though.

As I was eating, my system let me know someone was buzzing to be let up into my condo building. I frowned because I had no idea who it was. Only a select few knew where I lived, which was a mistake, but I didn't care since it wasn't people I worked with. Most bitches knew better, and would never try no shit with me.

I walked to look down out of my window, and saw it was Hayden's ass standing down there with her arms folded. I chuckled as I remembered her watching me leave with my shorty. Walking back to the bedroom, I shook Kimberlyn lightly until her eyes opened. She covered her naked body with the sheet, and then ran her fingers through her hair.

"I will be back in a little bit, aight? I got some shit to handle. If you wanna go somewhere, the keys to my G-wagon are by the door. If you crash it, I'm gonna crash that pussy. Actually, I'm gonna do that anyway, so have fun," I said making her laugh.

"Okay, don't leave me all day." She laid on her back as I walked to the bedroom door.

"I will do my best."

By now, Hayden was going dumb on my buzzer, so I grabbed my keys and phone before heading down. When she saw me walking out of the building, she stepped back so I could open the door.

"Fuck you doing? I'm leaving," I stopped her from trying to walk in.

"Is she up there?" she grimaced.

"Who?" I hit the alarm on my BMW 750i, and began walking towards it.

"The little girl that you stole from Gang, TQ."

"Oh, why does it matter where she is, Hayden? You know better than to question me, don't you?"

"Yes, but TQ, what the fuck? I haven't seen you in a week!"

"You just gave me some head four days ago, ma, what is you talking about?"

"And as soon as you came you made me leave!" she yelled louder than she'd intended to, prompting her to glance around to see who might have heard her.

"The point here is that you said you hadn't seen me, which you have. What you want from me? Where ya damn man at? Shit, I need this nigga to take you off my hands for a bit. You supposed to be his bitch but you stay in my face like you're mine."

"I want to see you tonight."

"Tonight ain't gon' work."

"Okay, what about tomorrow night."

"Aight, I got you. Don't hit me up though."

"Okay babe," she giggled and then rushed to her car.

To be perfectly honest, I wasn't even gonna hit Hayden up, I just said that to get her out of my sight. Strangely, Kimberlyn was enough for me.

I made it to my parents' home about thirty minutes later. I typed the code into the gate, and then drove downward to park underground. When I got inside, it was quiet, so I knew my mother and sister weren't there. Walking to the den, I put my phone on vibrate so it wouldn't disturb whatever the fuck we were about to discuss.

"Sup pops," I said to my father and sat down.

"Tarenz, who is this girl you're interested in again?" he squinted his eyes, trying to remember.

"Why?"

"It was brought to my attention that she belongs to someone else TQ, and that may cause some problems for me."

"So Gang ran to you like a little bitch because I took his girl?" I chuckled and shook my head. "I don't know what to tell you."

"TQ, you're not in love, we know that. Just give the girl back to the boy so we can continue making this money."

"What did he say?"

"He said he would look for another distributor. I could easily kill him, but he makes me a lot of money and I don't want to do that. Now, just send the girl packing, and all will be well." He lit his cigar.

"Nah, I can't do that."

"Seriously, son? You want to cause us to lose money over a girl that you don't even care for?"

"Don't worry about what I care for. I want her and I'm gonna keep her. Gang is gonna have to suck it the fuck up. I don' made my mark on shorty anyway, she wouldn't dare go back to him even if I did want to let her go."

"You're in love," he chuckled and puffed on his cigar.

"Are we done here? I have some shit to handle and take care of."

"Yeah we're done, but I mean it, TQ, get rid of her so we can get back to business. I don't wanna lose big money over some pussy that you *claim* you haven't even fallen in love with."

"Bye, Pops."

I left out and got in my car to think for a second. I refused to give Kimberlyn up, not only because Gang wanted her, but because I wanted her, and bad. She was mine, and wasn't shit about to take her away from me. I needed her it seemed.

I sped home, and when I walked into my condo, she was on the couch watching TV. She was wearing a red dress with no straps, and I could see up her smooth thigh. Walking over to her, I got down on my knees to look up into her pretty face.

"Who am I to you?" I quizzed and spread her legs to kiss her inner thighs.

"My boyfriend," she moaned softly once I reached the crotch of her lace panties to plant a kiss. I yanked her to the edge of the couch, and continued to kiss between her legs, gently.

"Which means you haven't been in contact with any other niggas, right? Not even when we had that little hiatus?" I looked up at her and she shook her head 'no' before caressing my fade.

I laid my head in her lap, and closed my eyes to enjoy the feeling of her soft hands rubbing my head. I couldn't lie, I enjoyed having someone to call my own. Smashing different bitches was tiring and monotonous. It hadn't become a problem until Kimberlyn and I broke up though. I realized I preferred fucking and sleeping next to the same girl, and not someone new every night. I guess my brother Rhys was right, it felt good to have someone to come home to.

"Why do you ask?" she questioned softly.

"I just wanna make sure I'm turning in my player card for the right girl."

"You are," she got down from the couch, and sat on the floor with me. "And I won't run off like I did before either. I'm gonna be around forever."

"Forever?" I grinned and she nodded. I caressed her smooth thighs before kissing her lips. "How do you know I want your little ass around me forever? I like change, shorty."

"I can tell. You like me and not just a little bit." She straddled my lap slowly. Damn, was it that obvious?

"I do. I don't know why, but I do. I thought about you everyday during the time we were apart."

"I thought about you too. I waited for you to call, but you didn't. Why not?"

"Pride. And honestly, I was attempting to make myself forget about you, and I thought it worked until I saw you last night."

"You tried to forget about me by smashing different bitches?" She shook her head and pushed her long hair from one side to the other.

"Yeah, I ain't gon' lie to you. I definitely was out there. You forgive me?" I asked and she nodded. Intertwining our fingers, I kissed her lips a couple times before pulling back to look into her eyes.

"You forgive me for hanging up on you?"

"Of course. As soon as I slid up inside you last night, all was forgotten," I replied and we laughed together. "I love your smile."

"Thanks."

I pulled her closer into me, and then kissed her hungrily before leaning her back onto the floor. I missed making love... I guess.

Chapter 27

SUMMER

I'D BEEN AT WORK ALL DAMN DAY, AND ALL I WANTED TO DO WAS COOK dinner and soak my feet while watching TV with my baby girl. I would love to include Rhys into the mix, but he was never home which in some cases I felt was best. He damn near lived in that hotel room that he kept booked just in case. It's like we both were holding onto a relationship that we needed to let go of, but something was stopping us. I think it's because we loved each other so much, too much, and even though our relationship was rarely happy, we couldn't let it go.

"Hey, you still here?" Hakim jogged over to me lightly as I packed up my things at the station. *This nigga is too fine.*

"Yes, but that's normal. I thought you left like thirty minutes ago?" I frowned, but was smiling on the inside. I was kind of happy he stayed behind for some reason.

"I was gonna leave but then I decided to hold off and umm, wait for someone."

"Oh yeah? Who? Nia and Renee just left, you missed them," I smirked and so did he, but not before he looked me up and down approvingly.

"Now you know I was waiting on you, ma, don't even play me like that."

"And why are you waiting on me?" I began to zip my suitcase up, and shut off my mirror lights.

"Because I wanted to ask you for your number. I want to get to know you better, but outside of this place. It's always someone around when I want to talk with you."

"Hakim, I have a boyfriend."

"Oh, damn, okay. Is it like serious? Or is this something new you've started?"

"No, it's serious, very. We have a daughter together, and we've been with one another for about ten years."

"Ten years?" he looked down at my hands and frowned. "And you don't have a ring? How old is he?"

"Why?" I folded my arms.

"I mean I was hoping his age would be the reason he hadn't asked you to marry him, but then again it shouldn't matter. Y'all have been together that long and have a child, I don't understand the hold up."

"Well, it's not for you to understand, Hakim. My boyfriend and I are working on some things and we want to get everything right before we walk down the aisle."

"How about you just take my number down, and if shit goes wrong, or if you need someone to talk to, hit me up. I don't bite, I just really like you and if there is a slight chance for me, I wanna take advantage of it, ya know?"

I wanted to say yes, but then I felt like it was wrong. But on the flip side, I was sure Rhys was still fucking with Lisa. I mean she was always making a big deal on social media about him, and she would somehow find out his new number every time he got one. He swore he didn't know how she was doing the shit, but I didn't believe that. I believe every time he got a new number, he was giving it to her. I turned my lip up at my thoughts.

"Okay, you can just have my number. I'm not a big first texter if you know what I mean."

"I do, and cool."

I read off my number to him, and smiled as I watched him store it. I was excited to get to know him, and hopefully he would be able to help me get over Rhys. I was tired of being wrapped around his finger. I wanted to be free, and I was sure Hakim would help me do that. The easiest way to get over one man is by getting with another.

"See you later, Hakim," I waved as we walked out of the building together and went our separate ways.

"I will be texting you soon!" he called after me.

I just half smiled and continued to my car.

As I was putting my suitcase into the trunk of my G-Wagon, I heard someone walking on the gravel of the parking lot behind me. I glanced over my shoulder, and saw the last person I ever expected to see.

"What the fuck?" I turned to her with a frown. She looked like she'd just stepped off a runway, which was weird as hell. This was the second time I'd ever seen this bitch in person, and neither time was good.

"I told you I wasn't gonna just let you have him," she grimaced.

"Lisa, you need a life." Now if he wasn't messing with her, why is she here right now? Still on his dick. I swear I hated Rhys and all the turmoil he caused me.

"Oh I have a life, but I can't say the same for you."

"What?"

POP! POP!

She sent two bullets into me, one in my shoulder and one in my hand, before rushing off through the parking lot and into the darkness. My wounds burned as I began to hyperventilate. Was this really happening? Did I really just get shot over this nigga?

I quickly dug into my purse with my good hand as I cried out in pain. I began to feel weak as I searched and searched for my phone, which was nowhere to be found it seemed. It began ringing, allowing me to locate it, and when I retrieved it I saw Hakim's name.

"Hakim! Co-come ba-back to the agency, I've been shot!" I screamed and fell to the floor, still clutching my phone.

"What? Summer? Are you okay?" he quizzed like a fool.

"Call 911, Hakim!" I cried as my arm and hand began to ache terribly.

I was losing blood like there was no tomorrow, and getting more light headed by the second. Hakim continued talking, but I was no longer able to hold the phone. Falling backwards onto the ground, I shut my eyes and fell into the darkness, unwillingly. My mother always said Rhys would be the death of me.

Chapter 28

RHYS

THE NEXT MORNING...

"Baby—"

"Shut up, Rhys," Summer gritted as she stared at the wall in her hospital room.

Last night I thought I was gonna die when I'd heard she'd been shot. Then when she explained to me who'd done it, I felt even worse. I was happy she told the police she didn't know who shot her, because I wanted to enact revenge on her behalf.

Lisa, in my eyes, was never anything harmful. I didn't pay her much attention, and always felt like Summer was overreacting when she would have me change my number repeatedly. See, I wasn't the type of nigga that you could bug by texting and calling all day. For one, I barely used my personal cellphone because I was always working and mainly used dummy phones. I didn't believe in dummy phone apps and such, that wasn't nobody but the damn government. Secondly, I was the type who just wouldn't respond. You can text me twenty-four hours a day, and I just won't say anything back, it's really that simple. I never understood people who could be bothered by something so small, like my brother Lendsey who hated to be blown up. Yeah I had a temper, but shit like that did nothing to me, surprisingly.

By saying that, the fact that Lisa always found my number every time I changed it somehow was slightly alarming, but a nigga didn't give a fuck. I killed people for a living so there were matters at hand that were more important. There were bigger fish I was frying, or so I thought.

"Summer, I'm gonna take care of her."

"You should have taken care of her a long ass time ago, Rhys! That's how I know you're still fucking her! Talking about you don't know how she gets your number! Bullshit! Ah!" she winced in pain and clutched her shoulder where she was shot. "Move the fuck away!" she yelled to me when I attempted to touch her.

"I ain't fucking with Lisa, shorty, I haven't fucked with her since the last time you caught me fuckin' up, I promise."

"No, Rhys," she began to tear up, and I just didn't know what to do. I wanted to hold her, but I knew she wouldn't let me. "What if Bryleigh was with me? Thank God she was with your parents!"

"I swear this is the last time she's gonna fuck with you, baby." I kissed her forehead. Just then I heard some footsteps. I turned around to see some nigga and immediately frowned. "Who the fuck are you?"

"I'm Hakim, I'm Summer's co-worker. I'm the one who called for help when she got shot," he replied, adjusting his grip on the flowers.

"Oh word? Well umm, thanks, but you can go now. And take yo' fuckin' flowers with you." He looked from me to Summer as if he were asking her if it was okay to do what the fuck I'd just said. "I said to get the fuck up out of here!"

He jumped slightly at the boom of my voice, and then began to back away slowly.

"Just go, Hakim," Summer sniffled.

Once he left, I turned my attention back to Summer who was still crying a little bit. That nigga coming up in here with flowers rubbed me the wrong fucking way. He'd better find another nigga's bitch to bring flowers to, because bringing them to mine would only get his ass killed.

"Fuck is he, Summer?"

"He just told you, Rhys, don't start. Calm down, Rhys!" she shouted as I paced the hospital room angrily; she knew my fuse was short to nonexistent. Something in my gut told me to just kill that nigga.

"I'm gone," I said before slipping out of the room.

"Rhys!"

I don't know what she and Hakim had going on, but I was gonna be watching very closely. If he thought he was about to move in on her, he would be deadly mistaken; yes, deadly. And Summer might end up buried next to that nigga too.

THAT NIGHT...

I was chilling in Lisa's house on her couch after discreetly breaking in. I really didn't know what the fuck was wrong with this bitch. Shooting my girl? Really? It almost made me want to let muthafuckas know what I did for a living so that they could save themselves. Only if Lisa knew that I wasn't the one to play with. I admit I should've threatened her when she first started her antics, and maybe she wouldn't have gone this far, but it was too damn late.

"How did you get in here?" she walked in and closed the door behind herself slowly. She was really stupid to still be living her life like she hadn't just tried to kill my shorty.

"How have you been getting my new numbers, Lisa?" I only wanted one answer before I smoked her ass.

"Rhys, how did you get into my hou—"

"Oh, don't play the little scared bitch now!" I hollered so loudly that I could damn near see her jump out of her skin. "Tell me how the fuck you were able to get my number, bitch." I towered over her and then slowly brought my gun to her temple.

"Please Rhys," she began to sob. "I wouldn't have done if it you hadn't have been ignoring me! I told you I had something to tell you but you didn't listen! She was the reason—"

"I'm gonna ask you one more time, Lisa. How the fuck did you get my number every time I changed it?"

"My friend, Maria, works for your service provider, so whenever you changed it she would look you up and give it to me. But it was only because I needed to tell you I had an abortion when we first broke up—"

PHEW!

I put a silenced bullet into her head. Initially all I wanted to know was how the fuck she was getting my number before I killed her, but hearing her say she had an abortion made me kill her before I could even think. Not like I wanted kids with her ass because believe me I didn't, but the fact that she killed a child of mine angered me. I think I felt a bit guilty because I remember when we first ended it, she was blowing me up saying she was pregnant. I just chucked it up to her being a woman scorned, but I guess I was halfway wrong.

Getting back out of her home, I climbed into the car I'd driven over there, and took the long way to the warehouse. Why was this shit bothering me so damn much? I didn't kill the baby, she did! *You should've believed her when she said she was pregnant man*, I thought, but then quickly shook it from my head. Lisa was the past and that was it. And she could've been lying about the abortion anyway.

As I was driving, I got a text from this shorty named Chenaye that I'd chilled with a couple times. That's all we did was chill. I had a feeling she was starting to like me, but I'd stated plenty of times that I just wanted a homie and nothing more. She said she was cool with it, so I continued to be her friend.

I preferred to have female friends because one, niggas were dick riders these days and always begging to be down. Two, women were better looking, and three, niggas were fake, yes faker than bitches, oddly. The only dudes I called my friends were my brothers, and even them niggas irked me every now and then. TQ's friend Jayce was cool, but lately I felt like his ass was on some fake shit too.

Chenaye: *Wanna come over? I have your favorite drink.*

Me: Fasho

I made it to her house after dumping that car off and getting my shit from the warehouse. Chenaye lived with her mother, but her mom was never home. She traveled a lot with her husband who was some well-known pastor. I'd never heard of the nigga, but then again, I hadn't been to a damn church in years. Maybe that was my problem.

"Hey boo," Chenaye smiled as she answered the door.

I walked into her home, and frowned at the picture of her and some girl. I saw the picture every time I came over, and it always made me frown because I couldn't remember where I'd seen the girl before. They were both little kids in the picture, so it was hard to recall. I didn't want to ask because I felt like getting to know her too much would mix in feelings... on her part.

"It smells good in here." I plopped down on the couch and looked down at my phone to text Summer.

Me: Goodnight baby. Will be at the hotel tonight, and back to see you in the morning. Make sure that bitch ass nigga don't show up. I will bring Bry with me tomorrow.

I knew she wouldn't respond, but I didn't care. I'd thought about spending the night with her in the hospital, but I just wasn't in the mood to bicker. Also, that nigga with the flowers still had me hot. So after I left here, straight to the hotel it was.

"Hello Rhys!" Chenaye waved her hand in my face.

"My bad, what did you say?"

"I was thinking we could go to the movies or something."

"Nah, I told you we ain't doing all that. We're just associates, stop trying to make this shit become more than it is."

"I just thought—"

"Well don't. If you want a boyfriend, look elsewhere, Chenaye. I have a woman; all I want is a friend."

She just sighed and nodded, before pouring some Jack Daniel's into my glass.

Chapter 29

GOLDIE

I needed a few things like body soap, shaving cream, and razors, so I decided to stop by Target since they were cheaper than drug stores. Surprisingly, I made it out after picking up exactly what I came for. The cashiers even congratulated me for spending less than fifty dollars. I chuckled at the thought as I neared my car.

As I walked onto the driver's side, a familiar smoke gray Charger with dark ass tint pulled up on the side of me. I sighed and hit the unlock button on my key remote, hoping to hurry up and get into my car. Unfortunately, he was faster than me, and stopped me from getting in.

"What, Ethan?" I exhaled.

"Baby, let me talk to you for a second," he smiled as if everything was peaches and cream. This nigga hadn't talked to me since his baby mama tussled with me, and that was almost two damn months ago.

"You need to go talk to Juanita, Ethan. You asked for a chance and I gave you one, even though I knew I shouldn't have. You fucked that up so get the fuck over it. You and I are just not meant; why can't you accept that?" I frowned. I really wanted him to see that he and I were just not on the same page, nor would we ever be, at least not at the same time.

"I wanna try though, Goldie. That was our problem, you gave up on me. I still want to see where this goes. I love you and I wanna try and see if we can work this shit out, ma."

"Ethan, you need to take all this effort that you're trying to put into us, and put it into your family. You have a baby, and you should try with that."

"Juanita and I aren't even together, she's just on some jealous bull-shit, Goldie!"

"I don't care what the hell she's on! And Ethan, let's not forget, I know you, boo. I saw all in her face how in love she was with you, and how desperate she was to convince me to leave you alone. I know because that used to be me at one point."

"Goldie—"

"Please, Ethan! I am begging you! I am begging you to leave me be. I don't want to be with you, and it has very little to do with Juanita and your baby. I wasn't feeling it this go 'round, I really wasn't. I was lonely and I gave you a chance that you didn't deserve. Now please, just forget about me."

He was just looking pathetic at this point. He should've been able to see that this time was different. There were no tears, I wasn't hitting him, I wasn't threatening him, and I wasn't blowing his phone up for answers. My actions were screaming that I didn't care, yet he refused to see that.

"Don't try to make me out to be some desperate ass nigga shorty! Talking about you're begging me! You were the one who was on my nuts for years, not the other way around! You ought to be happy I even gave yo' ass a chance! There were plenty of hoes I could've made my bitch, yet I chose yo' inexperienced ass who could barely go anywhere that wasn't church and bible study!" he snapped.

"Okay, cool," I waved him off, prompting him to grab my wrist and twist the fuck out of it. "Ethan, stop, that hurts!"

Because this was the Target on Boylston, it was a pretty busy area. I was embarrassed like fuck at the fact that he had me about to cry. He finally let my wrist go, and then back handed me so hard that my eye immediately swelled shut.

"Please!" I pleaded with him, because the damage he'd done so far was already too painful to bear. I could only imagine if he kept going.

"Bitch," he snarled and then walked to his driver's side, before hopping in and speeding out of the parking lot.

I hurriedly climbed into my car, and just broke down crying. I for real hated my life, and no matter how hard I tried I was miserable. I spent years loving a man who never loved me, and when I finally found the strength to press on, he goes nuts.

Sometimes I felt like no one cared for me outside of Kimberlyn and Matikah. My mother despised me because I wasn't the same church girl I was raised to be. She was my mom, and she never even answered my calls. The only person that she and her pastor husband cared about was my sister, because she paraded around like she was the Virgin Mary. My sister and I didn't get along at all because I didn't deal with fraud people, and she was jealous of the fact that until I rebelled, I was the favorite child. We didn't claim one another either. It was almost like we didn't exist in each other's lives.

As for my father, he paid my bills as an incentive to stay away from him. He had a new wife and he wanted to appear childless for her. It hurt to know his reasoning for not wanting me around, but at least he was the reason I was able to survive outside of my mother's home. My job at the local drugstore paid nowhere near enough for me to live on my own.

I said a prayer to God, asking for some sun in this storm that I called life, all the while begging him to forgive me for being ungrateful for the blessings I did have. I felt a little better after that, so I cranked my car and went home to chill.

My best friends were boo'd up, so I was going solo tonight. I guess it was a good thing because if either one of them saw my eye, they would want to murder Ethan. I didn't want that, I just wanted to never speak of or see him again.

Chapter 30

MATIKAH

"Did you enjoy the movie?" Lendsey quizzed as we walked through the parking lot holding hands.

"I did."

Lendsey had me ready to do all kinds of things, but I wanted to be his girlfriend first before anything. We'd been spending a lot of time together, and things have gotten pretty close to going somewhere sexual, but before it did I wanted to find out where we were.

The drive had been quiet so far, and all we did was exchange glances here and there while listening to the music. My palms were sweating because I was so nervous to inquire about what we were to one another. I knew what type of guy he was, and I never expected to be so into him when we started hanging out. Everything Goldie told me danced in the back of my mind, yet I still pursued him and now I had strong feelings for him.

"We're going to your house?" I quizzed and he nodded as he made a right turn. *He's so fine*, I thought to myself.

"That's cool, right?"

"Of course," I chuckled for some reason like an idiot. *Nothing is funny, why are you chuckling, Matikah?*

We made it to his home, and once he parked his car, I decided to take the plunge and just ask him what the fuck was up.

"Lendsey, are we friends?"

"I think so," he half smiled. No, that wasn't what I meant to ask. I needed to stop being scary and grow the fuck up.

"No, are we together? Are you my boyfriend? What's up? I mean we spend a lot of time together, and I don't know I'm just wondering. No pressure though," I half lied. I wanted to fuck him so there was plenty of pressure.

"You wanna be together? You ready to be my shorty?" he smiled and gripped my thigh in his hand.

"Yeah."

The way he asked me started to make me wonder, but I knew I wanted this. I've wanted this from the first time I laid eyes on his sexy ass. I stared at the side of his face as he looked out of the windshield, thinking. If he needed this long to make up his mind, then it couldn't be good.

"I didn't know it needed to be spoken on, but since you need to hear it then yes, you are my girl."

"Cool," I nodded nonchalantly even though I was clicking my heels like Dorothy from the *Wizard of Oz* in my mind.

We got out of the car and headed up inside his condo. Grabbing a bottle of vodka and some glasses, we tread to his room to start drinking. Thank God I ate before the movie, or else I would be drunk right away from intake on an empty stomach. After my third glass of straight vodka with no juice or chaser, my body began to warm up and I was feeling real nice.

"Come here," Lendsey bit down on his plump bottom lip. He'd just dimmed the lights in his room, and removed his shirt. Suddenly as he neared me, I became a little bit scared of what he was about to do. "Relax," he began kissing my thighs while running his hands up my dress.

I inhaled sharply once I felt his strong hands grip the waistband of my underwear. Before I could even process it, he was pulling them down slowly. Removing my sandals, he threw them across the room, then yanked me to the edge of the bed so that my bottom half was hanging off.

"Ah," I moaned softly once he put his warm mouth on my vagina. It was weird at first, and I didn't know what to do, but when the pleasure kicked in, my body relaxed.

The combination of the liquor and the way his mouth felt had me on one. This was so good that I wanted to scream out as if I were the lead in an opera. Instead, I just bit my lip to muffle the moans that were begging to escape. Not satisfied with my reaction, he buried his face deeper into my center and began attacking me like a lunatic. I had no choice but to cry out as if I were being stabbed repeatedly.

"Mmm, fuck," I gripped my curly hair as if I needed it to calm me down.

Suddenly, the pleasure between my legs intensified to a point where my body quivered violently. Liquid seeped out, as my legs and torso continued to jerk lightly. I came. I finally understood the hype that surrounded orgasms. I gripped the back of Lendsey's head as he continued to devour me like his life depended on it. I released two more times before he stood up to remove my dress completely. As soon as my C-cups were on display, he took my nipples into his mouth. After getting his fix, he took my hand and put it down his pants to feel his erection. My eyes bulged out of my head almost at how hard it was, because I didn't even know it could get to that point.

He knew what I was thinking because he chuckled at my facial expression and said, "Yeah, I've been waiting for this."

Standing up off the bed, he removed his jeans completely along with his boxers. His golden brown complexion was gorgeous, just like his six-pack. He kept eye contact with me as he rolled a condom down, and the lust in his eyes was at an all-time high. He climbed onto the bed and got between my legs before tonguing me down passionately.

"Are you a virgin?" he looked into my eyes with a confused expression.

"No," I lied and chuckled slightly.

"Then why are you so tense?" he pursed his lips and smirked, knowing I was lying.

I was scared out of my mind of what was about to happen, but I wanted this; I wanted him. He was my man, and I wanted to be everything to him so that he would never stray. I prayed that he would be everything to me as well.

"I'm a virgin," I whispered and waited for his reaction.

"Why you lie?"

"I don't know."

"You thought I wouldn't fuck with you if you were a virgin or some shit?" he frowned and I nodded slowly.

"You are kind of old to be pure, but it's all good," he grinned and so did I.

"Fuck you, nigga," I spat before he slipped his tongue back into my mouth. Embarrassingly, I jumped when I felt the head of his dick poking at my hole.

"Just focus on the kiss," he instructed.

Again, we began kissing passionately, and I tried to ignore him sticking me down there. A shock of pain went through my body as he finally began pushing with all his might to get inside of my body. Whimpering like a little poodle, I dug my nails into his muscular biceps, hoping it would somehow ease the pain.

"Shit," he groaned and began kissing my neck. "Damn, shorty."

His eyes were closed so I knew he was enjoying this way more than me. With every pump, there was pain. After a few minutes the pain began to subside a little, and I felt the same pleasure I felt when he had his mouth down there. Cupping the back of his head, I kissed him hungrily knowing another orgasm would be near once all the pain ceased.

"You good?" he bit down on his lip as he thrust in and out of me slowly. I just nodded while moaning since I couldn't talk. "You feel good as fuck, shit." He looked down to watch himself work for a couple moments before making eye contact with me again.

I finally released, and once I did he sped up his pace. Placing my legs in the nooks of his arms, he slammed into me, prompting me to cry out loudly. He was soon moaning as well, and finally we exploded together. Removing the condom slowly, he got out of the bed and I listened to him go to the bathroom.

"Matikah, come here!" he called out, making me jump.

I got out of the bed slowly since my pussy was sore, and made my way to the bathroom. I stood in the doorway and watched him run some water in the huge ass bathtub.

"Come in here, let's take a bath."

"Together?" I frowned.

"Yes together, you're my shorty so we can do this. And I know that pussy is hurtin'," he chuckled. I just smacked my lips and walked over to him. "How do you feel?" he quizzed once we were in the warm water.

"I'm okay. It hurt way more than I thought it would."

"You'll get used to it." He gripped my breasts in his hands and then kissed on my neck from behind.

I surely hoped so. I was more than satisfied with my decision, however... at least so far.

Chapter 31

KIMBERLYN

Matikah, Goldie, and I were out to lunch at No. 9 Park. I was treating them since TQ had given me some money. He gave me way more than I would ever need for anything, so I wanted to do something nice for my friends.

"I have something to tell you guys," Matikah smiled as her eyes went from me to Goldie.

"What?" Goldie frowned. I was anxious to know too.

"I made a charge on my V card," Matikah grinned.

"Huh?" Goldie and I said in unison.

"I'm no longer a virgin."

"Since when?" I bucked my eyes.

"Since a couple nights ago. After we went to the movies, we went back to his house and it happened. It happened three times actually," she chuckled before sipping her water.

"You're so nasty," Goldie laughed. "So have you spoken to him since?"

"Yes I have, and I'm gonna go back to his house tonight. We're boyfriend and girlfriend now, so we're gonna be talking a lot. Even though we pretty much spent every day together when we weren't together officially."

"I'm happy for you and surprised. You know Lendsey has a bit of a record, so the fact that you got him to settle down in a sense is dope," I nodded.

"I can say the same for TQ," Matikah raised a brow at me. She laughed when I threw my hands up in mock surrender.

"Well if he has changed for you, then cool, but I doubt it," Goldie shook her head.

"Sometimes all it takes is the right girl for a man to get his act together," Matikah cocked her head and then lightly hi-fived me.

"What's up with his brother though, Britain? Does he talk to anyone? I saw him with a girl, but she didn't look important to him," Goldie inquired.

"I'm pretty sure he has a girl. Why didn't you ask him yourself when you were eye fucking him at the party?" I put some food into my mouth. I was sure TQ told me Britain had a girlfriend, but she was never, and I do mean never around him when I saw him.

"Because I was too scared. He had a bitch in his lap every time I rounded up the courage to say anything to him."

"Well like always, another party is coming up. Their oldest sister Saya is throwing it, and TQ invited me. I will bring you along," I stared at Goldie with a smirk.

"Why are you looking at me like that?" she giggled.

"Because you talk all this shit, knowing damn well you like Britain. And to make matters worse, he's the worst one of them all," Matikah spoke what was on my mind.

"True, but unlike you two, I just want some dick," she smacked her lips and the three of us burst into laughter.

After lunch, we went to the mall on Huntington Avenue. This mall in particular had high-end stores, which is why we chose it. We entered the Louis Vuitton store, and the purse that I'd been wanting for years was staring me in the eyes. I gravitated towards it, and glanced down at the price tag, which almost gave me a heart attack.

"You gonna get it?" Goldie questioned as she eyed it along with Matikah.

"I can't, it's too much." I shook my head.

"I thought you said TQ put a lot of money into your account?" Matikah raised a brow.

"TQ, huh?" a voice called out, making us all look back. It was Peel's girlfriend Hayden with some other girl.

Hayden and I were never the best of friends, but she was cool. We'd hung out, not on our own, because she was Peel's girl, and I was almost Gang's.

"Yes, TQ," I turned to face her fully, along with Goldie and Matikah.

"He's giving you money?" she cocked her head and folded her arms as if she were confused as hell.

"I don't really think it matters. You should worry about who Peel gives his money too, boo," I raised one brow.

I knew she was watching TQ at those past few functions for a reason. I wonder how Peel would feel about that.

"And what the fuck is that supposed to mean, bitch?" she snarled.

"Just what I said. Worry about your nigga and his funds, and I will worry about mine, baby girl."

She burst into laughter along with her friend, and then turned her attention back to me. She looked me up and down while grinning widely.

"Boo, please don't tell me Tarenz Quinton has you thinking that you're his bitch," she snickered as if she just couldn't help herself.

"She is his bitch, *boo*," Goldie chimed in, surprising me. She was usually so against TQ's and my relationship.

"That's cute, Kimberlyn. You should've stuck with Gang, at least you wouldn't be getting played. Anyway, tell TQ I said what's up and that I had fun chilling with him the other day," she winked and walked towards another area of the store where the scarves were.

"She's probably lying, Kimberlyn," Matikah rubbed my back.

"Maybe she is, maybe she isn't, but I'm gonna find the fuck out. And for his sake, she better be lying like fuck!" I fumed. Because I was angry, I bought the purse and the matching wallet to go with it.

Afterwards, we left the mall and I sped to TQ's condo. I had a key, so if he wasn't home, I would just wait for him. To my surprise, when

I got up inside, he was dressed, eating a bowl of cereal. He looked so nice in a cream colored sweater with two horizontal stripes on the sleeves, light blue jeans that didn't sag too much, a black baseball cap, and all white Adidas. His jewelry was subtle but still sparkled here and there.

Throwing my bags onto his couch, I stormed over to him, prompting him to crack up. I'd never seen a man so fine in all of my twenty-one years.

"What the fuck is so funny?"

"You storming over to me like I'm supposed to be scared or some shit," he snickered.

"You're fucking Peel's girl?" I cocked my head and folded my arms, waiting for his answer. My fists were clenched, waiting to rock his shit. He was 6'5" so I wasn't sure how I would get to his face, but I would find a way.

He stared into my eyes with his beautiful blue ones and said, "I have. Why?"

"She told me she chilled with you the other day. Is that true? When did you fuck her last?" I barked, slamming my hand down on the counter.

"Aye, calm yo' little ass down. Don't be walking up into my shit going loco on a nigga. I was minding my business eating my fucking Cheerios, and you just come up in my shit acting a fool!" He made his way around the island in the kitchen, and started towards me, wearing a scowl.

"Tell me when?" I repeated although scared.

He lifted me up and sat me down on the island, before standing between my legs. His strong hands ran up and down my thighs as he stared up into my face with a smug expression. I hated his cockiness, but loved it at the same time.

"I fucked her like three weeks ago."

"Really, TQ? Just three weeks ago?"

"Yes, three fucking weeks ago. After you got stupid with a nigga I fucked around with her and a couple other hoes, but you knew that. Why does it even fuckin' matter? Only person I'm fucking right now is you. You got a key to the crib, the necklace, and a diamond watch with my initials in it, you should know the position you have."

"How many women have positions in your life, TQ?"

"Well, my mama—"

"I'm serious," I cut him off and he cheesed before licking his full sexy lips, and stroking his neatly trimmed facial hair. His caramel complexion was so smooth, making me want to kiss it.

"It's just you, I told you that shorty. I don't want you questioning me about any other girl ever. Don't let these hoes get in your head when you know you're sleeping next to me every night, aight? Have I ever not come home to lie next to you at night?" he quizzed and I shook my head 'no'. "Exactly. Chill out, Kimberlyn."

I gripped the sides of his face gently, and pressed my lips against his. The kiss turned passionate, making us both release subtle moans here and there. I just needed to be more confident in my position in his life. And from now on, I would be.

Chapter 32

HAYDEN FRANKLIN

"That was her, huh?" my home girl Ingrid asked as we plopped down on the couch in my apartment.

"Yes," I sighed and ran my hand down my smooth, slicked back bun. "I forgot you've never met Kimberlyn."

All I wanted to do today was go out and get some retail therapy. But no, I had to run into the little bitch who had somewhat ruined my damn life in a sense. TQ was mine, he always had been, ever since we met in high school. I know I have a boyfriend, but Peel is just something to do while TQ plays dumb. As soon as TQ got his shit together, I would be right there, ready to be taken.

In all honesty, I would have no problem if he was just fucking Kimberlyn, but from what I'd witnessed there was more. He was doing things with her that he'd never done for any of his other hoes; shoot, he was doing shit that he'd never done for me. In all the years that I'd known him, he'd never taken me to nice dinners, or bought me things, or given me money like he did her. Seeing that watch with his initials on her wrist, and that necklace saying *TQ* made my stomach drop to my ankles damn near.

The part that had me feeling the worst for some reason was that I knew Tarenz. He and I were super cool, and he would tell me all the time how he would never do the things that he was currently doing with Kimberlyn. He would straight knock the shit out of you if you tried to post him on social media, yet she was able to get a couple pictures with him for the gram. My ego was beat the fuck up and battered right now. I was beautiful, I was good to him, and I'd loved him for years, yet she just came out of nowhere and took him from me. I wasn't the jealous type who went around trying to start shit with niggas' girlfriends in hopes of winning him back, and I knew TQ wouldn't hesitate to bust a cap in my ass if I were to try.

"Hayden!" Ingrid waved her hands in my face.

"What? Shit," I snapped. I wasn't in the mood to hear her talk at all.

Ingrid and I had been friends since middle school, so she'd witnessed my whole relationship with TQ. It was embarrassing, to say the least, for her to know what he was doing to me. Ingrid knew how I felt about him, and for her to be front row watching him dis me had me feeling ashamed.

"You need to relax, Hayden. It's not like he's married to the damn girl. I'm sure he will be over it soon," she rubbed my back gently.

"You don't know him, Ingrid! This isn't like him, and I'm worried that he's gonna go even further with her," I began to sob, so she pulled me in for a hug. "What if he gets her pregnant? Or asks her to get married?" *That would ruin my future*, I thought.

"He won't, boo. Remember, you know him and you know he's not the type to be getting married and having kids and shit, Hayden. Didn't he tell you himself that he would never?"

"He did, but he also said he would never do the things that he's doing with her. Did you see the watch? The necklace? He gave her money," I cried harder on her shoulder. "I saw her holding his car keys!"

"It's a phase, Hayden. Just chill and let the time pass, and soon enough he will be back to you. Haven't you been fucking him this whole time anyway?"

I pulled away from her, and stared down at my feet, embarrassed yet again. TQ's antics had reduced my character. He had me lying and making things up that at one point in my life were true. I felt pitiful, when I wasn't even that type of girl. I always got the guy, and I was always the girl who the guy left everyone for.

"No," I finally responded in a whisper so low that it was almost inaudible.

"You said—"

"He let me give him head, and I found out it was only because they were on a break. Now that they're back strong, he won't even text me back. I'm too afraid to show up at his house again, because what if she's there?"

"What if who is there?" Peel walked in through my door. Why did I give this nigga a key to my shit? Sometimes I wanted to be alone, and lately he wanted to be up under me all the time.

"Hayden, I will talk to you tomorrow. We can visit the nail shop then." Ingrid kissed my cheek and then stood to her feet.

She didn't speak to Peel because she didn't like him. She thought he was weak as fuck, and told me every chance she got that I could do better. I loved Peel, I really did, but TQ was my first love. I was no virgin when I met TQ, but he showed me things and turned my little timid ass out. He had me doing all kinds of freaky shit, and just the thought of it made my clit throb. That was until Peel came into view.

Peel was an attractive guy, and the fact that he had money via Gang, made girls fall at his feet. He was light skinned, had deep brown eyes, wore a fade, and he dressed and smelled good all the time. He put you in the mind of a younger version of T.I. I enjoyed spending time with him, and he was good to me too, but he just wasn't Tarenz Quinton. I had a good man but was pining for an ain't shit nigga like TQ.

"What you crying for, babe?" he sat next to me and hugged me. I couldn't possibly tell him what was wrong with me.

"I'm just a little stressed out, Preston," I replied, using his real name. I sniffled and then wiped my nose with the back of my hand.

"Want some wine?" he quizzed and I nodded.

"It's already chilling in the fridge; you know where it is."

When he got up, I grabbed my iPhone and went straight to my

Instagram app. I typed in Kimberlyn's handle, and the first picture I saw made my heart ache. It was a burst picture of her being hugged around the neck by TQ. Both of their heads were cut off, but I knew that tatted forearm and hand anywhere. On his neck was a small gold chain bearing her name, and the caption read *That's mine.*

"Yo, why you always on her shit?" Peel roared, scaring me to the point where I dropped my phone onto the floor. He scoffed and set the wine glasses on my coffee table.

"I-I was just seeing how serious they were. You know Gang isn't feeling it, and I was just seeing if they'd broken up yet so I could tell him."

"Whatever Hayden, let me find out, ma. If you're fuckin' that nigga, we gon' have some problems."

Fuck.

Chapter 33

GOLDIE

THAT WEEKEND...

Tonight was the boys' sister, Saya's birthday party. The Quintons were always finding reasons to throw their exclusive ass parties, but I didn't mind at all. Tonight I would get a chance to be up close and personal with Britain, that's if I built up enough damn courage to do so. I needed to just remind myself that I only want one thing from him, and that would make things easier.

Britain Quinton was so fine to me and every other bitch in Boston. He wore long dreads, had smooth light caramel skin, and his eyes were so beautiful. He was tall as hell, dressed to the nines always, and was the perfect size. He wasn't too buff, but he had a lot of muscles and tattoos just like his brothers. The only thing I hated about him was his whorish ways and cocky personality, but it was also something that I was very fond of. His demeanor screamed that he had good dick.

I know only wanting one thing from him made me sound like a hoe, but niggas like Britain were only good for one thing. Niggas like Britain and his brothers were not the types that you tried to be a girlfriend to. That's all I was trying to explain to my friends, but they thought I was hating. I just didn't want them to waste their damn time on some dudes who would just hurt them. Kimberlyn and Matikah weren't like me, they were sweet and kind, so I felt I had to protect them sometimes.

"Have you ever met his sister?" I asked as Kimberlyn pulled up to the big ass condo building on West First Street in South Boston.

TQ had purchased her a Model S Tesla, so she was riding clean as hell. Slowly but surely, I was starting to believe that TQ was more serious about her than I'd thought. However, material things did not equate to love.

"Briefly. He took me to meet his mother, and she was leaving right when we walked in. We spoke but it wasn't anything major," she replied. "What about you, Matikah?"

"Nope, never, but I brought her a little gift," Matikah replied.

Getting out of the car, we made it inside the building, and took the elevator up to the condo. I'd heard that the condos in this building ran for one million dollars, and by the looks of it, I knew it was true.

"Okay, it's this one," Kimberlyn said as she looked down at her iPhone. "TQ is coming a little later with his brothers, but he wanted me to get acquainted with his family."

"Oooh, he must be serious," Matikah nudged her as we both chuckled. "Nah, Len told me the same."

Kimberlyn knocked on the door, and after a few moments, a beautiful girl answered the door. Her eyes were the same blue gray color as the boys, so I knew she was the sister. She was dark skinned, and had some long ass hair that swept across her ass. Her makeup was flawless, and she was so pretty that she looked fake.

"Hello ladies, you must be my brothers' friends," she grinned, flashing her pearly whites. "Kimberlyn, I remember you. But what are your names?"

"I'm Matikah, happy birthday," she handed her the gift bag.

"Thanks. Yes, I heard about you from Lendsey... be careful with that one," Saya said and then turned her attention towards me.

"Goldie, I'm not dating any of the guys though," I chuckled nervously when I saw her confused expression.

"Well come in ladies, the party is just getting started. You all are of drinking age, right?" she looked over her shoulder as we followed her in. We all nodded and said 'yes' simultaneously.

The condo was so beautiful and huge. There were a lot of people here, but it didn't seem crowded at all. There were bartenders and people walking around holding little snacks and champagne glasses too.

"Great, you guys can hang out and get a drink from the bar, or take a champagne glass. When you get settled, come sit at the table with my mother and me," Saya smiled and then switched off in her tight gold dress.

Tonight I wore a red number that was short and looked sexy against my smooth vanilla complexion. My golden brown locks were in a bun on top of my head, and I wore a few small pieces of silver jewelry. Kimberlyn wore a canary yellow tube dress that stopped mid thigh, with nude sandal stilettos. She was wearing gold jewelry, and her long dark hair was in a low ponytail. Matikah wore a turquoise number that was a halter style, and she had matching shoes somehow. Her beautiful long curly hair was flowing freely.

We got our cocktails from the bar, and a couple of shrimp puffs before taking a seat at the table with Saya, Summer, and Mrs. Quinton. Kimberlyn said that TQ's father was extremely busy, so he rarely had free time. That was probably why he wasn't here.

As for Summer, she looked really good despite her being shot some time ago. I guess it had been a while. And here I was thinking Ethan caused me problems, but at least I'd never been shot by his side chick. The story was all over Boston as a 'rumor', but my friends and I knew the truth since we were close with the family.

"Hi again, Mrs. Quinton," Kimberlyn smiled as we took our seats at the big beautiful table.

"Please, call me Josephine."

"I'm Matikah, L—"

"Lendsey's girlfriend," Mrs. Quinton cut Matikah off. "Yes, my son told me about you. Well no, he didn't because he doesn't want me prying into his life as he says. But I saw your name pop up on his phone so I crept into it," she giggled.

Mrs. Quinton was beautiful, and she kind of favored the actress Taraji Henson, just a bit darker. She seemed to have her personality too, because she was very upfront and spunky.

"Yes, I am his girlfriend. I'm happy you know because I wanted to make sure he was serious."

"Oh, if Lendsey so much as stored your damn number in his phone then he's serious. With the way he tosses women to the side, there is no need to store their contact in his phone. So when I saw your name, I knew it was something," she winked. "Now I know you two, but who are you?" she looked to me.

"Oh, I'm just their friend, Goldie," I nodded.

"Which one of my sons are you after? I hope it's not Britain because that boy has enough women problems." She bit down on a piece of scone of some sort.

"Oh, I'm not interested in—"

"Child please, there isn't a woman who can see clearly that isn't interested in one of my boys," Josephine said, making Saya, Kimberlyn, Summer, and Matikah laugh. "Even a blind woman knows they're attractive."

"I kind of like Britain," I half smiled.

"Thought so, good luck with him." She sipped her champagne. "Hey! Anthony! Refill boo!" she shouted and tapped her glass with a butter knife.

We chatted with each other for about thirty minutes longer, and finally the boys arrived. As soon as Britain entered the dining room, my heart rate sped up. He walked right over, and sat in the empty seat next to me. I thought I would faint just from the scent of his Jo Malone London cologne.

Chapter 34

BRITAIN

As soon as I walked in, I spotted that little light skinned shorty who'd been eyeing me the whole damn night at the last party, and every other time I saw her. Right then it hit me that she was the one I saw when I was at the car wash that day. The shit was hilarious to see how much she was feeling me, but refused to say anything. That was the hundredth time I'd seen her, and her eyes were locked onto me. I mean, if she wanted this dick all she had to do was say the word. Don't get me wrong, I was picky as fuck, but shorty was fine as hell and I wouldn't mind sliding up in her a couple times.

I decided to fuck with her and take a seat next to her. The party was already jumping, and I spotted a couple of oldies I'd smashed along with some new potentials, but I was more interested in the little light bright.

I could hear her inhaling and exhaling sharply because that's just how nervous she was. It didn't turn me off though, it only made my dick hard. I watched her home girls get up and go to the living room to dance with my brothers, but I stayed put.

"You need to speak as soon as you see me, boy!" my mother spat.

"Sorry Ma, hi how are you? And happy birthday, big sis." I smiled and grabbed one of the appetizers off of the silver platter in the middle of the table.

"Thanks, bro," Saya nodded as she stood up. Her nigga, Aries, walked in, and she had her eyes locked on him as she switched off. Aries was a cool nigga, but I still didn't like any muthafucka that was fucking my sister. I didn't care if she was older.

I looked to my mom to tell her to leave, but she raised her eyebrow at me like I had her fucked up. I just chuckled at her crazy ass and stood to my feet, pulling shorty with me. She didn't protest, so I led her to my sister's den area where everyone was in there dancing and shit. Pulling her down onto the couch with me, I was able to take in her appearance some more, and her body was perfection.

"What's your name?" I asked.

"Goldie."

"Why are you always staring at me? You want me to fuck you?"

"What?" she jerked her neck back. If she had a set of pearls she would've clutched them for sure. I couldn't help but laugh. I was serious though.

"Do you want me to fuck you, ma? I mean you stay staring at me, and I can see all the lustful shit going through your mind when you do."

"No, I don't want you to fuck me. I just have a staring problem," she lied with a straight face, and we both burst into laughter.

"Nah, girls as pretty as you don't have staring problems. You can't, because as soon as a nigga makes eye contact with you, he thinks he has a chance. I'm sure you know that." I bobbed my head to "U See Us" by Nipsey Hussle.

"I mean I'm alright, I'm not that pretty."

"I don't fall for that shit. I know you're saying that so that I will tell you that you *are* pretty. And since you're hella pretty, I will oblige. Goldie, you're beautiful as fuck," I bit my lip as my eyes drifted all over her from head to toe. I could tell she took care of herself, and her perfume was sexy too.

"Whatever, nigga," she sucked her teeth and waved me off.

I pulled her closer to me when I saw Aries' homeboy plop down on the couch next to her. I saw him looking at her from across the room, but I was already calling dibs on this pussy. Wasn't no nigga getting up in her before me, especially not if I knew their ass.

"You smell good, give me your number."

"How do you push two random ass thoughts like that together?"

"Because I'm Britain Quinton, now lock that shit in and it better be the right one or I'm gonna beat you up."

"Yeah right," she giggled as she typed.

"My bad, I meant beat *it* up," I said, making her clear her throat and re-cross her sexy legs.

"Sup, I'm Jamie," Aries' homeboy stuck his hand out to her like she wasn't damn near in my fucking lap already.

"Aye nigga, don't you see I'm fucking talking to shorty?" I hissed.

"Britain man, I ain't even notice, and you have a girl—"

"Shut the fuck up with that bullshit. As a matter of fact, get up off this couch and go sit somewhere else with ya bitch ass!"

"I ain't about to—" He stopped when he felt my gun at his temple.

Goldie tensed up, and so did a couple people who were right by us and could see. I wasn't playing; I would murk this nigga in front of everybody in this bitch and dare one of them to snitch. Rhys might have been the hitman of us four, but my dad made sure we were all handy with a gun, and never scared to pull the trigger of one.

"Aight, aight, chill," Jamie said holding his hands up in mock surrender.

I nudged his head with my gun before putting it back in my waist. He hopped his ass up and rushed through the people dancing to go to the other side of the room.

"Fuck y'all looking at?" I growled when I saw the few people by us still watching with their mouths ajar. They scattered upon hearing my question, and then I turned back to Goldie who was looking at me with a frightened expression. "My bad shorty, now where were we?"

I had plans for Goldie, and anyone who wanted to give me a hard time while trying to execute them would get stepped to, that included Tekeya. She was about to get the boot anyway; shit, you notice she wasn't invited to the last few family functions.

Chapter 35

LENDSEY

"Fuck you was blowing up my phone for, Dania?" I frowned. She and I were sitting in her apartment as I sipped on a water bottle.

Her ass had been calling my phone for two damn weeks now, and sending me texts saying we needed to talk. I didn't have time for the bullshit, and in a minute I was gon' knock her ass off. I was praying she wasn't on that suicide shit again.

"I'm late."

"Late for what?" I chuckled and took another sip of my water. I had a sister so I knew what being late meant, but I wanted to give her a chance to not sound stupid. She knew damn well there wasn't a chance that I'd gotten her pregnant.

"My period, Len, and I'm pretty sure I'm pregnant."

"Yo, Dania, if you're pregnant you know that shit ain't mine so I'm still trying to figure out why the fuck I'm here."

"Lendsey, you know you're the only one I've been with lately, so don't even try to play me like that." She shook her head repeatedly as tears flew down her fair cheeks. "Why did you have to start dating that bitch?" she began sobbing hysterically.

"She ain't no bitch, shorty."

"And now you're defending her? I've been down for you for two fucking years, Lendsey, and yet somehow you make this bitch a priority? Really? What about me, huh?"

"Dania, you know I got love for you but we had an agreement that shit was never gonna get serious like that. Why are you doing this right now?"

"Because you said you didn't want a relationship! I thought that when you did want to settle down I would be first in line. How the fuck did I get skipped over?"

"I didn't want a girlfriend, but shit just happened. I met her and I liked her. I felt something I have never felt before so I made her my girl." As soon as I finished my sentence, Dania started taking off on me. She landed a couple punches, but I was able to restrain her finally. "Calm the fuck down, Dania!"

"I love you, Lendsey! This is so fucked up!" she cried violently as I pinned her hands down at her side. "How can you say that you felt something that you've never felt before!"

I did feel a little bad, so I pulled her into a hug and just held her small body. She was weeping so hard that I could feel her soaking my shirt. I placed a light kiss on her neck, making her pull back to look up into my eyes. Before I could say anything, her lips were against mine and we were tonguing it up.

"Dania," I whispered as she put her small hand down my sweats to stroke my dick.

She began jacking it slowly, before dropping to her knees to take me into her mouth. Gripping the back of her head, I guided her up and down my dick just the way I liked it. Dania could suck dick like no other. She gagged a little bit, making my dick even harder, and a few moments later I was releasing down her throat. She hopped up ready to fuck, but I stopped her.

"What?" she frowned down at me.

"Move, shit!" I said more so to myself as I stood up and fixed my sweats.

"For real, Lendsey? I can't even get my nut?"

"Dania, I'll holler at you later or some shit." I rushed out and climbed into my car. Before I pulled off, I saw her standing in the doorway watching me.

My phone buzzed and I saw I was thirty minutes late picking Matikah up from her dentist appointment. I knew her ass was gonna be on me about fucking up, so on the way there, I tried conjuring up a good lie while ignoring her texts. I made it to the dentist office, and she was standing outside wearing a scowl. Storming over to the car, it seemed as if she locked eyes with me even though my windows were tinted.

"You forgot," she said once she closed the passenger side door.

"I didn't forget shorty, I was just running late and shit. Give me a kiss." I pecked her cheek but she pushed me away by pressing her small hand into my collarbone. "Oh, for real?"

"Yeah for real. You didn't think to call or text me to say you were running late, Len? You probably were out doing dirt."

I floored it out of the parking lot and turned my music up, because I really wasn't in the mood to argue with her. She was my first girlfriend in a sense, so I ain't even know how to go back and forth without sabotaging the relationship. These hoes out here didn't argue with me because frankly it was nothing to argue about. And if they did feel bold some days, I shut the shit down like I just did with Dania, until she opened that mouth to my dick.

Suddenly, the Big Sean song was turned down, and I looked over to see Matikah looking at me.

"Fuck you turn my shit down for, huh?" I furrowed my brows before pulling off at the sight of the green light.

"I'm sorry for saying you were out doing dirt. I guess I'm still slightly paranoid, but I'm gonna do better," she nodded as if she were talking to herself.

I pulled over on Peterborough Street, in front of this little Mexican food spot named El Pelon Taqueria and shut the engine off. After being quiet for a few moments, I turned in my seat to look at Matikah. Hearing her say that she was sorry for accusing me of something that I had in fact done made me feel bad. I was on the fence, wondering if I should admit my wrong or just take it to the grave. I mean what did she expect? I was a twenty-four-year-old man who was used to fuckin' any bitch that I liked. How did she expect me to change overnight? Then again, if I couldn't do it I shouldn't have told her I was down to be her nigga. Fuck!

"Baby, I get why you're paranoid because a nigga ain't got the best background and shit. But, I ain't worried about no other girl but you, I promise."

Technically, I didn't lie. Matikah *was* the only girl I was worried about. I didn't care about Dania like that, or any other hoe that may possibly come in contact with this dick. I was gonna try though, I really was. Being faithful was gonna be a true test, it would be like making a twenty-year crack head go cold turkey. It had to come down to how bad I really wanted shorty, and damn did I want her. Plus, her pussy was fire so I should be good... I hope.

"I know, and I'm only worried about you too."

"You better only be worried about me."

Just as I said that, my iPhone began ringing in the cup holder. Dania's name was right there on the screen, so Matikah picked it up, declined it, and then put my phone in her big purse that I'd just gotten her.

"Aye shorty, give me my phone."

"After we eat, and why are you so in a rush to talk to that bitch? Why are you talking to that bitch anyway when you used to fuck her? Don't she know I'm your girlfriend?" she raised her brow. She was so pretty that I had a temporary brain fart. "Hello!"

"Yeah, yeah she knows. And I'm not in a rush to talk to anybody, I just want my damn phone, Tikah." I reached for her purse but she moved back, wearing a smirk. "Give me my shit before I have to hurt yo' little ass."

"I might like that."

I bit my lip and let my eyes trail her full lips, as memories of me pounding that pussy last night invaded my mind. Just that quick, I had no care for my phone.

"Fuck it, keep it. Let's hurry up and get this food so I can take you back to the crib and fuck."

"Must you be so forward?"

"Yes, now hurry up." I hopped out of my car. Don't worry, I was gonna shower before I slid up in my shorty.

"You gon' trust me?" I panted as I rammed Matikah from the back, while pinning her arms behind her. This was my favorite position, because I loved seeing her face twist up as she looked back at me.

"Yes, yes baby," she whimpered.

My girl was still pretty inexperienced in the bedroom, but I loved that she never told me no. No matter what I told her to do, she was ready and willing. Ain't nothing like a pretty bitch who was willing to do anything to please you, but wasn't a hoe.

"Turn around," I told her after she came on my dick and I pulled out. Once she did, I slipped my dick into her mouth, and humped slowly until I busted. Like the freak she was slowly turning into, she swallowed it up, and then licked her full lips. "Come here," I pulled her into me as she breathed heavily. "I love fucking you baby."

"Really?" she quizzed as I laid on top of her, between her legs.

"Hell yeah." I began kissing her lips, then her neck, collarbone, and then her nipples. My dick was already coming back to life like them damn zombies in *Thriller*. "I wanna eat that pussy again."

She chuckled as I pressed her legs against her stomach roughly, and then began feasting on her center. Knowing this pussy was mine, intensified sex for me just like Rhys said it would. I was burying my face all in her shit, and moving my tongue like a maniac. Feeling her soft hand on my kinky hair really motivated me to get in there some more. I damn near sucked the orgasm out of her.

"Len, baby, shit.... Uuuh mmmm, oh, oh my gosh," she cried out.

After she came four good times, I decided to come up for air and kiss her hungrily. I never thought I'd say this, but I could fuck the same girl all day.

Chapter 36

TQ

"I have somewhere to be," I sighed as I sat in my father's office.

"Somewhere that's more important than handling business?" he raised a brow, and put the temple of his eyeglasses in his mouth.

"This ain't about no damn business, Pop, I can already tell. My schedule is set for the month, so I know today is about some bullshit."

"Watch your tone, Tarenz."

"I'm a grown ass man, I don't watch my tone for no damn body, and especially not when it's a person who is wasting my time."

The door opened, and my mother walked into the room. Behind her was none other than Gang. My mother kissed my face, and then left the three of us alone. I knew my dad was gonna do some shit like this because of my refusal to give up Kimberlyn.

"What's good, TQ?" Gang put his hand out to shake mine, but I just sucked my teeth and looked away.

His little gesture wasn't genuine, and if it was, he was a bigger bitch than I had assumed. He knew I was fucking his obsession, aka Kimberlyn, so why would he try to shake my damn hand? Fuck out of here.

"Now TQ, as I explained to you before, Gang makes us a lot of money," my father stated.

"So do other niggas on the East Coast," I replied, nonchalantly.

"Yes, true, but not as much as him. We need to keep him, TQ, and right now there is only one small thing standing in the way."

I burst into laughter as I thought about the reason that I was here. Did this nigga Gang really have my father call a meeting to ask me to leave *my* girl alone? Nah, this had to be a damn dream. Was it that serious? The nigga never even hit, so where did such an attachment come from?

"TQ, man, you don't even want her like that," Gang chimed in and smacked his lips.

"Nigga, don't speak up on me like we go way back or some shit. You don't know what the fuck I want, homie. Just know this, Kimberlyn is my woman, and if I find out you dropped by her house again, I'm gonna make yo' ass disappear, nigga."

"TQ!" my father barked.

"Fuck this, fuck him, and if you're on his side, Pop, fuck you too. I'm out. Don't contact her or show up again Gang, or I'm gonna go David Copperfield on yo' ass."

"Tarenz! Tarenz!" my father hollered after me but I was done already.

Kimberlyn was mine, and as much as I hated to admit it, I had some strong ass feelings for her. I couldn't quite explain them, but I'd never met someone like her before. Her demeanor and overall personality was something I wanted to see in a wife. I never pondered over the traits I wanted my future wife to possess until I met her. By saying that, I wasn't gonna give Kimberlyn up to no nigga, even if it was for all the money in the damn world. Damn, listen at me.

"Dog, I meet bitches, discrete bitches. Street bitches, slash, Cocoa Puff sweet bitches..."

My brothers and I were at the strip club, and currently there was some fine ass bitch on stage, popping her perfectly round ass to DMX. Crazy enough, I didn't feel the urge to put my dick in her mouth later like I usually would have. With the way she was looking into my eyes though, I knew she would be trying to bounce on it for me afterwards. Kimberlyn had completely seized my mind though, and just the thought of fucking another bitch at the moment had me feeling guilty and keeping a soft dick.

"What he say?" Britain, my little brother inquired. I was just putting them up on game about what my father called me to the house for earlier.

"Same shit he said last time, to leave Kimberlyn alone."

"Gang does make y'all a lot of money," Rhys commented and took a swig of his beer.

"And? Fuck that nigga. We make a good amount of money off the other niggas we distribute to as well, he ain't the only nigga," I barked but in a low tone.

"Is she worth losing that extra cash? And pissing Pop off?" Britain quizzed and looked at me.

This nigga valued no bitch, not even his so called girlfriend, Tekeya. He would give that bitch up in a minute if he were in my shoes. I used to be like him, never as bad, but now things were different for me. And if he kept questioning Kimberlyn's importance, he and I were gonna have some problems.

"Yeah, she is. I'm rich as fuck, and I'm gonna still be rich as fuck with or without Gang. I got enough money to quit this shit altogether."

The three of them were quiet as they processed my words. Because we all had different positions in QCF, this shit didn't affect them as much. We were all bosses of our own area in a sense. Losing Gang would do nothing to their pockets directly, because that wasn't their forte.

"I let Dania suck my dick," Lendsey blurted as he stared at the chick on stage, seemingly in a daze, but not because of her.

"So," Britain shrugged, wearing an irritated expression. I chuckled at him lightly.

"What happened to all that shit you were talking about Matikah, nigga?" Rhys furrowed his brows. This nigga was always angry. He would even get angry if you told him how easy it was to get him angry.

"It just happened. I went to talk to her because she'd been blowing me up. She told me she was pregnant, and then one thing led to another," Lendsey explained.

Like Britain, Lendsey was not built for monogamy. I don't know what shorty said or did to convince him to be in a relationship, but it caught us all off guard, especially because it happened so damn fast. I couldn't talk though. I just hoped she was prepared to go to war for this nigga like Dania had done plenty of times.

Anyway, I knew Lendsey was bothered as fuck by this shit because he was a man of his word. If Lendsey said he was gonna do something, he was gonna do it. The fact that he'd already broken his promise to his shorty clearly had him buggin'.

"Pregnant? You was sliding up in there raw?" Britain asked.

"Nah, I mean, not that I remember. I was careful, like I am with every bitch. But when she said that it got me to thinking, ya know?"

"So what, you gon' tell Matikah?" I inquired.

"Nah, you better not if you wanna keep her my nigga. Don't listen to TQ's ass, listen to a nigga who don' had a girlfriend for years. Plus, who knows if she really is pregnant?" Rhys answered for him, giving him advice in the process.

"Enough about this shit, I can't even concentrate on these beautiful specimens because y'all are talking so damn loud," Britain snapped.

"Which one you taking to the crib?" Lendsey chuckled, already knowing how Britain's ass got down.

Britain's girlfriend Tekeya was a nut job, yet he still strayed. Last time she caught him cheating, she threw a rock at this nigga's head and he had to get stitches. Yet, as soon as he was able to function properly, he was back to dickin' these hoes down. I laughed lightly at my thoughts.

We chilled at the club until 2am, and just like I'd predicted, shorty dancing to DMX was all in my grill as I was leaving. A couple months ago I would've drove her to a hotel nearby and beat her guts out, but I wasn't on that tip tonight, or any night as of late. Britain on the other hand left with two bitches, wearing a smile so wide his ears should've been wet.

I made it home, and when I walked to my bedroom I spotted Kimberlyn sleeping on top of the covers in one of my t-shirts. Her hair was all over the place, and her mouth was open. She was sleeping hella good.

I pulled some fresh boxers from my drawer, and then went into my bathroom to brush my teeth, floss, rinse, and then shower. Once I was cleaned to my liking, I climbed into the bed with her. Seeing her smooth golden thighs with not an imperfection in sight, brought about the urge to have them sitting on my shoulders.

Reaching under the t-shirt, I tugged down her red panties and threw them to the floor. My mouth began to salivate at the thought of tasting her center. I dropped my head down and got comfortable, before pulling her clit into my mouth. She stirred lightly, while I held her legs apart to go in.

"Tarenz," she whispered and then let out a light moan afterwards.

Feeling her small, soft hand caress the back of my head, only motivated me to devour her further. She was arching her back and squirming lightly, just the way I liked. Hearing her soft whimpers, tasting her, and inhaling her scent was the shit.

"Mmm, mmm," she let out a high-pitched moan that I could tell she was attempting to muffle, before releasing for the third time.

I finally decided to quit since her legs were all shaken up like Elvis. Staring down at her, I rubbed my hands up and down her small trembling legs. She looked up into my eyes and then pulled the big t-shirt over her head. I removed my boxers, and then laid between her legs to enter what I'd like to call heaven.

Her walls were so tight, wet, and warm, that it made no sense. If she charged me for this pussy I would pay top dollar. That meant a lot coming from a nigga who swore up and down that all pussy felt the same.

I took her nipple into my mouth and sucked hungrily, while groping her other breast. Hearing her moan and feeling her body begin to perspire only heightened the feeling. I continued sucking her nipples as if I was trying to get the last bit of juice out of a Capri Sun, and then finally picked my head up to kiss her full lips. I loved her mouth. It was wide and beautiful, which is why when she smiled she could light up a room.

Cupping the back of my head as I slammed into her gently while kissing her, she said, "I love you, Tarenz."

Chapter 37

RHYS

ONE WEEK LATER…

I MADE IT HOME, AND WHEN I WALKED IN IT WAS LIKE DÉJÀ VU. I smelled food and spotted Summer cooking breakfast in the kitchen. I was tired of the breakfast at the hotel, so I decided to opt out of it this morning, making a nigga hungry as fuck.

"Hey baby," I said dryly, not sure how *this* argument was gonna go down. "I can pick Bryleigh up from pre-school all next week."

"Hello and thanks," she replied as if she didn't have a care in the world.

"What are you making?"

"A scramble, would you like one?" she looked up from the skillet to me, and half smiled. I kissed her lips gently, and then kissed her shoulder wound. No matter how many times we fought, kissing her never got old.

"Yeah, I want one." I sat down at the bar after I removed my hoodie. "Where is Bry?"

"She's with my parents, they wanted to take her shopping."

"I just took her shopping."

"You took her toy shopping, Rhys, they're taking her for clothes."

"Kids don't like clothes," I chuckled and so did she. When I was younger, I hated to open a gift on Christmas morning to see an outfit. I wanted toys!

"May I ask where you were last night?"

"I spent the night in the hotel, I texted you that last night, Summer." I could barely have a regular conversation with her before she got to interrogating me.

Taking my business phone out, I scrolled through the information my father sent me on some people he needed me to take out since they'd done some dumb shit. I shook my head as I read one of the names, because he was some young cat that my dad had helped. He was living on the streets in Dorchester, and my dad took him under his wing. I guess since he was just one of the young runners, doing small tasks, he felt the need to turn on my dad. Now, he was about to die at only twenty.

As I prepared a killing schedule for him and a couple other victims, I heard light sniffling. I sighed while standing up, and then went to the bathroom to piss and clean my hands. I came back into the kitchen, and hugged Summer tightly from the back. As soon as I did, she began sobbing even harder. Turning the burner of the stove off, I made her face me and hugged her tightly.

"Who is she?" she hollered into my chest as I rubbed her back.

"Summer, there isn't anybody but you! Damn! Don't get upset over—"

"Don't get upset? Don't get upset over the fact that you didn't come home, and the fact that you make it obvious you were out cheating on me!" she pushed me backwards, and I rubbed from my baldhead down to my beard.

"Make it obvious? How the fuck am I making something that is completely false, obvious?"

"I spent the night at the hotel," she mocked me. "Whenever it's that vague it's a lie."

"Summer, I'm at that hotel every damn night almost! And this is why! Don't act like the hotel room is new shorty! Don't do it!"

"Stop always fucking yelling, Rhys!"

I took a deep breath and then sighed heavily. "So what you want me to do?" I yanked her back to me and then kissed her lips a couple times, sensually. I just really didn't want to argue. I loved this girl, but I was starting to forget why.

"Get rid of her and any other bitch that you feel the need to fuck with, Rhys! I swear, in a minute I'm gonna be the one not coming home." As soon as 'home' left her lips, I had her hemmed up against the cabinet next to the stove.

"Do that shit and it'll be the last thing you ever do," I gritted. "And like I said, ain't nobody to get rid of, baby. I love you Summer, even though you get on my damn nerves a lot, I love the fuck outta you. Can't you feel that?" I frowned and she shrugged. "We need to get along better, baby, that's all I want," I whispered.

"Pay more attention to me then."

"I will." I groped her ass in my hands while tonguing her down. I craved her crazy ass.

She began unbuckling my pants as I ripped her panties off like they were nothing. Running my fingers across her wetness, I could feel how ready she was, which only made my erection grow.

"I missed you," she said as I lifted her up slowly.

I brought her down onto my dick, and slowly pumped in and out of her. We were sucking one another's lips, and moaning like this was the best shit we'd ever felt; and it was. Summer and I may not have gotten along well, but we always made it happen sexually.

"I missed you too, I love you," I groaned as I continued to pump into her. She had that perfect combo, being tight and wet. You could hear her gushing on my rod miles away, and the shit was driving me crazy! "Damn."

"Mmm, shit, Rhys."

A few more hard, long, pumps, and I was nutting all in her body. We both shivered lightly as we attempted to come back from our orgasm. Our chests were rising and falling against one another as we kissed like long lost lovers. This was the type of shit I wanted to come home to, not her running her mouth and accusing me of shit I wasn't doing.

"This is what I miss, baby," I let her down and pecked her soft, full, lips. "If we can just stop arguing, we will be good. I don't want these girls, only you."

"I think we can make it work if you come home more, and control your anger, Rhys. I told you that you scare me sometimes."

"I don't have any fucking anger issues, Summer! See, you ruined the fucking moment with that bullshit!" I barked and rushed off to the back, holding my pants up.

These days I felt like we were beating a dead horse in this bitch.

Chapter 38

MATIKAH

Kimberlyn and I were supposed to go get our nails done together, but since she was a bit under the weather, I decided to go alone. I usually would have waited, but I was in need of a pampering immediately. If I waited any longer, I was sure that Lendsey would start to notice. I would be mortified if he did.

I walked into Treasured Nails on Boylston, and was instantly greeted by my nail technician, Trisha. Trisha was really bomb, so bomb that Kimberlyn, Goldie, and I all followed her whenever she moved. She'd been here for the last two years though, which was good. However, as soon as she left, so would the three of us.

"Okay, come soak your feet, honey," Trisha smiled and shook the remnants of the water off of her hands.

I did as she asked, removing my sandals and submerging my feet into the water. It was the perfect temperature, not too hot and not too cold. While I soaked, Trisha turned on the back massager so I closed my eyes.

"That's what I told the bitch," some girl spoke loudly as she entered into the nail shop.

She looked black, but also looked to have a bit of Spanish in her blood. Her body was tight, and she knew it, which is why she barely had any clothes on. My body was one to turn heads as well, but home girl could be in videos. Throwing her long dark brown hair over her shoulder, she spoke to one of the other ladies named Linda, before she and her friend took a seat one chair away from me.

She and her friend continued to talk to one another, as I just watched Trisha start to remove my nail polish. My phone buzzed, and I saw it was Lendsey calling, causing my skin to get hot and my heart to beat faster.

"Hello?" I answered.

"What you doing, shorty? I finished what I had to do earlier today."

"I'm getting my nails done."

"Who you getting ya nails done for?"

"For you, honey, who else?" I giggled like a little schoolgirl as I nodded my head 'yes' to one of Trisha's questions.

"Better be, ma. And thank you because you cut the fuck out of my leg last night when you kicked me in your sleep. Make sure she cut them bad boys down, I almost backhanded ya ass."

My jaw dropped as I attempted to contain my laughter. I prayed he was joking, but with Lendsey you never knew. I would always be scared to laugh because sometimes he would be serious. One time he told me his friend's cologne was so strong that it gave his aunt an asthma attack. I laughed but he was dead serious and I felt bad.

"That was so mean, I need to go home anyways this weekend."

"No you don't. The pain is worth it. But aight, hit me when you're done, I have to go get stitches," he sighed.

"Fuck you," I laughed before hanging up on his rude ass.

I felt the two girls looking at me, so I glanced over out the corner of my eye. They didn't say anything, so I just diverted my full attention back to my phone so I could reply to a text sent to me from Goldie.

"So is he still tripping?" the friend asked the Spanish one.

"Yes, but you know how Lendsey is, girl. He gets mad but then comes right back home where he *belongs*," she replied, and my stomach dropped upon hearing Lendsey's name. I looked over and she was watching me out the corner of her eye. "I like the color you picked out," she grinned and pointed to the bottle that was sitting next to Trisha.

Trisha looked up at me with a worried expression. Trisha and I were like friends, and she knew all about my new boyfriend that I was gone in the head for. By saying that, she was floored like me to hear Lendsey's name come out of this chick's mouth. There weren't too many niggas named Lendsey.

"Thank you, and did you say Lendsey?" I furrowed my brows.

"Yes, why?" She began putting her long hair into a messy bun on top of her head, wearing an innocent expression.

"Lendsey what?"

"Lendsey Quinton, again, why?" she cocked her head.

"Don't tell me you're messing with him?" the friend flared her nostrils at me, as she and the Spanish chick stared me down angrily. I swallowed the humungous lump in my throat when I saw Lendsey's name tatted on her left breast.

"Well I am. I mess with him heavy, and all night. Looks like he won't be coming home to you anytime soon," I fake smiled.

"Oh, he was home earlier this week. I'm not sure where you were though. Then again, like you said, you only get him at nights."

"No, I get him all day, and I'm not about to believe shit that comes out of your mouth, hoe. Don't mention Lendsey again unless you wanna get fucked up!"

"Little girl, who the fuck do you think you're talking to? Dania is Lendsey's bitch and always has been, where did you come from?" her friend hissed. Hearing her say the name Dania brought me back to the day Lendsey's phone was ringing.

"I came from the gutter, meaning I won't hesitate to fuck either of you up over my nigga. Now like I said, don't mention Lendsey. And Dania, stop blowing him up when I'm with him. I had to take his phone one day because you just couldn't take a hint."

The stare she gave me let me know that if she could kill me and get away with it, she would. I could tell from looking at her that she was in love with Lendsey. Her anger was a mixture of jealousy and broken heartedness. It made me wonder if I'd broken up a happy home, or just taken a man from a woman he was never gonna fully give himself to. I would find out though.

For the duration of the rest of my visit, Dania and I exchanged no words. By the time I was done, I felt like a new woman, and I immediately got into my car to call, Lendsey. He'd bought me a nice ass Infiniti Q70, and I was grateful to not be on foot any longer. I felt some type of way about accepting gifts from him so early in the relationship, but he said if I didn't take it, it would just collect dust because he wasn't returning it.

"Yo! Fuck you blowing me up for, shorty? I told you I don't like that," Lendsey finally answered as I pulled into the driveway of my grandmother's home. She'd been on Kimberlyn and I about not coming home and shacking up with TQ and Lendsey, so I wanted to show my face.

"I saw Dania at the nail shop today."

"And?" he asked with an attitude.

"She told me you came *home* to her earlier this week."

"You sound dumb."

"You must think I'm dumb, Lendsey! Did you fuck her this week? Have you been fucking her?"

"Nope!"

"So she just made that shit up," I scoffed and shook my head as I checked out my freshly waxed eyebrows in the sun visor mirror.

"Pretty much."

"Bye Lendsey."

"Bye baby."

I hated how nonchalant he was about the shit. As I sat in the car staring at my grandmother's house, I remembered I promised him I wouldn't be so paranoid. He was probably being short because I'd lied and broken the damn promise already. Removing my phone from the cup holder, I dialed him back.

"I'm sorry," I sighed.

"You good, ma, be at my condo in an hour, aight?"

"Aight."

I got out of the car and went inside so that I could see my grandmother. She was sitting in the living room, watching tennis like she always did. I smiled as I watched her sigh and suck her teeth when the girl she was rooting for kept fucking up. I made my way over slowly, and then plopped down next to her, prompting her to look over at me. Seeing her face light up made me sad. Kimberlyn and I had really been neglecting her, and I was gonna be sure that we stopped. I felt like she needed us, and even though we were with Lendsey and TQ, we needed her too.

"Well I thought I would never see you again," she set her bowl of soup on the coffee table. "Would you like some?" she asked.

"No, I'm okay." I shook my head and sighed lightly. Lendsey and Dania were still on my mind, making me feel some type of way.

"What's wrong?"

"It's Len."

"Already? What happened?" she frowned before sipping whatever was in her glass. It appeared to be apple juice.

"I think he's cheating on me, and the worst part is, I think it's the same girl every time."

"Meaning he has feelings for her."

"Exactly."

"Why do you think that, Matikah?"

"Because he was late picking me up one day, and Lendsey is a very prompt guy. He's never late and he always follows through. Then today at the nail shop, some girl that I remember calling his phone was in there discussing him. I don't know, maybe I'm just being extra because of his history."

"There is this thing called women's intuition, Matikah. If you feel in your gut that he's really being dishonest, he probably is."

Chapter 39

SUMMER

A COUPLE DAYS LATER...

RHYS AND I WERE DOING MUCH BETTER, ESPECIALLY NOW THAT HE'D been coming home every night for the past two weeks. However, I wasn't able to sleep with him as much because his trysts with Lisa, and God knows who else would enter my mind whenever he touched me. I didn't know how we would be able to move forward in this way, but right now I was too emotional to make any decisions.

I was placing my makeup kits into my work suitcase as he walked in wearing a towel around his waist. I glanced up at him, and like always, his gorgeous looks gave me a warm feeling all over my body. His beautiful deep caramel complexion, those blue eyes, that clean-shaven bald head, and that scruffy beard were all to die for. He and all his brothers were attractive in their own way, but Rhys was at the top in my book. He walked his tall, lean but muscular frame closer to me, and I could smell that he'd already sprayed on the cologne that he wore daily, Versace Eros.

"Going to work?" he sat down on the bed and watched me.

"Yes, it's a Saturday shoot." I jumped a little when he moved my dreads out of my face to look at me.

"You good?" I could tell he was frowning as I zipped up my suitcase.

"Yes, Rhys, I'm fine."

"Can I have a kiss?"

"I have to go; I'm running late already." I hopped up and then rushed out of the bedroom before he could protest.

I pulled up to the studio I worked for about fifteen minutes later, and rushed inside so I could begin setting up. I saw Paul eyeing me as I began to unload, so I knew he was a little perturbed that I'd come in so late. It was only six minutes, but Paul didn't play.

"Look who it is," Nia sang as she placed her makeup brushes into a little cup on her station.

I looked over to see sexy ass Hakim walking in. He was wearing a tight under armor top that showed his muscles, and some gray joggers. He was bobbing his head to something playing in his Dre beats, and just the sight of him had my clit throbbing.

"Morning, ma," he winked at me as he passed me by, headed to the back with the rest of the models.

"Shut it, Nia," I chuckled and so did she.

As soon as I was done setting up, Hakim was the first one in my chair. I was so nervous for some reason, even though I'd done his makeup plenty of times for plenty of different shoots.

He looked over, and when he saw Nia wasn't paying attention he asked, "Did you get my text this morning?"

"Yes, I don't think I can come though. My boyfriend has to work tonight but he will be expecting to see me when gets home."

"I will have you back early Summer, I promise. And from what you told me, he don't appreciate you anyway."

I know I should've never told Hakim my relationship problems, but I was mad, so I did. We'd texted here and there, and it was nothing too deep. That was until Rhys came home that last time and blew up because I mentioned his anger problems. When that happened, I blabbed to Hakim, and he was saying all the right things. If Rhys found out, he would kill me *and* Hakim.

"Hakim, I—"

"Anybody ever tell you that you look like Simone Battle? The singer that killed herself?" he quizzed, changing the subject.

"Yes, all the time." I gestured for him to close his eyes so I could put makeup on them.

"Beautiful, baby," he whispered, getting me wet that easily. "So what do you say? Meet me at the lounge tonight. If he can go be with other women, you should have the same privilege bestowed upon you."

"Fine," I cheesed and continued fixing him up.

About seven hours later I was off work. I rushed home so that I could shower and get ready to meet Hakim at this lounge on Boylston. His friend was performing, and he wanted me to watch the show with him. Rhys' mother already had our daughter Bryleigh since yesterday evening, so tonight was perfect. I was supposed to pick her up after work, but I would think of something to tell Rhys to explain why I didn't. I knew his mother wouldn't mind one bit; she loved Bryleigh.

Once I was all cleaned, it was time to get dressed. I picked out an all-black number that clung to my body like the perfect fitting glove. I wasn't thick I guess, but I had a nice round ass, and perfect C-cups to match. I smiled as I thought about all the compliments Rhys gave me on my body. One thing I loved about him was how much he praised my beauty. I just wish he felt the same about our relationship.

I decided to pull my long dreads up into a big bun on top of my head, and then spread some body butter all over my smooth brown skin. As I was putting my shoes and jewelry on, my phone buzzed.

Daddy: Can't wait to come home and see you baby, I love you. Tell Bry daddy has a surprise for her.

I smiled at Rhys' text, but then it quickly faded when I realized what I was doing. I contemplated not going until I remembered all the nights I slept alone, while Rhys was out doing him, or sleeping in a hotel as he would say. I knew he was in the hotel, I just doubted he was alone.

Also, Hakim was fine and I was starting to like him. Maybe he was better for me, even though I loved Rhys. Sometimes it's hard to let go of what you love, but sometimes it hurts more to hold onto it.

I spritzed my body with perfume, then I was out of the door. Arriving to the lounge, I gave the guy at the door my name, before he had someone escort me to the table where I saw Hakim sitting. He was dressed in a blue button up, black slacks, and some shoes that were too dark for me to make out in the dimly lit lounge. He smelled good too. Hakim was no Rhys, but because Rhys was so fine, you didn't have to be as attractive as him to still be cute.

"Sorry I'm late," I said once he handed me a drink.

"It's cool, she hasn't gone up yet." That was another thing about Hakim, he was calm and serene, whereas Rhys was a crazy psychopath. He was my crazy psychopath though. *Get it together, Summer.*

"So tell me why such a beautiful girl like you is with a maniac."

"He's not a maniac, Hakim, he just has a short fuse."

"Does he hit you?"

"What? No! Of course not!" I frowned at the thought.

Rhys was a nutcase, but he would never put his hands on me. That's why he was never home, because he had to remove himself before he pummeled me to the floor. I didn't like that Hakim was trying to make Rhys out to be some monster. Rhys was a good man, in certain lights, and I was the only one who could trash him. He provided for me, loved me, was phenomenal in bed, and we always had a good time together, but he just couldn't keep his dick in his pants or his anger at bay. I just wished I hadn't badmouthed him to another nigga.

"Not yet you mean," Hakim scoffed.

"Let's talk about something else, Hakim. I didn't come out for a therapy session but thank you very much for trying."

"I'm sorry, Summer, I ain't even mean it like that."

"It's cool."

Finally, his friend came on stage and performed a couple songs. It was like slow pop songs or something, not really my style, but she had a beautiful voice. During her show, Hakim and I kept up small talk, and I was starting to enjoy myself again. Because before she came out, I was ready to go home and wait for Rhys to arrive.

I met the friend, Carli, and we all chilled for about an hour before Hakim and I left. He asked me to come to his place for coffee, and since I was having such a good time with him, I decided to comply. He lived in a cool little home in Jamaica Plain, which was pretty nice from the outside.

We got out of our cars, and as we began to walk on the sidewalk, Hakim took my hand into his. I smiled shyly as we walked hand in hand like a couple. It didn't feel right because I was in a relationship with someone else, but I didn't want to let go. Maybe the longer I held on, the better it would feel.

Suddenly, the sound of a gun being cocked was heard, and Hakim immediately dropped my hand. I turned around to see crazy ass Rhys, holding a pistol to the back of his head. His face was so knotted up, that I didn't think he'd be able to untwist it.

"Fuck you doing, Summer?" he grimaced.

"Rhys, it's not what—"

"Not what I think? How? You're holding hands with this nigga!" he yelled and I saw a lone tear travel down his cheek. He got rid of it quickly. "And I'm cheating? No wonder you've been on me! It's because you out here doing dirt!"

"Look man, I-I- you don't ha-have to—" Hakim stuttered.

"Shut yo' ass up, homie! I'm ready to blow yo' muthafuckin' brains out!" Rhys seethed in his ear almost.

"Rhys, baby, relax. You know I would never cheat on you. Let's go home." I moved towards him slowly, and rubbed the side of his beautiful face a couple times, gently. He stared down into my eyes, and finally lowered his weapon.

WHAM!

Spinning Hakim around, he slapped the dog shit out of him with the gun, and then proceeded to whoop his ass right there on the sidewalk. Hakim was screaming out in pain as I begged Rhys to stop. Hakim looked like he was dying, and all I saw was blood. You couldn't even make out what he looked like anymore, and Rhys had just started.

"Holding hands with mine!" Rhys shouted as he beat Hakim to a bloody pulp. Hakim was no longer yowling, so I knew he'd either passed out or died.

"Rhys! Stop! We have to go!" I pulled on him but he was in beast mode and way too angry to stop. "Baby, please! You can't go to jail! Think about Bry!" At the mention of our daughter, he finally stopped assaulting Hakim.

"Be glad I didn't kill you, bitch," Rhys spat before we both got into my car to leave.

"How did you even get over here?" I quizzed while driving. Tears were coming out of my eyes. I hated to see Rhys act that way.

"Don't worry about it. And why the fuck are you crying!!"

"Because I'm scared! I hate when you act like a maniac!"

He just sucked his teeth, turned up the music, and then lit a blunt. This nigga was certified, and I wasn't sure how much longer I could deal. *Lord, please don't let Hakim be dead*, I silently prayed.

Chapter 40

KIMBERLYN

A COUPLE DAYS LATER…

TQ and I were out to eat at some Mediterranean restaurant named Mistral, and afterwards we would be going to the club with his brothers and my friends. So far, we'd only eaten appetizers, and the food was delicious. I'd never been here before, but TQ was always showing me new and fun places. I was in love with him, but I just wished I hadn't blurted it out that time we had sex. He didn't say it back, and it was obvious why. We acted as if it never happened, and frankly I preferred it that way.

The waitress set our plates of prime rib down, and as soon as she walked away, we held hands to say a prayer over the food. We stole glances every now and then as we dug into our dish. He looked so handsome, and the more time I spent with him, the more in love I was. I'd never met anyone like him.

"How is it?" he asked me, referring to the food.

"Really good, and tender. How is yours?" I smiled.

"Same. You look sexy as fuck, by the way. I've been meaning to tell you that, but every time I look at you I forget because of how pretty you are."

I blushed and pushed my hair behind my ears. He still made me nervous, especially when he spoke sweetly to me like that.

"Thank you," I finally replied. "Are you prepared to party?"

"Not really. We won't be long, I'm just showing my face. It's a couple cats in town that wanna meet me and see if we can work together, so that's what I'm there for. My brothers will party though. I just wanna go home and slide up inside you."

"Like every night."

"Yeah, like every night. I like spending my nights with you and nobody else, shorty."

"I know. It's almost like I live with you," I giggled and ate some potatoes.

"It is. I like having you close. I can protect you better. Is your grandmother feeling some type of way about you not staying with her much?"

"Sort of, she doesn't like the idea of shacking up," I responded and we laughed together.

"Well technically we don't live together, you're just at my spot all the time."

"True. I start school in two weeks, so I will be spending more time at home most likely. When I say home I mean my grandmother's home."

"Why?" he furrowed his brows.

"I don't know. I can't have my books and shit all over your house, plus I like to make tea and shit when I study."

"You can bring all your shit to my condo, shorty. And I will buy you what you need for tea."

"I have a feeling you don't wanna be away from me," I half smiled.

"It's true. I don't like being away from your weird, pretty ass," he grinned and so did I.

We continued to talk and eat, and then afterwards we ordered dessert. He paid the bill, and then we left out to the car so we could head to the club. The venue was only about ten minutes away, and as soon as we got there, TQ pulled up to the valet booth.

"It's straight, I got her," TQ told the valet guy who was about to open my door for me. I just smiled as I waited for him to come around and open my side for me. He helped me out of the car, and then kissed my lips gently before taking my hand into his.

I noticed as we walked to the bouncer, the girls were staring and talking like always. I used to be uncomfortable when that shit happened, but now it made me laugh. They were jealous because I had the nigga they all wanted, claiming me. I was gonna bask in this shit too. Right before we walked in, I nudged TQ and tilted my head back so that he could kiss me. He placed a nice one on my lips, sending vibrations all the way down to my clit.

We made it up to the VIP section, and just as I was about to text Matikah and Goldie, I spotted them swaying to the music. Summer was sitting down, seemingly in a daze as she sipped on some cocktail. TQ and I greeted everyone, and then he kissed me again before whispering in my ear that he was gonna talk to a couple dudes I saw standing by Rhys, Lendsey, Jayce, and Britain.

"Y'all look cute," I chuckled and pinched Goldie lightly on her back.

"Thank you, you know who I wore it for."

"Who? Britain?" I cheesed.

"Exactly," Matikah answered for her. "They've been texting, despite the fact that he has a girlfriend who is psycho."

"But she's never around or at any of these functions, so she must not be too important," Goldie waved Matikah off as she swayed to the music.

When Goldie set her mind to something, nothing could stop her. And if she wanted Britain, she was gonna have him. I just hoped his deranged girlfriend didn't try to do something to her, because I would be ready to go to war for my friend.

After dancing a little with them, I decided to go keep Summer company. Summer was really nice and pretty, and she and Rhys' daughter was so cute. She was a bit on the quiet side, but it seemed to be because she was always thinking. I watched as Rhys kissed her lips before joining TQ again, so I made my way over.

"Not having fun?" I quizzed.

"I am," she smiled. "I just have a lot on my mind."

"You seem to always have a lot on your mind."

"Do I? I guess I do. I'm always thinking about shit constantly. I guess because I've never really had friends, I just keep all my thoughts in my head."

"That could make you crazy," I chuckled and so did she. "But we can be friends. We *should* be friends since our men are brothers."

"I'd like that," she smiled widely, showing her deep dimples.

"Tarenz!" someone yelled out, prompting both Summer and I to look in the voice's direction. I watched Tarenz look over his shoulder at the pretty light-skinned girl, and then turn his attention back to the two men he came to meet. "TQ!" she shouted again.

"Aye, Amikka, go on with that shit," Lendsey said to her before sipping his drink.

"Who is that?" Matikah walked over with Goldie, before sitting in Lendsey's lap.

"I don't know, but I'm gonna find out." I stood up and moved my arm when Lendsey tried to grab me. I neared the edge of the VIP where TQ's security was standing, and got in the girl's view. "What you looking for TQ for?"

"None of ya business, aight? You can have the dick tonight, but tomorrow I call dibs, deal?" she laughed and clapped her hands together. Her New York accent was strong as hell, making me wonder why she was here in Boston.

WHAM!

I punched her and she flew back, falling down the long porcelain staircase and onto the dance floor full of people. There was a bit of commotion, and next thing I knew, I was being snatched up by TQ. I knew he was gonna be pissed. I could feel it in the way he rushed me out of the venue.

"What the fuck is wrong with you, Kimberlyn? I told yo' ass I had to handle business and you out here fighting?" he barked. We were in some alleyway, when suddenly I saw his Ferrari being driven up to us. One of his people that I'd seen before, hopped out and left the door open. TQ opened the passenger side for me and yelled, "Get in!" I complied because I was scared.

He sped off like a bat out of hell, and the sight of his jaw clenching was sexy. I knew I shouldn't have been getting turned on, but I was. He just looked so good when he was mad.

"I'm sorry," I whispered. "She said some things that I didn't like, Tarenz!" I whined.

"Like what? Huh? What the fuck did she say? I'm hoping it will help me understand why you felt the need to stoop to the level of some loud mouth hood rat."

"She said she was gonna fuck you tomorrow night."

He began laughing angrily as he dipped through traffic going about ninety. This Ferrari was lightning fast. My window was down, and the wind was viciously slapping me in the face so I rolled it up.

"Kimberlyn, what the fuck did I explain to you? What have I *been* explaining to you, huh? You don't need to fight these hoes, shorty! You know I'm not gonna be fuckin' her tomorrow so why even do all that?" He turned his lip up in disgust as he parked his car at his condo.

"I know. I just get so angry," I twisted my face up making him snicker. "What?"

"You look cute, not intimidating. But shorty, I love you not them, so don't even let them get to you."

"You love me?" I turned in my seat to look at him.

"Yeah I love yo' ass. I feel like I need you to make me whole sometimes. Don't tell nobody I said that shit."

"Tarenz!"

"I'm kidding, baby." He leaned over his seat, and as soon as our lips touched, my breathing became heavy. I rubbed the side of his face gently as I relished in the kiss we shared.

"I love you, TQ, I almost thought you didn't love me."

"Nah, a nigga love you, and I only love you, aight? Don't sweat these bitches, Kimberlyn, I'm your nigga."

"You damn right you are," I kissed him again, and then toyed with the TQ necklace he'd gotten me. He said he wanted it to be the first thing niggas saw when they approached me. He had a *Kimberlyn* necklace, and to my surprise, he wore the shit faithfully; he even slept in it along with his other small gold chains.

Ah, the feeling of being in love...

Chapter 41

GOLDIE

A FEW DAYS LATER...

TONIGHT, BRITAIN WAS COMING OVER TO MY APARTMENT TO CHILL SO we could get to know one another better. We'd been texting a lot more than I expected, and I was even more interested in him than I was before. I really thought he would give me more of the cold shoulder, considering that he had a damn girlfriend and because of who he was, but that wasn't the case. We'd even talked on the phone, and sometimes we'd FaceTime when he traveled out of town with his brothers. He was so nice, and I assumed he'd be an asshole. I mean, he was an asshole still, but not to the point where it was unattractive or annoying. I enjoyed getting to know him, which I didn't think would be the case with a guy like him.

He was so smart, and I thought it was adorable how he loved numbers and math. Upon seeing him, you would think he was some drug dealer but he wasn't. I was surprised to hear that he just assisted his father in balancing books. That's all he would tell me anyway.

The fact that Britain was only fifty percent of what I thought he was like had me thinking about the way I'd come at Kimberlyn and

Matikah about TQ and Lendsey. I thought I knew these guys based off what I'd heard numerous times, but clearly I didn't know shit but the stuff the hoes they threw to the side told me.

I finished combing down my fresh press, and looked over myself in the mirror. Since we were just chilling at home, I chose to wear a simple tube dress. It wasn't overly dressy, but it wasn't sweats and a top either. The last conversation we had was last night where we talked on the phone until 3am. He was out in North Carolina with TQ for a business trip, so of course he used his free time at night to talk to me, and *not* his girlfriend, Tekeya.

I did feel some type of way about talking to him since he had a girlfriend, but I'm sure I wasn't the only one, and Britain claimed that they were on the brink of breaking up. He said she was way too crazy, and always trying to put her hands on him. I wasn't sure if I believed him, but it's not like I was trying to make the nigga my man or anything.

KNOCK! KNOCK!

I heard someone knocking at the door of my apartment, so I rushed to answer it. Although I knew Britain was a thug all the way, my neighborhood Mattapan was not one to play with. It was night-time and a little hot, which meant niggas would start acting a fool. The longer I kept him waiting outside, the more likely a problem would arise. People feared he and his brothers, but it was nothing for one idiot to act out and cause shit.

I answered the door, and there he was looking so damn good. He wore dark blue jeans that sagged just right, black and white chucks, and an all black hoodie. His hood was on, pushing his dreads to the front. His lips were so sexy, which made me realize I had yet to kiss them.

"For me?" I grinned as I took the boxed bottle of Patron from his hands.

"For us, fuck you mean?" he chuckled and stepped into my apartment, allowing me to inhale his cologne. He embraced me and I was sure that I'd came all in my panties.

After getting him settled on my couch, I rushed to the bathroom to wipe between my legs. My pussy was on that hoe shit, even when I wasn't. After wiping myself up, I placed a liner in some fresh panties just in case my juices began to flow again. I washed and moisturized my hands, before double checking my appearance and coming back out. He looked so bomb as he frowned his face, searching for something for us to watch.

"Come," he patted my couch once he'd noticed that I had returned. I smiled and sat down. I was so nervous that my leg was quivering, so I had to tuck it behind me. "You look good, shorty," he licked his lips.

"Thank you. So do you."

Right when I said that, my phone chimed, and Ethan's name popped up. We both reached for it, but unfortunately Britain was much faster than me.

"Who is dude?" he questioned as he read whatever text Ethan had sent. *I knew I should've listened to Kimberlyn when she told me to turn off the text preview feature*, I thought.

"He's my ex boyfriend."

"Ex, why? You never mentioned him."

"I don't like talking about him. And he's my ex because he and I don't want the same things, you know? He wanted an open relationship, and at first I was okay with it but after awhile it didn't feel right."

"He allowed you to fuck other niggas?"

"I mean yeah, I could, but I only did once, and I felt disgusting afterwards."

"Yo," he burst into laughter. "No fuckin' way I would allow my girl to bust it open for a random." He shook his head repeatedly.

"I feel the same about my man, but I didn't really have a choice in that area."

"So why is he still calling you, does he know you're mine? If not, you need to tell him." *Nigga what?*

"Yours? How am I yours when you have a whole girlfriend who lives in your house, Britain?"

"She lives in the house I bought for us to live in together, but I'm never there, you know that. I'm always out of town working, or at my condo in Brighton."

"Well no matter where you sleep, you have a bitch. I'm not trying to be your side chick or anything."

He stared at me for a couple moments, and then tugged me closer to him. Caressing the side of his face, I leaned up a bit to kiss his soft lips. A few gentle pecks turned into hardcore kissing, and soon our tongues had become entangled. Feeling his big strong hand rub up my smooth thigh was life! Pushing my dress up, he grabbed ahold to the top of my panties, but I stopped him, not wanting him to see my panty liner.

"No, no, shorty, please," he whispered before shoving his tongue back into my mouth, and roughly yanking my panties down.

Lucky for me, he threw them and didn't even look at them. He then pushed my dress up over my head, leaving me butt ass naked. He just stared at my naked body, and ran one of his fingers between my breasts, and down my stomach. His mouth latched onto one of my nipples and sucked hungrily, and I just ran my hands through his dreads as he got his fix on them. Once he did, he picked me up and carried me to the back bedroom. Lying me down, he again admired my physique while removing his clothes. Standing at 6'5", his body was in perfect condition under his beautiful light caramel complexion.

"Damn," I whispered once his dick was exposed.

He smiled at me, and then set the condom in his hand on my nightstand. I just laid there, not knowing what was next, but I was dripping like crazy. Dropping to his knees, he pulled my body to the edge of the bed, and began devouring my kitty. He placed his hands on the backs of my thighs, and lifted my legs a little while holding them apart, as he continued to feast on me.

"Mm, shit," I whimpered as I grabbed the back of his head. "Fuck," I called out as my body jerked from releasing. He didn't stop though, he kept sucking the fuck out of my clit, making my body feel amazing! "Britain," I sniveled as if I were about to cry, just before I exploded again. He stopped sucking, and then planted soft kisses on my pussy before swiping his tongue between my folds a few times. I thought he was done, but he dove right back in until I begged him for mercy.

He stood to his feet, licking those full lips of his as his dreads hung down. This was hands down the sexiest nigga on the East Coast, and that was fact, not an opinion. He brought his dick to my mouth since my legs were too weak to get to him myself.

I was hesitant so he said, "I don't fuck any girl raw, not even her."

I nodded and took him into my mouth, then began bobbing up and down it as if my life depended on it. I'd been wanting to suck this dick for a while now, and I was gonna enjoy it. I sucked it sloppily until I felt it harden even more. He shot his seeds down my throat, and I swallowed, surprising myself. I massaged his dick, and it got hard again instantly.

"Lay back," he demanded.

I laid in the middle of the bed, and he crawled between my legs, kissing his way up to my lips. Despite his demeanor and personality, he was gentle with me. He sucked my nipples hungrily again, and then reached for the condom to open and slid it down using only one hand. His member invaded my body, ripping me in two it seemed. I unintentionally dug my nails into his biceps as he pumped in and out of me.

"Damn," he whispered into my mouth before kissing me. I was whimpering like a little bitch, because it hurt but felt good as fuck at the same time.

The way his big hands groped me, the way he moved in and out of me, I knew I didn't want this to be the last time. This felt way too good, way better than I thought it would have, and I began lightly tearing up because I knew I was already attached. I was attached to a nigga who was attached to someone else.

Placing my legs in the nooks of his arms, he stood on his knees and plowed into me until we both came hard as fuck.

"Damn, shorty," he panted, dropping down on me to kiss me passionately.

I just tossed my arms over his shoulders, and hugged him tightly as we continued to kiss. For the rest of the night we fucked, licked, and sucked one another. He didn't go home, and I wasn't about to make him.

Chapter 42

LENDSEY

Matikah had been acting real weird these days, and I didn't know why. She didn't like me touching her that much, and she was spending the night at home with her grandmother most nights. I would have to damn near beg her to sleep here with me, which wasn't the type of nigga I was at all. Her attitude had me feeling uneasy as fuck though.

After brushing my teeth and showering, I wrapped my towel around my waist and exited the bathroom. I smelled waffles or pancakes, I wasn't sure which one, so I smiled thinking Matikah's mood had improved. Entering the kitchen, I saw her setting a plate of food on the counter, before she hopped onto the stool. She was wearing some little ass shorts and a tube top, making my dick perk up. I hadn't fucked in two days, which was a long ass time for a nigga like me. And the fact that Dania had been hitting me up made it no easier to keep my dick in my pants. I hadn't touched her ass though.

"What you got?" I asked, even though I could see what was on her plate.

"Belgian waffle." She stuffed a strawberry into her mouth, refusing to make eye contact with me.

"Shorty, what's wrong? Why you acting all cold and shit?" I frowned. I was irritated now and ready to say fuck this relationship. This monogamy shit wasn't me anyway.

"Did you fuck Dania while we were together? Yes or no? Len, do not lie to me. It would be better for you to be honest with me." She set her orange juice down after sipping it.

I stared into her pretty face for a few before saying, "I didn't fuck her, she sucked my dick and that was it."

"Wow," she chuckled and shook her head as she stabbed a waffle slice. "I knew it! I knew it!" she threw her fork at my head, but I moved just in time.

"What the fuck, Matikah? You said it would be better if I told the truth and now you're tripping? I'm confused!" I hissed.

"You stupid muthafucka! You lied to me and said you hadn't touched that bitch the day you were late, and I knew you had! You had me looking stupid in that nail shop, going off like I had a nigga who was about something!" she hopped down off the stool.

"Matikah! Matikah, chill the fuck out. Look, I got some head, but when she was ready to fuck I stopped her."

"Oh, and that's supposed to be better, Lendsey?" she bucked her eyes and stared up at me.

"Hell fucking yeah it's better! I came from fucking a different bitch every day of the week, to only slipping up once and getting some head! You ought to be grateful!"

She had me fucked up! I was not the type of nigga to be faithful, shit, I wasn't even the type to get in relationships, yet she was mad because I fucked up once! The old me would've fucked Dania all over her damn apartment, and then fucked two other bitches later that day! In my eyes, she needed to appreciate the fact that I was even trying to be good to her ass.

"I ought to be grateful," she chuckled and threw her plate into the sink with food still on it. She knew that was something I hated, so I was sure she did it on purpose. "It's a wrap, Lendsey, you can go back to being a bachelor." She began tearing up and stormed out of the kitchen.

I tried to play it cool, but it was starting to settle in. I didn't wanna break up with her. For some odd ass reason I liked being her nigga, and only hers. Her little ass must've put voodoo on me or something, because I was changing right before my eyes. The old me would've been helping her pack whatever shit she had over here, but this new nigga she had turned me into wanted to beg like Keith Sweat for her to stay.

"Baby, hold up, I ain't mean what I said." I walked into the bedroom.

"Doesn't matter. You cheated on me and I'm done."

"I can't make it up to you? Me pushing her off don't mean anything?"

"First of all, nigga, you shouldn't have been over there in the first place! You were my man, you had no business being over that bitch's house, Lendsey!"

"I only went over there because she was fucking blowing up my phone and shit! When I got there she was talking about she was pregnant and—" I stopped mid sentence, wishing I hadn't said what I said.

"Pregnant?" she moved back from me as her chest moved up and down from breathing so hard.

"Matikah, no that bitch—"

"No, move!" she shoved me when I tried to pull her into me. "You belong with her ass, and I hope you're happy," she sobbed hysterically as she began shoving her shit into a duffle bag.

"Matikah." I got down on the floor with her and hugged her from behind while kissing her shoulders. She continued to cry and tried to nudge me off, but her little ass was no match for me. "Matikah, I'm sure she was lying, and I promise that was the first time I'd even seen her in person since we made things official."

"Move, Lendsey!!!!" she hollered loudly as fuck as she rammed her small elbow into my abdomen in hopes of getting loose. "Moooovvve!" she wept. "I knew I should've never let you get to me!"

I didn't say anything. I just held her tightly as her body jerked violently from crying so hard. What was I supposed to say? I needed to hold her here with me until I could think of something to convince her that I wasn't on that tip anymore. Right now she was too angry, and if I let her go she would dart out of here and never come back. This shit was so new to me, and I had no idea what to do.

Chapter 43
TARENZ

I had to meet with a potential business partner, like fuckin' always, but this time at least it was in Jamaica. And since it was, I wanted to bring Kimberlyn with me. I wanted to bring my girl with me. I liked the way that shit sounded for some reason. Hilarious. My mama always said, the right woman will change the wrong nigga. I didn't think it would happen, but it definitely was happening.

"You ready?" I asked Kimberlyn as we walked out onto the runway where my private plane was.

"Yes," she nodded nervously as I took her bag from her so she could walk up the stairs and onto the aircraft.

I secured the bags, and when I headed back towards the front, I saw her sitting down in the regular seat, near my back-up pilot, Primo.

"What you doing, shorty?" I grinned.

"What do you mean? I'm sitting down ready to take off."

"Nah, I'm flying right now, and Primo will take over when I get tired. Come up here with me and be my unofficial co-pilot."

"No TQ, I—"

"Aye, what did I say to you last night?"

"That we're partners," she sucked her teeth and rolled her eyes, causing both Primo and I to laugh.

"Exactly, now come on."

She unbuckled herself, and followed me to the nose of the plane. I showed her a couple controls as she rolled her eyes and sighed, saying she wasn't gonna remember. To annoy her, I kept going and explaining things to her. Unfortunately for me, she began to get into it and ask more questions. I guess it was cool that she was interested in something that meant a lot to me.

"Why didn't you fly us when we went to Connecticut?" she asked once we were both buckled in.

"Because that was a date, and riding the plane together was part of the date. This right now is just two people in love spending time together."

"I love when you tell me you love me," she said in a low tone, before rubbing the back of my hand on the shift like knob.

"Whatever, you ready?"

She nodded, so I began to circle the runway, and soon enough I picked up enough speed to ascend into the air. Her face was hilarious as we went higher and higher into the clouds. I could see her breathing hard, and low-key thought I could hear it too.

"How can you even see where we're going, Tarenz?"

"Because I use this, remember?" I pointed to the monitor with little green dots all over the place. "And if it were night time, there would be little lights around to help me see."

"I would be so scared to do this," she half smiled. "What if we get into an airplane collision with another plane?"

"Won't happen shorty, relax."

Once we got close to where we were landing, I began descending. I quickly put it on autopilot for a moment so I could get her up. I tugged her up out of her seat so she could fly it with me for a bit, and the look on her face was priceless.

"Wha-what are you doing?" she frowned when I placed her small hands on the controller.

"Fly it," I smiled and kissed her cheek as she sat in my lap.

"I can't!" she bucked her eyes.

"You already are, look."

It was quiet as we descended the plane together, taking in the sight of our destination. I'd never been to this part of Jamaica before, so it was new for me as well. After about five minutes, I finally let her get back into her seat so I could land the aircraft completely.

I landed the plane, and we were now in Kingston, Jamaica. Since the flight was short for me, I didn't need Primo to take over. Kimberlyn was a good co-pilot in the sense that she didn't go to sleep while I was flying. She stayed up the whole time, and all we did was talk. She told me naughty funny jokes that she'd learned, and although corny, I enjoyed hearing them muthafuckas. Even though we were five years a part, it didn't seem like it. I didn't feel like I was trying to raise her or make a little girl become a grown woman. Funny enough, she was way more mature than girls my age, even Hayden.

Because I was forced to mature quickly and get into business with my father, I found women around my age to be immature and for lack of better words, dumb as fuck. They only wanted to talk about their shady ass home girls, celebrity gossip, reality shows, how good their most likely trash ass pussy was, and the newest trends. I didn't give a fuck about none of that shit, and neither did Kimberlyn, making us a somewhat perfect match. And if she did enjoy any of that shit, she knew not to talk to me about it.

After getting off the plane, we were taken to our hotel in Port Antonio. It was a big beautiful suite made of wood, and there were trees and plants all around, giving that official Caribbean feel. Primo was staying somewhere else for the time being, and I knew he was planning to take advantage of all the sexy Jamaican women here.

"How long are we staying, TQ?" Kimberlyn questioned as she circled the place. I followed behind her since I'd never been to this particular hotel either.

My potential business partner wanted to meet in Port Antonio, so I just chose the nicest place to stay in that city. I also heard this area was romantic, which is exactly what I wanted.

"I need to stay two days, but it's open ended since I flew us here. How long do you wanna stay?"

"Forever," she beamed and then walked closer to me to wrap her arms around my torso. "I'm kidding, maybe five days?" she squinted her face to see what I thought about that.

"That's cool, but that's all the way up until you start school ain't it?"

"Exactly."

Since we left the U.S. at 4am, it was around noon here in Jamaica. I just changed into a t-shirt and some khaki shorts, while Kimberlyn changed into some sexy ass red one-piece bathing suit. The shit had cut outs everywhere, showing areas of her body only I needed to see. She put her hair into two braids like Pocahontas, and then slid her pretty feet into some sandals. I watched the whole time like some thirsty nigga.

"Ready?" she smiled.

"Yeah, when did you get that bathing suit?"

"When you took me shopping for this trip," she replied as she looked into the mirror.

"I bought that shit?" I frowned, trying to remember her picking that out.

"Yep!" I needed to start paying more attention to the shit she picked out instead of just footing the damn bill.

After she threw on this little see through jacket thing, we went out to the beach to chill, but ended up playing in the fuckin' water. That shit was weak as fuck, and I didn't want to do it, but it turned out to be fun. We then came back to the room to change, before going out to have some lunch. We ordered all kinds of shit off the menu just to try it and see what we liked. That bill was sky high, but it was worth the enjoyment, and seeing my shorty smile and shit.

We finally made it back to the hotel, after sight seeing, so we got into the shower together, and then climbed into the big ass bed.

"You had fun today?" I asked and she nodded with a smile.

"A lot of fun. I've never traveled outside of Boston before."

"No? That's crazy. I've traveled all of my life. Part of what I do is traveling. It gets tiring sometimes though, when you just wanna be still for a moment."

"I couldn't imagine, but I guess if I was always on the move like you, then that would make sense."

"Yeah, sometimes I just want to chill in my city for a month straight, but that ain't possible. The money is good though, because I can afford to do things like this for you, for us."

"All of us?" she scooted closer to me and kissed my lips.

"That's a weird way to say it, but yeah."

She nodded, but I could see in her eyes that something was bothering her. I slipped my hand between her legs, and the heat coming from it felt so damn good. Slipping my tongue into her mouth, I got on top of her and in between her legs. Pulling off her sleep shirt, I threw it to the floor before removing my boxers and doing the same.

"I love you," she whispered as I forced entry into her body.

It was dark in the room, but we could still see because of the sliver of light the stars provided. The faces she was making, and the soft moans she let out were my favorite parts. She exploded on my rod, so I slid out of her while sucking her nipples. I then put her on all fours, pressing the side of her face into the pillow.

As I entered her slowly from behind, I sucked her lips gently. She whimpered lightly and balled the sheets into her small fists as I began to thrust in and out of her walls. Being inside her was the greatest feeling in the world. I'd had a lot of good pussy, but I think because there were deep feelings involved, it made it better for me.

I rubbed my hands up and down her small sweaty back as she cried out. Gripping her ass cheeks, I sped up my thrusts, pounding her as she begged for mercy. Soon after, I was spilling inside of her body. Pulling out slowly, we both moaned. I then went to get a warm towel for us both, using one to clean her, and one for myself.

We got back in the bed, and drifted off to sleep together. As Ice Cube once said, today was a good day.

In the middle of the night, I opened my eyes to see that Kimberlyn was gone. This was the fourth or fifth time she'd left the bed in the middle of the night. Tonight I wasn't too sleepy to go in search of her though.

I got up, and then grabbed my boxers off the floor to put them on. I saw the bathroom light was on despite the door being closed, so I made my way to it. I heard her weeping faintly, and that shit caught me off guard. I racked my brain trying to think of the day's events, and what could've made her react this way. Before I could come up with anything, she was coming out and bumping into me.

"Tarenz," she sniffled and quickly wiped her eyes.

"Why are you crying?" I was now angry, wondering if someone had done something to her. She stared up into my eyes, and then looked off, still silent. "Kimberlyn."

"I'm pregnant," she responded in the lowest tone she had.

I didn't reply right away because I didn't know what to say. I didn't know if I was happy, angry, or what. Nah, I knew I wasn't angry, but I just didn't know how I felt.

Tears continued to ski down her smooth cheeks, so I brought her into me and hugged her tightly. I kissed her cheek even though it was wet, and then pulled back a little to look down into her face.

"How am I gonna finish school?" she cried.

"You're gonna finish, shorty, don't worry about that, okay? Let's be happy about it. At least the baby is coming in the world to two people who love each other, and not to two people who had a one-night stand, aight?" I said, and she chuckled and nodded.

She tightened her grip around my torso, and we stood there just kissing for a few moments. Kimberlyn had changed my life and me in more ways than one, and now a nigga was gonna be someone's daddy. And to think just earlier this year I was on my how to be a player shit.

Chapter 44

MATIKAH

ONE WEEK LATER...

I danced in the passenger seat of my grandmother's car to "Rich As Fuck" by Lil Wayne as she cracked up at me. She hated rap music, so anytime it came on the radio, I made sure to turn it up and dance to annoy her.

"Turn that shit down before you burst my already sensitive ear drums, Matikah," she chuckled as she turned into the driveway.

I laughed while twisting the knob, and once she parked I unbuckled my seat belt. As we brought the groceries up the porch steps, we realized it was completely covered in bouquets of roses, and in the middle of the circle were two gifts.

"What the hell is all this shit?' my grandmother frowned, saying exactly what I was thinking.

I bent down a little to snatch one of the cards off the flowers, and when I saw it was a card with Lendsey's name in it, I immediately threw it down to the ground.

I hadn't talked to or seen his ass since the day he told me that he cheated on me, and that was two and a half weeks ago. I was done with his ass, and when I started to feel the need to call him, I would occupy myself with my friends, if I could. Lately they stayed boo'd up, even Goldie, which I don't know how she did when Britain had a girlfriend.

"It's Lendsey?" my grandmother questioned as she moved some of the flowers to the side so that we could get to the door.

"Yes," I sighed.

"You don't wanna talk to him?" she quizzed further once we got inside and began unpacking the groceries.

"I really don't. I haven't even thought about him until just now when I saw all of the roses out front."

"Sit down, Matikah." She pulled a chair out at the table in the kitchen, so I obliged. She sat down herself, and then stared at me for a little bit. "Be honest, I know you."

"I am being—" I stopped when she gave me that look that Tami from *Basketball Wives* makes. "I do want to talk to him but why should I? There isn't anything to talk about. He slept with someone else and then to make matters worse, he tried to justify it because of his past."

"He slept with her?" she cocked her head.

"Well no, he let her umm, you know, put her mouth on his private parts. He said he stopped her after that, but I don't believe it. And even if he did, that doesn't make a difference."

"Is this the first time he's reached out?"

"No, he calls me all the time, every day! He texts me nonstop, and he even made an Instagram to DM me on," I chuckled at the last part, along with my grandmother. "Look, here he goes." I slid my phone to her so she could read the text.

Don't Answer: *Did you get home? If so I hope you like the gifts baby. I swear I've learned my lesson already. I don't need much punishment.*

My grandmother giggled before pushing my phone back to me.

"That boy is desperate."

"He even had his mother call me and try to convince me for him."

"Really? And you're sure you don't want to try it out again? I thought you said you were falling in love with him?"

"I was, but it wasn't real."

"Why do you say that?" She got up from the table to get what she needed to make dinner.

"Because if it were real this wouldn't have happened," I frowned because she should've known that.

"That's not true, honey. Relationships aren't perfect. Now I'm not saying what he did was okay, because it wasn't at all. But what I'm saying is if you feel in your heart that you want to be with him, and that he has actually learned from his mistakes, then give it a try. But if you think he's doing all this just to get you back and mess up again, then by all means, keep away from him."

"Grandpa never treated you this way," I fidgeted.

"Your grandfather treated me very well just like Lendsey treats you. He had his moments though, and I contemplated leaving plenty of times, but I didn't. Then the one time I finally did, I was gone from him for a month. And when I finally decided to come back, honey, he was a new man. I think it's good that you're showing him early on what you won't accept. I think if I had have left your grandfather earlier, he too would've shaped up quicker. But that only happens when the man is a good man, if he isn't a good man, then nothing you do will improve him."

I was surprised to hear that my grandfather cheated on my grandmother, but I understood what she was saying. The problem was, I wasn't sure if Lendsey had actually turned over a new leaf. I mean what about the saying, once a cheater always a cheater? Yeah, no, if I go back to him he will think he can do what he wants to me. I was gonna continue to be strong until I was over him. Then again, the fact that he was trying so hard made me think. I knew he wasn't the type to give a fuck, and the fact that he did had me blushing a little.

"I don't know. I admit I'm surprised by his pleading," I sighed.

"He's probably never come in contact with a woman like you, Matikah. He needs you. He needs a woman who will keep his ass in line."

I watched my grandma start dinner, and then I remembered the gifts on the porch. I went out to retrieve them, as well as two of the many rose bouquets. Rushing to my room, I plopped down on my bed to open the big one.

Inside the big box were the Rihanna Puma slide ins in pink. I remember telling him I wanted them but they were sold out. I slipped them onto my bare feet, and twinkled my toes as I looked down at them. I then grabbed the slightly smaller box, and opened it to see a pretty gold bracelet with two diamond charms hanging from it. One charm was my initials, and the other was a pretty diamond heart. I looked further into it and saw there was a small folded note. I opened it up and it read, *add this one only if you want to.* He was referring to the diamond charm with *LQ.* I put the note and charm back into the box before locking it up. I then put the bracelet on, and laid back with my slippers still on.

Grabbing my phone, I went to our text conversation to respond.

Me: Thanks for the gifts Len, but I'm sorry, I just can't be with you anymore.

I backed out of my text app, and when I saw he'd texted back, I just locked my phone and silenced it. Ten minutes later he was calling, so I turned my phone face down so I wouldn't be tempted to answer. I knew if I responded he would think he had a chance; he was very mistaken, however.

Chapter 45

BRITAIN

SATURDAY AFTERNOON...

TODAY, THERE WAS A LITTLE AFTERNOON FUNCTION AT THE PARK. Everybody was gonna be there, and I couldn't wait. Usually my brothers and I didn't like going to open invitation functions, because niggas were haters and niggas were also thirsty. By saying that, we either would encounter a tiff, or sometimes niggas would follow us around trying to be down with whatever it is we did. The funny thing about that shit was that niggas had no idea what my family and I were into, they just knew we had money, plenty of bitches, and that our name almost meant as much as the president's.

"How do I look?" Tekeya spun around to show me her fit.

I swear my shorty's body was the truth, and it almost made me want to fuck her. Too bad I'd been fulfilling my needs elsewhere, and with the same chick. Usually I cheated with multiple women, but for some reason I was always hittin' Goldie's phone.

"You look sexy as fuck, ma," I smirked and hit the bedroom light to cut it off.

I spent the night in the house with Tekeya, attempting to maybe rekindle what we had, but it didn't work. I ended up sleeping in the guest room and getting on FaceTime with Goldie. I knew it was shady that I was fucking around with the same girl, but I couldn't help whom I wanted when I wanted them. Cheating with multiple women didn't seem as bad because it showed that Tekeya was number one, but now that I'd only been messing with one, that showed feelings were involved. That's the only reason I was trying to even spark up what Tekeya and I had again, to prove to myself that I wasn't feeling Goldie as much. It didn't work though.

"I can't wait to walk up in there on your arm," Tekeya chuckled as I opened the front door for her. I just shook my head. Was I her nigga or a new pair of red bottoms?

We made it to the park about twenty minutes later, and I parked a little ways down because I didn't want my whip right up front. Like a sucker ass nigga, I immediately began searching the function for Goldie. She told me she was coming with Kimberlyn and Matikah, so I was planning on seeing her... from afar.

"There are my brothers, come on." I walked over, holding Tekeya's hand as she basked in the moment, showing off to the girls that we walked by and that spoke to me.

I declined to say anything back to them, because one, I had already fucked most of them, and two, I didn't wanna hear Tekeya's mouth.

I dapped my brothers up, and then sat down with them. Tekeya sat right next to me, and for some reason I was just annoyed by her presence. I hated to feel that way but it was true. I wanted her to go mingle or some shit. I honestly didn't want Goldie seeing her next to me as crazy as that sounded.

"Aye, there goes Angelica," I pointed to Tekeya's home girl.

"Oh, I will go talk to her in a second," she typed on her phone.

"Go make me a plate shorty, please."

"Okay, babe." She kissed my cheek, and then switched off towards where the food was.

"Aye, when is Kimberlyn coming?" I asked TQ, and he, Rhys, and Lendsey burst into laughter. "Fuck is so funny?" I frowned. I glanced at Jayce who was staring off into space looking drunk than a muthafucka.

"Waiting for Goldie to get here? You know it's gonna be some shit when she shows up," Rhys laughed, as Summer sat in his lap shaking her head with a half smile. She'd been really quiet as of late, and that was strange.

"Nah, I was just asking a fucking question, you know, making conversation. I know y'all niggas are too stupid to know what that is," I hissed, knowing they were right.

I looked over my shoulder, and that's when I saw the three ladies walking in. Kimberlyn walked right up to TQ, and them niggas started kissing like they hadn't seen each other in years. I chuckled as a couple of his hood rats sucked their teeth and talked shit. Matikah sat on the other side of me, and awkwardly only spoke to everyone but Lendsey's lovesick ass. He was staring at her looking like his damn dog died. Goldie flashed me a sexy smile as I looked over her body and beautiful face. She and her friends all had on little ass jean shorts and tops with no straps, they just had different colors on. Kimberlyn's top was in white, Matikah had on red, and Goldie had a gold one on. It was funny that her mama named her Goldie, and that was her favorite color. She said her mom's favorite color was gold as well. Look at me remembering shit she'd told me. Anyway, her golden brown hair was hanging down her sexy back, and her smooth light skin was glowing. Damn. I tucked my bottom lip in as I recalled the nights I was inside her.

"What's up?" she finally asked while smiling.

"What's good?" I bit my lip again, and looked over her smooth legs, wishing they were wrapped around my head, right when Tekeya showed up with my plate.

"Excuse me," she low-key snapped at Goldie, wanting to get by.

"Come on, let's get food," Goldie told her friends, and they all sauntered off, including Summer.

They came back with their plates, and one for their nigga, excluding Matikah, so everyone began to eat. The party started to get even more fun when people began to dance. Kimberlyn was dancing in TQ's lap, because my brothers and I were not the type of niggas to be out on the dance floor winding like Omarion. Summer was doing the same, and Matikah just sang along as Lendsey watched like a bitch. Jayce had some hoe with him, but it wasn't unusual for him to have a new girl for every day of the week with his twisted ass. Since his wife died, he wasn't looking for anything serious.

My sister, Saya, her boyfriend Aries, and his same homie, Jamie that I pulled a gun out on, walked up to our table and sat down as well. The nigga Jamie smiled at Goldie, and then said something to her. They stood up together, and then walked to where everyone else was dancing in the park to begin fucking it up. That shit had me hot, and I didn't know why.

I tried to look away but I couldn't. Moving Tekeya out of my lap, I told her I had to piss, and rushed off towards Goldie and Jamie. I swiftly grabbed her arm, and took her further away from the party towards my car.

"Get in!" I barked, before looking around to make sure no one was looking. Thank God I parked a little ways away.

She sucked her teeth and then got in. I went around to my side, slipped in, and then slammed the door. It was quiet, but then she burst into laughter.

"You cannot be serious right now, Britain. You brought your girlfriend here, and you expect me to behave? I thought we were just friends?" she raised her brow. This girl was pretty as fuck.

"You know how I feel about you Goldie, so kill all that. Don't be dancing on another nigga in my face!"

"Oh, but she can dance on you? I got it."

"You fuckin' other dudes too?" I grimaced.

"No I'm not. And again, you can fuck her but I can't do what I want with my own vagina." She folded her arms and stared out the windshield. I was scowling while admiring her side profile.

"You knew I had a bitch, and for your information, I haven't been fuckin' her, only you. And that's my pussy," I squeezed her smooth thigh, prompting her to smack my hand.

"You're right, I did know you had a girl. I'm okay with the rules,

Britain, you're the one who isn't. Either we're gonna be just friends or we're gonna be more, but you cannot have both." She started to get out but I pulled her back and kissed her hungrily.

"Close the door," I said in between kisses. She did as I asked, and I began unbuttoning her shorts. Yanking them down along with her thong, I threw them to the back, and then released my dick. "Hop on."

"I don't have a condom," she said.

In all my years, I have never wanted to raw dog someone so badly. The last time I did I was seventeen years old, and I hadn't done it again since. Tekeya and I never went without, no matter how many times she'd tried to convince me. I didn't want any babies, especially not with her.

"Just hop off before I cum."

She looked away as if she was thinking, so I tugged her over gently until she was straddling my lap. I swear when I got inside of her I thought I was gonna bust. I gripped her waist to guide her up and down, and we resumed kissing like we loved each other.

Something told me to look over, and when I did, I spotted Tekeya and Angelica storming to my car.

"Hurry up and put your bottoms on!" I told Goldie.

"What?"

"Put your shit on!" I grabbed her stuff from the back and shoved it into her.

She hurriedly hopped into the passenger seat and slipped her panties up. She was buttoning her shorts as fast as possible, but Tekeya had snatched the door open already so she knew what was up. Before I could protest, Tekeya snatched Goldie up out my car by her hair. Both Tekeya and Angelica were going in on Goldie, but surprisingly she was holding her own. Next thing I knew, Matikah came over and started fucking Angelica up. Kimberlyn wanted to get in, but for some reason, TQ was holding her ass back. She was crying; that's how badly she wanted to fight. I saw Summer approaching, but she stopped when she realized that Matikah and Goldie were on the winning side. I could see in her eyes that she was waiting for any moment where it looked like they were losing, because then she would hop in.

My brothers and I were finally able to break it up, and to say Tekeya and Angelica lost would be an understatement. For as long as I'd known Tekeya, she'd never lost a fight, but I guess she was no match for Goldie, and poor Angelica was no match for Matikah. Angelica always lost though, ever since high school. She stayed fighting and getting fucked up. At least the bitch had heart.

The ladies had calmed down after being held back for a little bit, so we began pulling them in separate directions. Matikah snatched herself from Lendsey and rushed off, and his ass followed her like he was Forrest Gump. The look Goldie gave me told me she was done with me, and oddly I cared. That nigga Jamie caught my eye, and I peeped that evil smirk he was wearing. I would bet my bottom dollar that he tipped Tekeya off about Goldie and I being in the car. Taking Tekeya to my whip, I forced her inside, and then got in before peeling out.

"Fucking a bitch in a car while here with me!!! Really Britain!" she screamed and started wailing on me even though I was driving. "You stupid muthafucka!" she cried as she hit me. "You don't even touch me but got the nerve to be fucking that bitch!"

I was finally able to pull over and stop her from hitting me. Once I did, she sunk down in her seat and continued to sob hysterically. I didn't know what to say to console her, and frankly I didn't care to. I was for real holding onto something that I didn't want. Maybe it was time to throw this fish back into the water.

Chapter 46

SUMMER

Because Hakim's face was how he made his money, he hadn't been to work in weeks. I have to admit I felt bad, because this was all my fault. I knew I shouldn't have been out with another man when I had a crazy ass boyfriend. Rhys could track down anyone; I mean he got paid to do so.

Today, Hakim was at the agency after being gone for the longest, so once he got done talking to Paul, I wanted to have a word with him. I didn't text him or anything because I didn't know what to say. Honestly, I wanted to just sweep the incident under the rug, but guilt took over me eventually. I needed to apologize or something.

"Hey, Hakim," I waved him down as he came out of Paul's office slowly.

"Hey," he sighed and then looked away.

His face looked pretty damn bad, and I'm sure this was an improvement on how bad his injuries initially looked. His somber demeanor was heartbreaking to say the least.

"Hakim, I want to apologize for—"

"Really? Now? Now you want to apologize?" he frowned and moved closer to me. "Look at my damn face, Summer!"

"I told you I had a boyfriend! And I told you he was crazy, but you insisted that I went out with you!"

"This is my fuckin' bread and butter, ma!" he began to tear up a little.

"Hakim, I know and I feel terrible. I really didn't know what to say before, which is why I didn't text or call you. But seeing you today just made me feel like I needed to apologize and say thank you."

"Thank you for what?" he turned his lip up.

"For not calling the police on my boyfriend. We have a family, and his daughter needs him—"

"I really don't care about any of that. That nigga is out of his mind, Summer, and you need to move on. It may not be with me, but it needs to be someone else other than him. Look what he did to me? And then some girl he was cheating on you with shot you, ma! What more do you need to see that he ain't the one?"

"Hakim, I can't just leave him. I'm the only one who can calm him down when he gets like that. If anybody else were there that night he attacked you, they wouldn't have gotten him to let up."

"So you're saying you're only with him because he's a charity case?"

"No, I'm with him because I love him and I want to work on what he and I have. As far as me getting shot, he took care of that and—"

"I'm sorry, I can't stand here and listen to you defend a man who will be nothing but the death of you. If you really cared about your life and your daughter's life, you would get the hell out of there. I like you Summer, a lot, so when you find the courage and the smarts to let him go, I will be waiting for you. Just call me. He didn't run me off," he half smiled and so did I.

"Thanks for the offer, Hakim, but I don't think I will be using it. Relationships are work, and I want to work on mine."

"Like I said, when shit hits the fan, and it will, I'm only a call away, ma." He walked off towards the exit of the agency and left. I watched him until he disappeared, and then went to the back to use the restroom.

I was hoping Rhys and I could really work through this if I just trusted him more, and tried to keep our arguments to a minimum. I loved that nigga more than anything excluding Bryleigh, and I just didn't want to let him go at the moment; not while we're doing good, at least. However, if he did one more thing, it was over. I put that on everything. There is only so much a person can take.

After using the bathroom and washing my hands, I went to collect my things so that I could go home. Grabbing my phone to check the time, I saw I had a text message from my friend, Lydia.

Lydia: *Look what I saw when I was at China Sea in Mattapan.*

I clicked the picture attached, and my head began to ache as I took in the photo. There Rhys was, standing and talking to some bitch. All this time I thought Lisa was the only one, but clearly this nigga had a whole bunch of bitches. The thought alone made my stomach twist up. Not to mention that they were at our favorite Chinese food spot.

Me: *This was today? Who is that? If you know.*

Lydia: *Yes girl, like five minutes ago. This holy bitch named Chenaye.*

I couldn't do this shit anymore. I was gone. Done.

Chapter 47

RHYS

TEN MINUTES EARLIER...

I'D FINISHED A JOB I HAD EARLIER THAN EXPECTED, SO I WANTED TO GET some food from China Sea and surprise my shorty when she got home. She loved their food, and she loved me, so what better way to welcome her home. I knew she expected me to be gone all day, so this would be perfect.

I ordered the food, and then stepped outside to wait. It was too crowded in there, and I was not trying to be shoulder to shoulder with all them damn people. My irritable ass would fuck around and smoke a nigga for brushing against me too roughly. As soon as I stepped out, I regretted it, because I saw Chenaye switching her ass over. Recently, since I was trying to be one hundred percent on the straight and narrow, I'd cut off all communication with her and any other women I conversed with. I had to admit though, she looked good enough to eat. Too bad I was off her and trying to work on my shit with Summer. And besides the fact that I was no cheater, I only ate my girl's pussy.

"I knew I would find you here," she spat as soon as she got to me.

"Oh word," I stated nonchalantly as I slipped my hands into my pockets.

"Yeah word, where the fuck have you been? I haven't seen you in almost a month, Rhys!"

This killed me. I told her I just wanted a friend, yet she was acting like I'd told her we would be something. Even when honest, they still made you look like the bad guy.

"I told yo' ass I couldn't talk to you no more. My girl ain't cool with me having friends, I told yo' ass that and you know it, so don't come up here acting a fuckin' fool, Chenaye."

"Wow, so now you wanna do what she says? I thought we were supposed to be cool! How you just do me like that!" she started crying on the last part. I didn't give a fuck how much a bitch cried, it would never faze me unless it was Summer.

"Aye kill all that crying shit. You was cool with my decision when I hit you up that day, so what's the difference now?"

"Because I thought you were just bullshitting, but now I know you're serious. My mama told me this shit would happen! She said that you were talking all that just being friends shit for a reason!"

"Should always listen to ya mama," I shrugged right when the clerk called my number. I went in to grab my food, and when I got back outside, Chenaye started going in.

I continued to my car as she followed me, going off. Finally having had enough, I put my food into the car and gripped the fuck out of her bicep.

"Look ma, heed to this warning right here. Back the fuck up off me and keep it pushing. I ain't the one, and I have a little feeling that you know that already. I ain't worth the pain you may endure if you keep pressing me, shorty." I threw her back and she stared at me, slightly frightened for a bit, before turning on her heels and switching off.

I sped home, and when I got inside, I saw my daughter sitting on the couch watching TV already. I guess I got home later than I'd planned, but it would still be a surprise nonetheless.

"Daddy!" Bryleigh hopped off the couch and ran to me, hugging my leg.

"Hey pretty, where is your mommy?"

"She's in the back packing our things."

"Packing your things?" I frowned and she nodded.

"She said we're going on a vacation for a while to Grandma's!"

Sitting my baby down, I went to place the food on the bar before rushing to the bedroom. Sure enough, when I walked in Summer was packing her shit up into a suitcase rapidly.

"Yo, where the fuck you going?" I went and stood in front of the closet that she was yanking clothes from. Her face was tear stained, so I knew it was some shit.

"You worry about where the fuck your other bitches are going!"

"Well I'm not! I'm worried about where the fuck you're going! And why the hell are you crying, ma?"

"Because I'm done! I cannot do this anymore! I've taken way more shit from you than I should have and I am done, Rhys! This is the second time I have caught you fucking around on me! Some bitch named Chenaye? Really? Who else is there?"

"I ain't fucking with Chenaye, Summer, what is you talking about right now?" I was so damn confused. Chenaye would never go behind my back to contact Summer, and secondly, I *hadn't* been fuckin' with Chenaye.

"Then what is this?" she shoved her phone in my face, and I sighed when I saw it was a picture of Chenaye and I talking about forty-five minutes ago.

"Summer it—"

"Save it, Rhys. I'm done. This is done. We can figure out a schedule for you to see Bryleigh, but as far as you and I?" she zipped her suitcase. "It's a wrap, boo. Now you have all the time in the world to spend with Chenaye, and any other bitch!"

"Summer!" I tried to grab her as she rushed to the living room with her bag. "I have not been with Chenaye or anybody else! She showed up and—"

"Bye Rhys!" she grabbed my daughter's hand, and like that they left.

I rushed outside after her, after standing there perplexed for a bit, but by the time I even made it outside she was gone. In all the years I'd been with her, she'd never left me. She'd never even said it. And the one time I was on my shit, through and through, she did. I didn't know what to think at this point, but maybe it was time to just let this shit go.

Chapter 48

KIMBERLYN

Since TQ was out of town, Matikah and I decided to invite Summer and Goldie over to my grandmother's house so we could have an adult sleepover. I was still having morning sickness at times, but all I had to do was run some water while I threw up. I didn't want to tell my friends just yet. My grandmother knew, but that was about it until I hit my third month. She told me that was the way to do things in case something went wrong.

"Okay, what movie?" Goldie questioned as she picked up the remote to monitor the Apple TV in my room.

"Something with love, and a lot of sex!" Matikah smiled.

"Ain't nobody trying to see that shit, all it's gonna do is make me miss something I shouldn't be missing," Summer said.

"So you're really done with Rhys?" Goldie asked.

"I sure am. I wanna block his ass in my phone, but I can't because of Bryleigh. When I took her over there this afternoon, he was trying to talk but I shut that shit down."

"Damn, you sound like Matikah," I chuckled.

Matikah still hadn't taken Lendsey's ass back, and he had yet to give up either. He was starting to get me on his side. I'd never seen a man so desperate, and a part of me knew he was slowly breaking her down.

"That's the best way to be. I feel like a new woman now that I'm done with him," Matikah smiled.

"Yeah right!" Goldie sucked her teeth and we all laughed at Matikah's lying ass. She may have had us fooled for a little bit, but I think we were all getting hip to her facade; she missed Lendsey.

"All them niggas can stay in the trash, right along with Britain's ass," Goldie rolled her eyes.

Britain was harassing Goldie on the low, or at least he thought it was on the low, but she showed us all his begging ass texts. This dude had a bitch but was chasing Goldie. I shook my head as I thought about it.

We finally chose a movie, *The Wood*, and began to watch it. Halfway through the film, the UPS man beat on the screen door, before dropping a package. I hated that he did that shit because it always scared the fuck out of me.

Since I'd recently placed an order online, I hopped up and went outside to get it. Closing the door behind me, I walked out onto the porch to grab the box. I then went down the steps to go into the mailbox to make sure we'd gotten all the mail from earlier.

WHAM!

As I was looking into the mailbox, I was suddenly struck across the back of the head with a heavy ass object. Tears immediately came out of my eyes as I became dizzy. Right when I was about to turn around, I collapsed to the floor in pain, listening to the attacker pant heavily. I then tried to adjust my sight so I could see who it was as I turned over.

WHAM!

Another strike from the blurry figure dressed in all black. They kicked my leg, and before I could say anything, I blacked out.

BECOME A VIP READER!

*To join my mailing list text **SHVONNE** to **66866** and stay up to date! Also, join **Shvonne Latrice Reading Group** on Facebook!*